PASSION'S SWEET SURRENDER

What Reviewers Say About Ronica Black's Work

Freedom to Love

"This is a great book. The police drama keeps you enthralled throughout but what I found captivating was the growing affection between the two main characters. Although they are both very different women, you find yourself holding your breath, hoping that they will find a way to be together."—*Lesbian Reading Room*

Snow Angel

"A beautifully written, passionate and romantic novella."—*SunsetX Cocktail*

The Seeker

"Ronica Black's books just keep getting stronger and stronger. …This is such a tightly written plot-driven novel that readers will find themselves glued to the pages and ignoring phone calls. *The Seeker* is a great read, with an exciting plot, great characters, and great sex." —*Just About Write*

Flesh and Bone—*Lammy Finalist*

"Ronica Black handles a traditional range of lesbian fantasies with gusto and sincerity. The reader wants to know these women as well as they come to know each other. When Black's characters ignore their realistic fears to follow their passion, this reader admires their chutzpah and cheers them on. …These stories make good bedtime reading, and could lead to sweet dreams. Read them and see." —*Erotica Revealed*

Chasing Love

"Ronica Black's writing is fluid, and lots of dialogue makes this a fast read. If you like steamy erotica with intense sexual situations, you'll like *Chasing Love*."—*Queer Magazine Online*

Hearts Aflame

"Sleek storytelling and terrific characters are the backbone of Ronica Black's third and best novel, *Hearts Aflame*. Prepare to hop on for an emotional ride with this thrilling story of love in the outback. ...Along with the romance of Krista and Rae, the secondary storylines such as Krista's fear of horses and an uncle suffering from Alzheimer's are told with depth and warmth. Black also draws in the reader by utilizing the weather as a metaphor for the sexual and emotional tension in all the storylines. Wonderful storytelling and rich characterization make this a high recommendation."—*Lambda Literary Review*

"*Hearts Aflame* takes the reader on the rough and tumble ride of the cattle drive. Heat, flood, and a sexual pervert are all part of the adventure. Heat also appears between Krista and Rae. The twists and turns of the plot engage the reader all the way to the satisfying conclusion."—*Just About Write*

Wild Abandon—*Lammy Finalist*

"Black is a master at teasing the reader with her use of domination and desire. Black's first novel, *In Too Deep*, was a finalist for a 2005 Lammy. ...With *Wild Abandon*, the author continues her winning ways, writing like a seasoned pro. This is one romance I will not soon forget."—*Books to Watch Out For*

"This sequel to Ronica Black's debut novel, *In Too Deep*, is an electrifying thriller. The author's development as a fine storyteller shines with this tightly written story. ...[The mystery] keeps the story charged—never unraveling or leading us to a predictable conclusion. More than once I gasped in surprise at the dark and twisted paths this book took."—*Curve*

"Ronica Black, author of *In Too Deep*, has given her fans another fast paced novel of romance and danger. As previously, Black develops her characters fully, complete with their quirks and flaws. She is also skilled at allowing her characters to grow, and to find their way out of psychic holes. If you enjoy complex characters and passionate sex scenes, you'll love *Wild Abandon*."—*MegaScene*

"Black has managed to create two very sensual and compelling women. The backstory is intriguing, original, and quite well-developed. Yet, it doesn't detract from the primary premise of the novel—it is a sexually-charged romance about two very different and guarded women. Black carries the reader along at such a rapid pace that the rise and fall of each climactic moment successfully creates that suspension of disbelief which the reader seeks."
—*Midwest Book Review*

In Too Deep—*Lammy Finalist*

"Ronica Black's debut novel *In Too Deep* has everything from nonstop action and intriguing well developed characters to steamy erotic love scenes. From the opening scenes where Black plunges the reader headfirst into the story to the explosive unexpected ending, *In Too Deep* has what it takes to rise to the top. Black has a winner with *In Too Deep*, one that will keep the reader turning the pages until the very last one."—*Independent Gay Writer*

"...an exciting, page turning read, full of mystery, sex, and suspense."
—*MegaScene*

"...a challenging murder mystery—sections of this mixed-genre novel are hot, hot, hot. Black juggles the assorted elements of her first book with assured pacing and estimable panache."—*Q Syndicate*

"Black's characterization is skillful, and the sexual chemistry surrounding the three major characters is palpable and definitely hot-hot-hot...if you're looking for a solid read with ample amounts of eroticism and a red herring or two you're sure to find *In Too Deep* a satisfying read."—*L Word Literature*

"Ronica Black's debut novel, *In Too Deep*, is the outstanding first effort of a gifted writer who has a promising career ahead of her. Black shows extraordinary command in weaving a thoroughly engrossing tale around multi-faceted characters, intricate action and character-driven plots and subplots, sizzling sex that jumps off the page and stimulates libidos effortlessly, amidst brilliant storytelling. A clever mystery writer, Black has the reader guessing until the end."—*Midwest Book Review*

"Every time the reader has a handle on what's happening, Black throws in a curve, successfully devising a good mystery. The romance and sex add a special gift to the package rounding out the story for a totally satisfying read."—*Just About Write*

Visit us at www.boldstrokesbooks.com

By the Author

In Too Deep

Deeper

Wild Abandon

Hearts Aflame

Flesh and Bone

The Seeker

Chasing Love

Conquest

Wholehearted

The Midnight Room

Snow Angel

The Practitioner

Freedom to Love

Under Her Wing

Private Passion

Dark Euphoria

The Last Seduction

Olivia's Awakening

A Love That Leads to Home

Passion's Sweet Surrender

PASSION'S SWEET SURRENDER

by

Ronica Black

2020

PASSION'S SWEET SURRENDER

ISBN 13: 978-1-63555-703-9

This Trade Paperback Original Is Published By
Bold Strokes Books, Inc.
P.O. Box 249
Valley Falls, NY 12185

First Edition: September 2020

CREDITS
Editor: Cindy Cresap
Production Design: Susan Ramundo
Cover Design By Jeanine Henning

Acknowledgments

Thanks to the entire Bold Strokes team for all their hard work.

Thank you to my editor, Cindy Cresap. Cindy, your never-ending faith and encouragement keep my head above water in the stormy seas of self-doubt. Thank you!

Chapter One

Saturdays in Puerto Tranquilo were not what the town's name implied. There was no peaceful haven to be found. Which was why Camille Santiago usually avoided venturing into the heart of town at all costs on weekends. Especially during the warmer months when the market was crammed with summer tourists. The majority of them sun-scorched visitors from Arizona, seeking an oceanside reprieve. They came to Mexico for the white sand beaches but also enjoyed the abundance of cheap beer, a vast array of wonderful, local food and, of course, the shopping.

Today seemed to be no exception and Cam could see dozens of tourists from her Jeep as she neared the market. They were wandering from one street vendor to another, eager to get a glimpse of the local goods and souvenirs for sale. Cam couldn't blame them for their excitement, because the deals *were* good and the items *were* unlike anything they'd find in the States. So, she didn't necessarily have anything against the onslaught of seasonal visitors. She just hated crowds in general.

She preferred going into town during the week when most of the tourists were either back home in the States, pleasantly satiated from their weekend getaway or happily tucked away in whatever beach resort or rented condo they were staying at. And even though her town had yet to completely blow up and commercialize like a couple of others along the western coast of Mexico, it had slowly been gaining popularity among the visitors, mostly due to curiosity and spill over from the neighboring booming beachside towns. She was grateful though, at least for the time being, that her town still had some semblance of calm, even if she did have to wait for the off-season now to really experience it.

The old, low-key fishing village, which was where Cam was headed today, seemed rather sleepy in comparison to the market, despite the market's close proximity. People, she reckoned, didn't tend to linger when they came looking for seafood like they did when shopping for material items.

She shoved her '84 Jeep Wrangler into park on the dunes sandwiched between the market and the fishing village after finally giving up on finding an available parking space in the paved lot. She slipped off her canvas deck shoes before climbing out of her doorless vehicle and walked through the heavy sand away from the sounds of loud chatter and commotion and headed instead toward the hungry, aggressive shrills of the seagulls. The thick, salty smell of the sea and the strong, overpowering smell of freshly caught fish hit her hard as she slid back into her shoes and began walking along the worn planks toward the pier where she hoped to find her friend.

"Santi!"

"Hola, Santi."

Cam waved at a few of the fishermen as they said hello, referring to her by her well-known local nickname. Some of the fishermen were tending to their boats, while others worked in their corrugated steel huts, selling their daily catch to hungry tourists. She'd known many of the townsfolk for years, from her early visits to the area as a child, and they'd always treated her like a local, even before she'd moved there to live full-time.

It was still difficult for her to believe that this once quaint little seaside town, raw and rugged with the coastal beauty of the Sea of the Cortez, was well on its way to becoming a thriving, bustling tourist destination. She'd still decided to call it home, regardless of its probable future as a booming beach town. This place had always meant a lot to her. The salt, the sea, and the people were in her bones. This town had always been her haven, where she'd spent countless summers soaking up the sun, the surf, and the community. It was where she'd always felt the happiest, the safest. So, it had only made sense to her to finally make the move and call it home.

She'd just made sure the house she'd bought wasn't very close to town.

Because peace and tranquility were what she was all about these days.

"Hola, Santi. Necessitas una cerveza?"

She smiled at her friend Marco and waved off the bottle of beer he was offering from his tiny fish taco stand.

She continued toward the pier where she found the man she was looking for, her friend Tomas.

Tomas, however, was busy. He was in his brother's fishing hut surrounded by the large coolers containing their daily catch. He was talking with a woman, most likely a customer, but strangely, he didn't appear to be his usual jovial self. Cam stood off to the side, politely waiting for the woman to finish her business with Tomas. Cam assumed, by the look of her, that the woman was a tourist. Albeit an extremely fit tourist from the look of her well defined arms and legs. Her tank top with the name of a popular Phoenix marathon run for charity allowed Cam to notice that. It was her freshly pinked cheeks and shoulders that sold Cam on her being a tourist, however. That, along with the rest of her, like her perfectly creased navy shorts and spotless Nike trainers, sealed the deal. The strong scent of the sunscreen glistening on her skin was, at that point, irrelevant.

Cam had no interest in the woman's transaction with Tomas and stared off into the mildly tempered turquoise sea, concentrating on the warm breeze as it ran its fingers through her short hair. Occasionally, it brought the mist of the water along with it, pricking her with cold tingles, just enough to chill her for a few quick seconds before the sun baked them into her skin.

"Excuse me," the woman next to her said. "Do you know anything about the shrimp for sale around here?"

Cam turned to look at her, surprised and a little disappointed at being pulled away from her tranquil state.

"No, not—"

Cam's words fell, toppling into the sea as she properly took in the woman for the first time. Cam stood motionless, mouth hanging open. She was awestruck. Completely awestruck by the woman's beauty. And then came the shock at being so awestruck. It had been years, *years* since she'd been so strongly affected at the sight of a woman. It had been so long she'd totally forgotten how powerful and uncontrollable those feelings she'd long thought dead were. Now, in a flash, they were back, having dug their way to the surface from their graves to run amok inside her, wild, free, and hungry. And what was worse, she seemed to have no way to capture them, to wrangle them up and cage them. There was no sheriff coming to the rescue to help her round them up either. No Wyatt Earp was going to ride in and save her.

God, help me.
What is happening?

CHAPTER TWO

I was hoping you could help," the woman continued, obviously clueless to Cam's overwhelming sense of shock and awe. "I think there may be a language barrier."

Her pink lips parted, as if she were intending to speak again. As if she were waiting to respond to whatever Cam was going to say. But Cam couldn't say anything. She was too busy thinking how very much her lips looked like a bow, an archer's bow, turned on its side.

Would kissing those lips feel like the piercing of hundreds of tiny arrows? Sweet, sultry, honey dipped arrows launched from the most exquisite mouth she'd ever seen?

The bow-shaped lips closed, bringing Cam back to reality. Below the woman's dark, stylish sunglasses, the tips of her sunburned cheekbones appeared to have darkened to a deeper shade. And then her brow creased. She was obviously upset, apparently at Cam's lack of response, but all Cam could do was think about pressing her mouth to the small ball at the base of her jaw as it flexed.

"Never mind."

The woman turned back to Tomas, her short, brown layered hair, which was stacked in the back with a stylish cut, swayed from her sharp movement. Her frown was evident, even from the side, but it did nothing to detract from the perfection of her profile.

"Maybe we should try again," the woman said to Tomas. "I don't want the blue shrimp, I want the brown."

"No brown, miss. No, mas."

"But I *need* the brown." She rubbed her forehead. "I have to have the brown. Yo necessito…" she trailed off and Cam could sense her struggling to find the correct words in Spanish.

Cam intervened, growing frustrated herself. She spoke to Tomas in Spanish, and he explained that he'd already sold all the brown shrimp he'd had for the day. He only had the blue and the lady didn't seem to be willing to accept that. He also relayed that she'd been standing there arguing with him for more than twenty minutes.

Cam directed her attention back to the woman, who was now standing with her arms folded across her chest, waiting, not so patiently, for Cam to say whatever it was she was going to say.

"He doesn't have any more brown," Cam said, staring into the abyss of her black lenses. "He's sold out for the day."

She made a small noise of disbelief. "I don't see how that's possible. With all these fishermen? All these boats? You're telling me they're *all* sold out?"

"Tomas is, yes. As for the others…"

"I've already been to two others." She sighed and rubbed her forehead again. "I'm tired. I don't want to have to track down every fisherman here for some freaking shrimp. I don't understand how they could be out."

"It is late in the day," Cam said. "And weekends here are crazy busy, especially now with the beginning of shrimp season."

"Lo siento, miss," Tomas, said, apologizing. He held out the icy bag of blue shrimp. He told her she could have it for free.

"He said he's sorry, and he'd like you to have the blue for free."

She shook her head and laughed. "I can't take the blue. That's what I've been trying to tell him. But he doesn't seem to get it."

Cam felt herself frown as the woman's incredible beauty began to fade and give way to her attitude. She actually sounded kind of snotty, like maybe she thought Tomas was somehow too dense to understand her.

"He speaks English," Cam said, eager to defend her longtime friend. "And he has the ability to think and reason. So, he understands what you want. I can assure you of that. But what he doesn't understand, is your refusal to accept that you aren't going to get it."

She reared back a little and her mouth opened again. Cam could tell she'd struck a nerve so she quickly spoke, trying to douse the growing flames between them.

"Have you had the blue shrimp before?"

"I—no, I have not. My friend, the one who wants the shrimp, may have, I don't know. She loves to cook and she's very particular about her ingredients. She specifically asked for the brown." The question had seemed to throw her off balance. Her anger, now confusion.

"The blue shrimp is just as good. In fact, a lot of people like it better. It's kind of what we're known for around here. Your friend might like it too. I'm sure she can adjust whatever it is she's making to accommodate for the difference in taste. And Tomas, who is one heck of a great guy by the way, is offering it to you for free. So, what do you have to lose in accepting it? You don't like it, come back earlier tomorrow for the brown."

She scratched her head and sighed. "It's not as easy as that. My friend said the drive from her house to town is quite a ways. Which is why we stopped here to stock up on our way in. But yes, okay. I guess I don't have much of a choice, do I?" She dug in her pocket and pulled out some folded bills. She thumbed through them and held some out for Tomas. It was a generous amount. "For your time," she said, the venom finally gone from her voice. He looked hesitant, as if afraid she still might bite.

Cam assured him it was okay to take the money. He took it and nodded at her, thanking her. He handed her the bag of shrimp.

She thanked him, gave Cam a quiet, unreadable look and wished them both a nice day before she turned and walked away. The breeze came off the sea again, toying with the woman's thick hair like a child trying to cheer up a sad friend. Cam's gaze fell to the pebbled ground where the breeze was also playing with something else.

"Oh, no." She quickly knelt and snatched the fallen twenty-dollar bill and hurried after the woman.

"Wait! Miss, wait, please."

The woman turned with alarm but as soon as she seemed to recognize Cam, that alarm hardened to what looked like contempt.

"I'm not a jerk," she spat as Cam slammed to a stop.

"What?" Cam almost looked over her shoulder, convinced she was speaking to someone other than her.

"Your friend," she continued. "Tomas. I knew what he was saying. I—understood. I just wasn't sure he understood me. Not because I thought he was less than me or uneducated, or whatever else it was I could tell you were thinking. But simply because English isn't his first language and Spanish isn't mine. So, I was just trying to talk to him. To explain my situation, hoping he may have some sort of a solution. Like maybe he knew someone else who may have the shrimp. I don't know. Granted, I've had a very long, very shitty day and I know I'm frustrated and probably more than a bit cranky, but I am not an asshole. And I don't appreciate you assuming that I am. Got it?"

She lifted her sunglasses above her eyes and pierced Cam with a gaze that felt as hot as the sun but matched the cool turquoise color of the sea.

"Yeah," Cam said, stunned breathless, this time from her eyes. But the conflict she'd felt earlier returned and it had intensified. It seemed that one second she was lost in an awestruck delirium by the woman's beauty and the next she was dodging the flying daggers of her words. Her mind couldn't keep up, couldn't make sense of an enchantment that only seemed to lead to danger.

Cam held out the twenty-dollar bill. "You dropped this."

The woman stared, seemingly confused. The stone-like set to her face softened ever so slightly.

"Oh." She took the money and shoved it in her pocket. "Thanks."

"No problem."

She started to turn but halted halfway. "You shouldn't assume things about people, you know. Especially when you don't know what they've been through that day." She dropped her shades back in position over her eyes.

She had thrown one last dagger and this one had hit its mark. And Cam did not like the way it felt as it sliced into her skin.

"Really? That's how you're going to walk away? After making sure you got in one last jab? Making sure you got the last word?" She laughed and tugged off her own sunglasses and pinned the woman with a fiery gaze of her own. "I could say a lot of things to you right now. But I'm choosing not to. I left all that petty shit behind when I moved here, and I don't allow tourists to bring it back, regardless of what they say or how they behave. So, I'm just going to kindly suggest that you follow your own so-called advice. To maybe, instead of thinking about yourself, think about Tomas and consider what all he may have gone through today before he encountered you. Because I can guarantee you, whatever it is you went through, in one damn day, is nothing compared to what he goes through each and every day. And I mean *every* day. He doesn't get the benefit of a beach vacation, where he can spend endless hours lounging in the sand, drinking ice cold margaritas while being waited upon by others. He—" She stopped and shook her head. "What am I doing? Why am I wasting my time?"

The woman dug in her pocket again and retrieved the twenty-dollar bill. She shoved it toward her. "You're right. I should've considered him and his life and his feelings. Give this to him, along with an apology."

Cam didn't take it.

"Don't give him your money. Give him your respect."

The woman clamped her mouth closed and crumpled up the bill in her fist. The scarlet on her cheeks deepened once again.

"You don't know me," she said. "You—don't." She turned on her heel and walked away.

"And I don't think I want to," Cam whispered as she watched her walk away. "Even if you are the most beautiful thing I've ever seen."

CHAPTER THREE

I can't believe it. Is this it? It's—Oh, my God, you weren't kidding were you guys?" Blake Livingstone leaned forward from her position in the back seat to look through the windshield. She, along with her good friends Sloane and McKenna, had just emerged from the long bumpy dirt road through the dunes to turn down a new, smoother path, that seemed to stretch for miles along an endless row of beach houses. But it was what could be seen between the houses that had Blake nearly bouncing with excitement.

"This is it, all right," McKenna said from the passenger seat.

Blake kept staring as they bypassed more houses, getting quick glimpses between them of what Sloane and McKenna had been trying to describe to her back in Phoenix.

Soon they pulled into the sandy but cemented drive of a small, off-white bungalow style house with a low roof and wood trim. They parked parallel to a front entry garage, and from what Blake could see, the main door to the house appeared to be down from the garage on the side of the house.

Sloane turned off the engine to her Toyota Highlander. "She needs some work, but all in all, we think she's worth it." She smoothed her fine, shoulder length blond hair behind her ears and adjusted her red and white Arizona Cardinals ball cap. Then she smiled back at Blake. "You ready for the best beach vacation you've ever had?"

"I'm not on vacation, remember?" But she was unexpectedly excited and she couldn't restrain the grin that gave that away.

McKenna also looked at her from the front seat. "Oh, yes, you are. You're going to take some time to relax while you're here. That was the deal. Remember?" She playfully mimicked Blake.

Blake almost argued with her, wanting to reiterate that she and Sloane had things to do. Important things. This trip wasn't about a vacation for her. She didn't do vacations. But by the look on her friends' faces, Blake knew there would be no reiterating tolerated.

"Everybody loves a beach vacation," Sloane said. "And this one, I promise, will even win you over."

Blake was about to agree to at least try to do some relaxing while she was there, but words she'd heard earlier, about an hour ago, impeded upon the voicing of her good intentions.

He doesn't get the benefit of a beach vacation.

McKenna, who had climbed from the vehicle, opened Blake's door as the words from the stranger in town replayed. The distress they caused must've been apparent on Blake's face, because McKenna's clouded when she looked at her.

"What's wrong?"

McKenna looked at Sloane, who was still focused on Blake, as they waited for her reply. Blake was aware of the look that passed between them, and though she was too zoned out to directly witness it, she knew it had to be one filled with concern. Sloane and McKenna were the happiest, most well-adjusted couple Blake had ever known and they were extremely intuitive. With each other as well as others. And in particular, with Blake.

Blake slid off her seat, determined not to let a perfect stranger ruin her trip, and stepped onto the thick, soft sand next to McKenna. She hugged her tall, thin, frame and felt strands of her auburn hair flick against her arms as they were stirred by the breeze. "Nothing's wrong. Absolutely nothing." Blake drew away and tried to reassure her. "I'm on a beach vacation, right? So, what could possibly be wrong?"

McKenna studied her with her clear blue eyes. "I don't know. You were unusually quiet on the drive in from town." She cocked her head. "You're not still thinking about that rude woman are you?"

The tiniest of lumps formed in Blake's throat and attempted to grow. But she refused to let it. "Nah, just a little tired."

And discombobulated.

And really pissed that a woman I don't even know had and still is having such an effect on me.

And she was so presumptuous and pious and...freaking gorgeous.

McKenna threw her arm around her, graciously killing the lingering thoughts of the stranger, and led her along the side of the house where Blake noted the deep brown front door nestled in a small covered entryway just past the length of the garage.

"Flat tires in the middle of nowhere do tend to wear people out," McKenna said, referring to their very eventful and very unfortunate drive in from Phoenix.

Blake laughed. "Do they?"

Sloane hustled to join them and she, too, slid an arm around Blake.

"Close your eyes," she said.

"But I—" Blake saw the enthusiasm in her eyes. Even though they were a darker blue than her partner's, Sloane's emotions never had been difficult to discern, and Blake readily did as she requested, Sloane's enthusiasm contagious. "Okay."

McKenna and Sloane led her forward, guiding her through the deep sand. When they came to a stop Blake felt the weight of a strong breeze. "God, I can smell it," she said. "The ocean. Smelled it the second McKenna opened my door. And I can hear it. Hear the waves crashing. Like it's right in front of me. We can't possibly be this close to the ocean. We can't."

"Open your eyes and see for yourself," Sloane said.

Blake opened her eyes and there was the sea. Vast, blue-green and shimmering, like a gem, reflecting the colors of the setting sun.

"Oh, my God."

"Come on," McKenna said. The three of them hurried through the white sand to a slight decline where the sand went from soft, white, and thick, to a firmer, darker consistency that continued down to mushy wet sand the ocean had recently left behind as it pulled away from the shore. They walked on toward the water's edge, dodging a few small tide pools.

"It's so close," Blake said, glancing back up at the house. She'd been to the beach before, a few times in her life, but she'd never stayed at a place literally *on* the beach. Hotel or otherwise.

"Wait until high tide," Sloane said, staring out at the retreating sea as if it were calling to her. "Then you'll really be amazed at how close we are."

"But even at low tide it's just as incredible," McKenna said. "There are tide pools full of crabs and starfish, and seashells galore."

Blake took in the beach around her. To her left, it seemed to stretch into oblivion. The row of houses, the brown sand and the crashing waves, all of it. To her right, she found the same. It seemed never-ending.

"It's incredible," Blake said as she looked to her left and right again and saw the long stretch of sand and houses. "And endless." She shaded her brow against the setting sun, watching as four children played in the teasing surf. They were so far away she couldn't even hear them. She looked back to her left again and saw several people on the beach in the distance there as well. A handful at most. "And there's hardly any people."

"It's a private beach," Sloane said. "You can't be here unless you're in one of the homes."

"Oh, right," Blake said. She laughed a little. "I know you tried to tell me about all this, but I think I needed to see it for myself to truly understand."

"Summer's coming to an end," McKenna said, slipping out of her shoes. "So, there will be less and less people as the days go by." She took a few steps and shrieked softly as the water rushed toward her and enveloped her bare feet.

Her glee was infectious, and Blake, too, slipped out of her sneakers and peeled off her socks to step into the water.

"It *is* cold," she said as the water spilled over her feet and wrapped around her ankles. But the chill was welcome after a long, blistering hot day in the sun. Sloane and McKenna had assured her though, that the summer heat would soon begin to dissipate. According to them the nights were already growing cooler.

Sloane picked up an errant shell and side-armed it back into the sea. She brushed her hands on the sides of her shorts. "You ready to see the house?"

"Sure." *But there's no way it will beat this.*

CHAPTER FOUR

They picked up their shoes and headed back up to the house. When they reached the thick sand again, Sloane walked off in the direction of the car while Blake and McKenna continued to the covered patio that spanned the width of the back of the house. They stepped onto the cool cement of the patio and McKenna began uncovering and unstacking deck chairs. Blake helped and they arranged some around a patio table and then the rest on the opposite side where anyone who wanted to could sit down, prop their feet up on the low patio wall, and kick back with a killer view.

Just as they finished, the Arcadian door slid open and Sloane, who must've entered the house through the door along the side of the house, handed McKenna a small plastic tub and then backed out with a gas grill and rolled it into position at the edge of the patio near two of the chairs.

McKenna turned on a spigot beneath the large back window and filled the plastic tub with water. Then she placed it by the door and stepped inside it.

"Gotta clean your feet," she said. "To help keep the sand out." She stepped out and allowed Blake to do the same. Then she waved her into the house after Sloane.

Blake entered the hot, cozy-small bungalow and took in the living room to the right, where a sofa, coffee table, and two chairs sat across from a stone-walled fireplace. The furniture was neutral in color scheme and older, but still in good condition. In time McKenna would no doubt work her magic as far as the decor, but it was obvious the main concern or attraction wasn't the interior of the house. It was what was outside, just beyond that patio that everyone would be focused on and rightfully so. The kitchen was to the left, where Sloane was fiddling with the light switch and mumbling to herself. There was an L-shaped countertop with off-white cabinetry above and below. The sink was beneath the far window, which appeared to have a view of the front door and the side of the house. At the other end of the counter there was a refrigerator and beyond that, closer to Blake, was a round table with chairs. It was a simple, modest layout, complete with bright yellow linoleum flooring and a single domed light centered in the ceiling. A light, it seemed, that Sloane was having trouble turning on.

"Something's wrong with the lights?" McKenna asked.

Sloane continued to mumble, and she crossed to the living room and tried the lamps, which also seemed unwilling to cooperate.

"We gotta have lights, babe," McKenna said, hurrying into what Blake assumed to be the two bedrooms in the back.

"I know, Kenna," Sloane said. "I'm on it."

McKenna returned to the living room. "No luck."

"Great." Sloane removed her ball cap and ran her hand through her hair.

"Did you try the breaker? In the garage?" McKenna asked, heading for the front door.

"Yes," Sloane said. "I did that as soon as I came inside and noticed the entry light and the others wouldn't come on. I was hoping that fooling with the breakers would've somehow worked." She slapped her cap against her leg. "Guess not."

McKenna rubbed the back of her neck. "I don't understand. Everything worked fine a couple of weeks ago."

They'd moved in only a few weeks before. And from what they'd told Blake, they still had a heck of a lot to do, despite bringing down a moving truck full of furniture and necessities and a few friends to help. But they'd also said that the house was ready enough for guests, and Blake assumed that electricity was one of the things they'd considered ready.

"Is there anything I can do?" Blake asked. She felt bad enough at having come so soon after they'd moved in. Even if it was at their insistence. She felt like she needed to do something to help. It would be dark soon and they were miles from town. They needed a plan. "Light some candles, maybe?"

"Candles," McKenna breathed. She looked to Sloane with wide eyes. "Do we have candles?"

"Not unless they're leftover from the previous owner."

"Oh, wonderful," McKenna said.

"We got flashlights," Sloane said. "But that's it." She rested her palm on the Arcadian door. "We can live without power for a night, but I'm worried all the food we brought won't fare so well overnight in the coolers." She wiped her brow with the back of her hand. "Not with the limited ice we have."

They'd had trouble finding ice in town to replenish their coolers for the remainder of the drive in. It seemed to be as popular as the brown shrimp. Blake winced as she once again recalled her exchange with the stranger in town.

She groaned and shoved her out of her mind.

McKenna and Sloane looked at her.

"I wasn't groaning about this," she hurried to explain. "I was thinking about something else."

McKenna snapped her fingers. "What about our neighbor?"

"What neighbor?" Sloane said. "The house next door is vacant and the other one, she never seems to be home."

McKenna smiled. "She's home now. There's a Jeep in the driveway. I saw it when we pulled in."

Sloane seemed to light up. She tugged on the bill of her cap. "I'll be back." She slid open the door and dashed off to the neighbor's.

"Sorry about all this," McKenna said.

"Woman, please. You lured me to paradise on a private beach. I'll sleep outside in the sand if I have to in order to stay here."

She offered her a smile, wanting to ease her anxiety.

"You really like it?" McKenna asked, worried about everyone else's happiness as was her typical fashion.

"If I say yes will you start in with the 'I told you sos?'"

"I might."

"Then forget it."

McKenna laughed.

"Let's go unpack, shall we?" Blake said.

McKenna nodded and they began unloading the Highlander, bringing in luggage and boxes and coolers. Blake wiped her brow after she placed one of the last boxes on the kitchen table. McKenna had opened some of the windows to cool the house and now she was staring through the one in the kitchen.

"Sloane's coming. Looks like the neighbor is with her. I sure hope she can help."

"I'm sure she can," Blake said. "I'm going to go get the last box." She walked back outside and retrieved the last box from the SUV. She heard voices as she came back inside. Three of them. She expected one of them to sound unfamiliar. But it didn't. She was almost in the kitchen before that sank in.

Why do I know that voice?

She glanced up, searching for the source, and the box fell from her hands and crashed to the floor. She saw McKenna rush to her, heard Sloane ask if she was okay, but that all seemed surreal. The only thing that did seem real was the woman standing before her. The woman with short, midnight hair, tanned, olive skin, and dark, flashing eyes. Eyes that were taking her in intensely. Eyes she'd thought she'd never see again.

CHAPTER FIVE

Blake tried to tell herself it wasn't the same person, just someone who closely resembled the stranger from town. But the woman had on the same faded green pair of board shorts and the same snug fitting matching tank. She had the same T-shaped shoulders and strong, toned arms. Blake trailed her eyes back up to her face and saw the same pink scar just below her hairline on her forehead that she'd seen before and the other, less noticeable one on her cheek.

She couldn't deny it now. No matter how badly she wanted to. This was her. The woman who had insulted her, enraged her, and, if she were being honest, left her mind completely spinning.

And I won't even acknowledge how my body reacts to her.

McKenna touched Blake's arm. "You okay?"

Blake blinked and forced a smile. "I just lost my grip," she said, kneeling to help McKenna pile everything back into the box. She tried to take it when they finished, but McKenna wouldn't let her. She carried it to the kitchen counter herself as if she were worried Blake was too weak or incapable.

Sloane spoke as Blake stood alone, feeling awkward. "Blake, this is Cam. She lives in the house next door. Cam, this is my good friend, Blake. She's going to stay with us for a while for a much, *much* needed vacation." Sloane winked at her, but Blake was burning under the scrutiny of Cam's stare.

Cam came forward and offered her hand. Blake took it and found it to be surprisingly warm and soft. Her handshake was firm, confident. But Cam pulled away before Blake had the chance to squeeze her hand fully in return.

"We've actually already met," Cam said, holding Blake's gaze.

McKenna's face brightened. "Oh?"

"At the fish market," Cam said. "Earlier today."

McKenna stared at Blake, her eyes now wide with recognition. Blake had given her a quick rundown of what had happened on her trek to buy shrimp, leaving out the very noticeable fact that Cam was gorgeous. A fact that did not seem to be lost on McKenna, based on the shit-eating grin that had spread across her face.

McKenna crossed her arms across her chest.

"So, you're the woman from the fish market?" she asked Cam. "The one who helped with the shrimp?"

Cam sank a hand into her pocket. If she was unnerved, she wasn't showing it.

"I am indeed."

"Interesting," McKenna said, looking back at Blake. "Very interesting."

"Can someone fill me in here?" Sloane asked.

"I will later, hon."

"Fine, whatever. Cam, come with me." Sloane and Cam went from room to room and then eventually out the front door. Blake tried to hide her nerves by sifting through the boxes, trying to find things to put away.

"She seems nice," McKenna said.

"Yeah, she does, doesn't she?" Blake carried boxes of whole wheat pasta from the table to the countertop. "Where do you want these?"

McKenna pointed to the cabinets next to the fridge.

"She doesn't seem at all rude to me."

Blake slid the pasta into place. "Perhaps I was mistaken." She crossed back to the table and gathered more goods.

"Maybe." McKenna joined her at the table. "Rude or not, she certainly is a looker."

Blake fumbled with a jar of organic marinara sauce. McKenna caught it just as it slid from her grip. She held it out for her, smirking.

"And by the sudden reappearance of your butter fingers, I'd say that's something you've noticed as well."

Blake jerked the jar of sauce away from her. "You'd be wrong."

"Oh, Blake, my dear, when it comes to reading you, I'm never wrong."

They continued unpacking until they heard Sloane and Cam come back inside. McKenna once again crossed her arms over her chest as they entered the kitchen.

Blake gave her a pleading look, silently begging her to let whatever intentions she had go. But she merely shrugged, leaving Blake's nerves on edge. And catching a glimpse of Cam didn't help matters any. A thin sheen of sweat coated her skin, accentuating every sinewy muscle visible. Blake swallowed with difficulty and looked away quickly as Cam ran her lean fingers through her short, pixie cut hair. Blake couldn't help but imagine running her own fingers through that hair while locked in a passionate, writhing embrace, hungrily kissing, tasting…

"The electricity's shot," Sloane said. "Not sure why and we won't be able to get anyone out here to take a look until tomorrow. Cam knows someone who'll help us out. In the meantime, she's going to lend us some propane lamps and store our perishables at her place."

"The lamps are pretty old, but they still work fine. I'd offer my generator," Cam said, "but a friend is using it."

"You're doing more than enough," McKenna said. "We greatly appreciate it."

"It's no trouble," Cam said.

"We're getting ready to make dinner," McKenna said. She looked at Sloane. "Assuming the grill still works, we're going to have shrimp."

"We're probably a little low on propane, but other than that it should be fine," Sloane said. "But the way our day has gone, who knows."

"We'd love it if you'd join us," McKenna said, shifting her gaze to Cam.

Blake singed a look into her, but McKenna was too focused on Cam to notice.

"Maybe some other time," Cam said. "It sounds like you've had a very long day and I'm not exactly in the mood for shrimp this evening. But thank you for the invitation."

Blake stole a glance at her, her reply sounding sincere, kind even. The inflection of her voice when she said she wasn't in the mood for shrimp, however, was very evident to Blake. She couldn't believe McKenna hadn't picked up on it.

"We'll hold you to that," McKenna said.

"We better get busy," Sloane said. "The suns about to wink out for the night." She retrieved the bag of shrimp from one of the coolers, gave it to McKenna, and then she and Cam carried the two coolers containing the rest of the perishables out the Arcadian door with Blake and McKenna staring after them.

"Mm, cute butt too," McKenna said when Sloane and Cam were out of earshot.

"Stop," Blake said.

"Oh, not a chance, sweetheart. I'm gonna ride this bucking bronco as long as I possibly can."

That's what I was afraid of.

Chapter Six

Cam shifted the sizable tank of the propane lamp in her arms as she followed Sloane back through the sand to her house. As she neared the house she began berating herself for always being so helpful.

Why do I do it? Why do I go the extra mile for people? People I don't even know?

Because it's who you are.

You wouldn't feel right not helping.

So suck it up and deliver the lamp.

They reached the patio and Cam saw the reason for her inner turmoil, the reason why she was suddenly questioning the very core values that made her who she was. How could a woman she'd just met be causing her to question herself? Why was she letting her?

If she'd had her way, she wouldn't have returned with the lamp, preferring instead to avoid Blake altogether. But the probability of being able to avoid Blake completely was unlikely. According to Sloane, Blake was going to be sticking around for a while, so unfortunately, she did indeed have to suck it up if she wanted to venture outside her home at all for the next few weeks. This was the perfect opportunity for her to try her hand at it. Blake was on the patio, messing with the grill.

She stopped when she heard them and hurried to open the door.

"Thanks," Sloane said as she grunted her way inside with the twin to the lamp Cam carried.

Cam was right behind her. "Thank you," she said as she walked through the door.

"No problem."

Cam paused as the familiar phrase registered. She stole a glance at Blake unsure if Blake was mocking her from their earlier exchange in town. The smug look on her face confirmed Cam's suspicion. Blake, it seemed, wanted to make sure she knew it, too.

Cam bristled, feeling the need to hold her ground. She held Blake's stare and was careful not to even blink before she walked on. Blake wasn't going to intimidate her. This beach was Cam's home. No one was going to make her feel uncomfortable here. Not even Blake. Her temporary nuisance would be like an annoying gnat is all. Gnats eventually move on. Blake would as well. Until then, there was no way she was going to get the best of Cam.

"Can you put that one on the table next to the couch, Cam?" McKenna asked, as Cam stepped inside the house and turned her attention to her. She pointed toward the living room. Cam rounded the couch and situated the lamp, turning it on to ensure it worked. The soft glow of light and the subtle hiss of the propane were oddly soothing. Her aunt and uncle had used the lamps in their home in Puerto Tranquilo when she was a child. Back before electricity was available to many of the outlying beach residents. She used to sit up at night reading when she visited her aunt and uncle, the hissing lamp her faithful companion.

"Thank you so much," McKenna said.

"Yes, thank you," Sloane said as she emerged from one of the bedrooms where she'd placed the other lamp. Cam could see the light spilling out of the doorway behind her.

"It's no trouble, really," Cam said. "You sure you don't want me to go get the other one?"

Sloane waved her off and dug in the deep pockets of her cargo shorts to retrieve the two thick candles Cam had given her. "These will work fine for tonight."

"We can rough it a little," McKenna said with a laugh. "It won't kill us. It might even be a little…romantic."

Sloane grumbled and rolled her eyes. "Only you would think that spending a night without power is romantic."

"It can be. Don't you think, Cam?"

"Uh—"

"You don't have to answer her," Sloane said.

McKenna grimaced as if she were offended and swatted Sloane's behind as she walked past her into the kitchen.

"If you change your mind, you know where to find me," Cam said, relieved at not having to discuss her opinions on romance at the moment. Especially considering her current predicament involving the woman outside.

"Is there any way I can change your mind about dinner?" McKenna asked.

"Yeah, it's the least we can do," Sloane said.

A loud curse came from Blake out on the patio. Cam could see that she was still fidgeting with the grill.

"Thanks, but no. Should you happen to need anything though, don't hesitate to come knocking."

"Actually," McKenna said as she turned and slid open a kitchen drawer. "There is one last thing you can do." She crossed to Cam and handed her a stick lighter. "You can give this to Blake on your way out. I asked her to light the grill but forgot to tell her she'd have to use the lighter. The starter switch doesn't work."

Cam took the lighter but felt her face heat slightly at the thought of having to speak with Blake. And if she wasn't mistaken, McKenna seemed to be studying her closely as if she could somehow see it.

Cam nodded, lighter in hand. "See you two tomorrow."

"Night, Cam," Sloane said.

Cam stepped onto the patio and slid the door closed. She approached Blake from behind, listening to her as she cussed at the grill.

"What the hell is wrong with this thing?" She was kneeling in front of it, messing with a red button and then the valve to the propane tank.

Cam could hear the hiss of propane, so she knew Blake had the valve open okay. When she pushed the red button to light the grill, however, it just made a clicking noise. Cam wondered how long Blake had been at it and she immediately became concerned at the amount of propane that had probably been released. Quickly, she knelt next to Blake and closed the valve.

"What are you doing?" Blake demanded as she straightened to a stand. Her eyes were fiery and full of obvious accusation and what looked to be…embarrassment.

Have I hurt her pride?

"Trying to prevent you from blowing yourself up," Cam said matter-of-factly.

Blake stammered, as if she were taken aback by her candidness. "I'm just trying to light it. I think I know what I'm doing."

Cam held up the lighter, somewhat amused that this stubborn and defiant woman seemed to be squirming a little. "McKenna forgot to tell you that the lighter on the grill doesn't work. You have to use this."

Blake squinted toward the windows like she was expecting to find McKenna standing there watching them. Cam recalled the way McKenna had been studying her a minute before and for a brief moment, she wondered the same. But there was nothing to be seen at the window. Only the reflection of the ambling sea.

Cam turned her focus back to Blake and Blake quickly tried to take the lighter from her hand. Cam pulled it away.

"You need to wait a few minutes," Cam said. "You've released too much propane."

"I realize that," Blake said with contempt, Cam obviously having insulted her intelligence. "I wasn't going to use it right away." She attempted to grab it again, but Cam wouldn't let her have it. She was agitated now and that pissed her off. She didn't do agitated anymore. But somehow Blake had brought it out in her in a matter of seconds.

"What are you doing?" Blake asked.

"Helping you," Cam said with a voice that revealed her own contempt.

"I don't need your help."

"I disagree."

"Yeah, well, I don't really care."

Blake bored a look into her eyes as they stood toe-to-toe and Cam flat out refused to look away.

How long before she finally caves and breaks eye contact?

Will it be before me? Before my mind does its damndest to tempt me into kissing those alluring lips?

Cam blinked the thoughts away, both surprised and appalled at where they'd gone. But Blake intensified things by leaning closer, as if she were taunting Cam and her refusal to look away. She leaned in a little more, their breath mingling. Seconds stretched into eternity and Cam's gaze fell unknowingly to Blake's lips. Blake seemed to have noticed before she did because she took full advantage by reaching around behind her, wrapping her fingers around the lighter and quickly snatching it away.

Cam felt the shock and betrayal wash over her face before she regained control of herself and put on a mask of indifference.

Blake gave a short, overly satisfied laugh, however, seemingly to let Cam know that she was wasting her time in her attempt to mask her feelings. Cam's agitation grew, this time with herself for being so mercurial and so easily discernible. But what soon became more unsettling to her was the way she'd felt when Blake's body had been mere inches from hers. There was something there. Something powerful. Blake had felt it too, Cam was sure of it. The tough girl act she was continuing to put on couldn't mask her feelings any more than Cam's did hers. Nevertheless, Cam continued with her act, too angry and spiteful now to give in.

"Okay then," Cam said, forcibly calm with a hint of sounding blasé. "Show me how you're going to use that to light the grill."

"What?"

She pointed to the trophy Blake was holding ceremoniously in her hand. "Go on, show me."

Blake opened the lid to the grill as if she were demonstrating the most obvious procedure in the universe. She aimed the lighter between the grates. "In here."

"Wrong."

Blake reddened beyond the pink tinge of her sunburn. "What do you mean *wrong*?"

Cam took the lighter from her and knelt. "You have to slide it into this hole near the base and then pull the trigger." She showed her, as if Blake wouldn't be able to figure out how to insert the lighter into a hole, and stood. "If you do it your way, you'll get burned."

"Fine. Thank you. I think I got it."

Cam raised an eyebrow, feeling a little better now that she'd turned the tables a little. "Do you?"

"Yes."

"You're sure you don't want me to do it?"

Blake narrowed her eyes. "I'm sure."

Cam extended her hand and opened her palm. Blake retrieved her trophy like it was highly valued property. Property that Cam had intentionally stolen.

"Then have a good night, Blake. Don't…blow yourself up."

She stepped off the patio into the sand, leaving Blake standing there with the stick lighter in hand, held like Lady Liberty's torch.

Chapter Seven

Cam slid a bottle of wine from the cooler next to her refrigerator without even checking to see what kind it was. She was unconcerned with the things she usually, and sometimes obsessively, paid mind to, like labels and flavors and aromas. She was currently seeking out the comfort the wine never failed to deliver rather than the ambiance. She was finally home for good for the evening, leaving Blake behind at Sloane's. She may have left her behind in the physical sense, but it was the emotional sense she was now concerned with. The wine, hopefully, would help with that.

After opening the bottle effortlessly, she carried it, along with a glass, into the living room. She set them on the end table, sat lotus style on the couch, and then poured herself a full glass.

The first sip tasted like the remainder of the radiant sunset she could see just outside her picture windows. She could taste each individual color as they exploded to paint her mouth just like they were painting the sky. Red, orange, and pink on her tongue. Purple on her throat, a strong finish that lingered after she swallowed. The wine was well on its way to becoming the best fucking piece of art ever created.

Painting her from head to toe.

Yes. This was what she needed.

The sips she took were too big and the time between them too short. But the warmth and wooziness that came very soon thereafter, was...bliss. She stared endlessly out at the surface of the ocean, watching as the colors of the sunset changed like a kaleidoscope. She was usually entranced by the restlessness of the water and its impressive rendering of the evening sky. But tonight the beautiful brilliance created by nature could not hold her attention. It was the beautiful woman next door who still had hold of that, whether she wanted it or not. Cam was sure it was the latter, because that was how she felt as well. But neither of them seemed to have a choice in the matter. They were under each other's skin.

Cam closed her eyes and tilted her head back. She had to think Blake away, but the task seemed impossible, despite the effects of the wine. She kept replaying their face-off on Sloane's patio and what it had felt like being that close to her. She recalled Blake's impassioned stare and the silent battle of wills it had evoked. It had caused a noticeable heaviness to the air as the unintentional chemistry between them intensified. Cam could almost imagine the tiny sparks that had been firing off all around them. Cam didn't think anything could surpass the power of that moment until Blake took the lighter from her. The way the contours of her body felt as they'd pressed against hers was something she knew she wouldn't be able to forget. Blake had unknowingly done something to her. Opened a door Cam long thought closed. It wasn't all Blake's fault. Cam had done well in shielding herself with Blake. But that stare. The longer she'd looked into her eyes, the weaker her resolve had become, eventually giving way to what Cam could only call a failure.

She blamed it on loneliness and lack of adequate time spent around beautiful, single women. Which, she had to confess, had been her own doing. And that, it seemed, had helped to keep her in that deep, dark hibernation for four years. Now that Blake had flung open the door and forced her to awaken, she was stirring back to life and stumbling some as she took her first steps back into the bright, blinding sun.

Yeah, so don't be so hard on yourself.

I just…slipped up.

Let my guard down.

Got caught up in her exquisiteness as a woman.

And, for a second, imagined she was just as exquisite on the inside as well.

And her lips, beseeching as they were, made that all too easy to do.

She refilled her glass and toasted the end of the day as the sun dipped into the sea. Night was on the prowl now, chasing away any remaining light. Bruising the sky with black and blue, allowing for only the tiniest and sharpest of diamonds to begin to wink through. It was the same process every evening and she usually watched it from start to finish. Watched as the night tried to control the relentless arrival of the stars. Only to ultimately give in in the end, too many of those damned determined diamonds to contend with. It was just easier to let them keep coming and coming, piercing their way through until the dark sky was awash in glitter.

No one has control.

Not even the night.

Something always gets through.

Good. Bad.

Doesn't matter.

Something will always find a way.

She swallowed more wine, depressed at having to forge through, what she was sure would be, another restless evening. Sleep was unlikely to come knocking. It had been bypassing her door, thumbing its nose at her off and on for a long while now. She never knew when it would choose to pay her a visit, so there was no predicting or planning of her nights. There was just acceptance and the kind assistance of the costly liquid that came in a bottle.

The wine soothed and sedated, but it did not make her sleep. She knew it had the ability, but she never drank enough to give it a chance. Drinking herself into a temporary oblivion was acceptable, necessary even. But drinking herself into a drooling coma was not. If she was going to go that route, she would've done so four years ago after—

She set the glass on the table, grabbed the remote and thumbed on the sound system. She found some music she could tolerate and traded the remote for her pen and leather bound journal. This was her daily routine, or should she say nightly ritual?

First, sunset.

Then wine.

And then, the journal.

One. Two. Three.

The only things that varied were the length of time she spent scribbling in the journal and what happened after she finally decided to give up. Those two things were as unpredictable as the taunting S.O.B. everyone else referred to as sleep.

She massaged her brow with her pen in hand, the white pages staring up at her. Oftentimes they seemed to be mocking her, daring her to tear through the cobwebs of her creative mind and rummage through tattered, dusty, unlabeled boxes and yank something, anything, old or new, out and hold it up into the light and believe in it enough to actually write it down.

But the dozens of blank pages attested to the rarity of her finding anything worth putting to paper. The endless rummaging was too exhausting. It often turned her mind to mush. So even if she did happen to find something, chances are, she might not even have the wherewithal to accurately relay it from her mind to her pen.

She took a deep breath, knowing she had to try. Before the nightly ritual with the wine, before she lost...everything, this was how she coped. This was how she got through. Thinking. Dreaming. Creating.

Writing.

She cleared her head, let the music penetrate.

An image came.

Blake.

Her instinct was to fight it, but her defenses were drunk on the wine. Finally, her faithful elixir was working.

So, she went with it.

Allowed Blake to stay.

Allowed her to speak.

Allowed herself to listen, even though she didn't like it.

She scribbled down the words. The ones Blake said and then the ones that came from her in response. Those words led to feelings. And suddenly she couldn't write fast enough. She filled one page and moved on to the next, the words flowing like a raging river. She had so much to say, so much to describe when it came to Blake.

She wrote until her hand cramped and continued through that, until the stream of words trickled to a stop.

She closed the book, feeling breathless, like she'd just flat out sprinted until her body gave out. In a way, that's what she'd done. Her mind had flat out sprinted until it gave out. And just like an unconditioned body, it hadn't been able to take her very far.

But it was a start.

It was *something.*

And now her blood was thrumming, her synapses were firing, and she was ready for another sprint. She left the wine and took the journal. She walked into her den, switched on the soft light of her desk lamp, and sat. Then she unzipped her computer case and pulled out her laptop. She had to plug it in to get it going, but once she opened it up and saw the stark white screen come to life, there was a rush of adrenaline and she could almost feel her pupils dilate as if she'd just injected a hit of something highly powerful and addictive into her veins.

Her hands hovered above the illuminated keyboard.

Blake materialized in her mind again and she began typing, pecking away madly at the keys. She realized she didn't have to reread what she'd written in the journal. There were just words there. Adjectives. Short, straightforward descriptions and depictions. Reactions and ruminations. But those words had opened the gates to the meatier goods. And now that she had access once again she was running wild, gathering all that she could like a crazed holiday shopper on Black Friday.

She kept the hurried pace up for a while, worried her access might once again be denied. Eventually though, she began to relax, growing more and more confident that the key she'd been given would continue to work from this point on. She fell into a comfortable rhythm as she created a new world. A world inspired by the woman next door. A world unlike anything she'd ever created before.

As she continued to write well into the night, the woman who'd inspired her was probably sleeping peacefully in the house next door, having no idea what she'd done.

Having no idea she'd shaken Cam back to life.

Shaken her back into existence.

Chapter Eight

The muted gray of dawn was shattered by the golden light of the rising sun as Blake slowed from her early morning run on the quiet beach. The salty air cooled her moist skin as it blew in off the sea. Her surroundings were serene, almost like a dream. A dream she couldn't yet seem to fully appreciate.

She'd pushed herself on her run, challenging herself to maintain a stride that was beyond her usual limit. Now, as she struggled to steady her breathing and calm a body that was beginning to ache, she searched for a reason for this newfound determination.

Why today of all days? The first day of her so-called relaxing vacation?

She rested her hands on her head to open her lungs and inhaled deeply as she walked along the firm, wet sand. The stabbing stitch in her chest subsided and her muscles went from burning to twitching. Those were the telltale signs she was going to be sore, and she knew she was lucky she hadn't hurt herself.

So, why did I force myself to run like the devil himself was chasing me?

A dog barked from the perimeter of the houses, slicing through the serene silence. Then another dog joined the first, and their volume increased and she realized they might be alerting to her approach. She shaded her brow and scanned the homes. She was nearing Sloane's, which was only three houses away. A tiny thought pricked her brain. Cam's house was just ahead. She had to pass it to get to Sloane's. She'd ignored its presence altogether when she'd set out on her run earlier. She hadn't given Cam or her home a second thought, or a second glance.

Two dogs appeared in the soft sand ahead. Their tails swished back and forth in excitement. She headed up the slight incline, warming at the prospect of petting them. She hadn't had the chance to interact with a dog in months, and she couldn't help but feel as excited as they seemed to be as she approached. Her own dog, Rascal, had been taken by her former girlfriend, Felicia, when she'd up and left. They'd adopted Rascal, an adorable brown terrier mix, together and she'd honestly been more heartbroken at the loss of him than she was over Felicia.

Guess that says it all.

The dogs standing in front of her looked to be border collie mixes. One was black and tan, the other a red and white. They remained where they were, waiting for her to come to them, something she found unusual. Most dogs would've already bounded up to her.

"Hey, guys," she said as she reached them. She held her hand out for them to sniff. They licked her enthusiastically but they didn't jump up on her and they didn't overwhelm her. They just bounced in place. "You're very polite," she said, noticing their leather collars and dangling ID charms. "Extremely polite. Someone has taught you manners." She knelt and massaged their fur. They were both clean and smelled as if they'd recently been shampooed. "Yes, someone loves you very much. Where are they, huh? Where's your owner?"

She'd yet to see another soul on the beach thus far that morning, and she hoped the dogs weren't wandering around unsupervised.

"Boys, come," a smooth voice said.

Blake perked, along with the dogs. She stood and the dogs took off, racing through the sand to join another similar looking black and tan dog whom they greeted affectionately. Then the three of them turned and trotted to the one who'd called for them.

Blake felt her smile fall.

Cam.

At once, the reason she had been searching for, the one spurring her newborn need to test her limits, became clear.

It wasn't the devil she'd been running from.

It was Cam.

After all, she was the one who'd kept her up all night, tossing and turning, unable to settle enough to sleep. She was the one relentlessly infiltrating her mind, with her caustic but well-composed and calmly delivered words. Along with her enigmatic stare and her dangerously enticing looks.

"I hope they didn't bother you," Cam said in that same infuriating easy manner of hers. It quickly and effectively smothered Blake's rising temper though, as well as the fury she'd felt as soon as she'd realized that it had done so.

Blake's bite was disabled and it had been done so effortlessly by the woman standing barefoot in front of her, wearing an unassuming outfit of gray, frayed cotton capris and a white, soft-looking shirt that showed off her forearms thanks to her having pushed the sleeves up. The wind tousled her hair, but it couldn't seem to cause the chaos it was intending. Because when it finally gave up and stopped, she looked the same. Casual. Natural. As if she'd just stepped out of bed, slipped on some clothes she had strewn over a chair, ran her fingers through her hair, and walked outside looking infallibly perfect. As if she never gave her appearance a second thought.

Blake wanted to be envious. Jealous even.

But she was too enraptured by her unintentional perfection. Too moved by her mere existence.

She didn't know a woman like that walked the face of the earth. A woman who not only didn't seem to care about her looks but had absolutely no need or reason to.

"They're not used to someone being on the beach so early," Cam said.

She sounded clueless to Blake's analysis of her.

She just stood there, hands in her pockets, looking so relaxed and carefree, almost like she had no bones to rigid her body, and Blake wondered if she might just suddenly ooze down into the sand. The dogs sat at her feet, tongues out, tails sweeping the sand, gazing up at her, as if they, too, were mesmerized by her tranquility.

"They didn't bother me," Blake finally said, walking once again toward Sloane's, which also meant she was headed for Cam. "They're cute and very well-mannered."

"They didn't scare you, then?"

"Oh, no. They were perfect gentlemen. And besides, I'm not afraid of dogs. I—love them, actually." She was contemplative as she smiled.

Cam studied her and Blake thought she saw something different in her eyes. A surfacing curiosity perhaps, like she wanted to ask her something. But the return of the breeze seemed to have blown it away.

"They know better than to leave the patio without permission. So, rest assured, I'll make sure they don't disturb you again."

"No," Blake said. "There's no need to—they didn't bother me."

"Even so I can't have them running after people, barking like that." She whistled and the dogs followed on her heels as she climbed the few steps to her patio.

Blake felt a sense of loss at her absence and she almost called out to her, to somehow bring her back. But she caught herself and watched her go, taking the opportunity to look beyond her to examine the details of her house without her being aware. It was a Spanish style bungalow with a flat roof with red tile. The stuccoed walls were painted a shade of rose, and the patio in which Cam was now standing had a large arched entry with two more arches on both the left and right perpendicular sides allowing for full view of the entire beach. The waist-high wall enclosing the patio was covered in colorful decorative tile that matched the Spanish flair of the home. It really was quite impressive. A lot of time and energy had gone into every detail. Were the decorative tiles hand painted? They were beautiful and set off the deep green fabric of the patio chairs.

Sloane had said that Cam's home wasn't much larger than the one they were in, but that it was a lot nicer due to all the renovating. Apparently, Cam had done all of that renovating herself. Blake had overheard all this as she'd gotten ready for bed the night before. The wall separating the bedrooms was thin, something she'd been reminded of again a couple of hours later when she heard the unmistakable giggles and sighs of love making. In regard to what she'd heard about Cam, she'd tried not to allow any of it to remain in the forefront of her mind as she'd crawled into bed. But despite those efforts, Cam came to her all night long, insisting on being the center of her thoughts just like she'd insisted on "helping" her light the grill. Blake had never encountered someone so self-righteous and rude.

She kept her attention on Cam, searching for any sign of the boorishness she'd displayed previously. But Cam seemed calm, at ease. Not at all bothered by the fact that Blake could possibly be watching her. She settled into one of those dark green, thickly cushioned chairs, propped her feet up on a matching ottoman, and crossed her ankles. The dogs rested beside her and she scratched their heads and spoke to them before she leaned back and reached for a hardbound book.

Blake tried not to stare, but she was bewildered by her reading and suddenly very curious about her, wanting to know why she was up so early, what it was she was reading and what kinds of things, other than reading and home renovation, she found interesting.

She'd thought she'd had her pegged just by her interactions with her the day before. But now she was questioning her judgment.

Have I missed something?

Could there be more to her than the brutish behavior and irritating apathy I saw yesterday?

She wasn't sure.

But she'd be damned before she'd make an effort to try to find out.

Some stones were better left unturned, regardless of their appeal.

CHAPTER NINE

B lake combed her wet hair in front of the bathroom mirror. She'd just showered, quite quickly, since they had a limited supply of water. Which, according to Sloane, was delivered by truck weekly. Nevertheless, she felt clean and refreshed from her morning run, even if she was already beginning to feel stiff and sore.

"Hey, look at you." McKenna was in the doorway, arms crossed, devilish grin on her face. "Already up and at 'em and pretty as a peach."

Blake rolled her eyes and secured the towel around her body. "Yeah, I'm a real stunner. Total heart stopper with my wet head, makeup-free face and old beach towel wrapped around me."

"I know someone who might think so."

Blake scoffed. "Don't even. And no, she would not think so. Trust me on that."

"I don't know, Blake," she said, her voice growing higher. "She sure seemed interested yesterday when Sloane and I told her all about you."

"What?" Blake fumbled with her toothbrush as she turned to look at her. Then, just as quickly, she tried to downplay her reaction. "Oh. She was probably just being nice. But when, exactly was this?"

McKenna seemed amused and Blake cursed herself for asking.

"Mm, I don't remember exactly. Sometime yesterday."

"Like when I was screwing around with that damn grill? Thanks for that, by the way. Setting me up by sending me out there knowing good and well I wouldn't be able to get it to work without the lighter. I know you did it on purpose."

"I had to do something to get the two of you alone together. And she seemed more than willing to help when I eventually pointed out my absentmindedness."

Blake brushed past her, angry in hearing firsthand that McKenna had purposely intended for Cam and her to interact alone, and in remembering just how fierce that interaction had been.

She entered the bedroom she was staying in and dug through her clothes in the dresser drawer. McKenna followed and hovered in the doorway.

"Just what, pray tell, happened out there on the patio last night? Seemed pretty intense from the little that I saw."

"Little you saw? You're saying you didn't spy on us and overhear every word we said? I find that hard to believe."

"No, Sloane and I retreated to the bedroom and did some unpacking."

"Yeah, right."

"So something did happen."

"As if I'd tell you." She started shoving clothes aside, frustrated that she couldn't seem to find anything she wanted to wear.

"Why not?"

"And reward your behavior? Nuh-uh. Don't think so."

"Okay, smarty-pants. Then I won't tell you what was said to Cam about you. Nor what all she seemed interested in knowing."

Blake shook her head. Laughed. "Wicked, wicked woman." She grabbed a lavender T-shirt and a pair of gray sweat shorts and tossed them on the bed. Then she slammed the drawer and opened another for panties, but chose to forego the bra. What was a vacation good for without a little freedom? "But I'm not falling for it. Not going to rise to the bait." She shrugged. "Because I couldn't care less."

"Uh-huh," McKenna said. "I can tell. You seem very calm about the whole thing and completely in control." She leaned against the dresser as Blake turned from her to drop her towel and dress. "So, I guess I'll leave you to it then. Just leave you to dress without telling you what all I learned about Cam. Seeing as how you don't care and all."

Blake paused.

Know about Cam? She hadn't mentioned she had info on Cam. But really, what all could she possibly know?

She glanced over her shoulder. "Fine, whatever."

"Okay."

"Yep, okay."

"Okay, well, seeing as how you're already showered and dressed, you can be the one to go over to Cam's to get the food for breakfast."

Blake whipped around in her T-shirt and panties. "Wha—no. Oh, no. No way. You're not doing that to me. I'm not going to be a pawn in your little game."

"If you truly don't care, Blake, then it shouldn't be an issue for you to go over there, should it?"

Blake clamped her mouth closed.

Damn you, Kenna. You wicked, wicked woman. Clever as hell, you are.

"Okay, fine. I'll go. But she may not be up yet, she—" But McKenna cut her off in the midst of her attempt to fib.

"Oh, I'm sure she is. See, that's one of the things I learned about her. She gets up before sunrise. Doesn't sleep very well apparently, and seeing the sunrise every morning has become something she looks forward to."

"Why doesn't she sleep—?" The question slipped out before she could catch it, which only seemed to please McKenna.

"So, anyway, she should be up." She started to walk away. "Don't be too much longer changing outfits and what not, worrying about how you look. I'm hungry."

"I'm not going to change—" But she glanced back at the bed at her sweat shorts and then down at her chest. She needed the bra.

Damn.

She started tugging off her shirt. "I'm ready."

But McKenna was gone. Blake hurriedly put on a bra, slipped her shirt back on and pulled on a different, albeit nicer pair of shorts, hoping McKenna wouldn't notice. Then she rushed into the bathroom and frowned at her hair and the dark circles beneath her eyes. But she couldn't primp, because she didn't care, right?

Who cares what a woman I hardly know thinks anyway?

She ran some mousse through her hair, tousled and crimped it with her hands, and then headed for the back door where she was faced with another decision.

Shoes or no shoes? If she wore shoes it may imply that she'd put forethought into her visit, something she didn't want Cam assuming. The shoes would also undoubtedly fill with sand and she really hated the way those minuscule grains ground their way into the soles of her feet.

She looked to McKenna who was sitting at the kitchen table, staring out at the sea.

"Do you think I should wear—?"

McKenna looked at her, waiting for her to finish.

"Never mind." She opened the door and crossed the patio in her bare feet. She walked through the deep sand to Cam's while repeating a mantra in her mind.

She's just a neighbor.

Just a person, like anyone else.

Though the words replayed on a continuous loop, sometimes even coming out upon whispers, they weren't able to stop the acceleration of her pulse as she neared the steps to Cam's patio. By the time she was standing at their base, staring up at the small, framed, Mexican art hanging between the two large windows, her heart was thudding harder than it had during her morning run.

She scanned the remainder of the space, took in the raw wood of the rustic accent tables, the rug with the elaborate Aztec design, the lush plants in terra-cotta pots in the corners. They were beautiful details that her mind was absorbing but she knew she wouldn't be able to process them properly until later. Right now she was too overloaded with anxiousness to do anything but struggle with the next insurmountable decision.

Should I call out to her from here or walk up onto the patio?

Why aren't the dogs barking? Haven't they seen me yet?

Should I wait for them to see me or should I knock on the door?

Normally, she'd have no issue whatsoever in bounding up to someone's patio to knock on their door. But with Cam it was different. She wasn't sure she was welcome. She took a tentative step up, then another, until she stood quietly on the rug. She waited. Listened. Noted the unusual designs of patina copper in the framed wall art.

But as far as movement from inside the house, there was nothing.

She looked at the large windows, wondering if Cam was watching her from behind the reflective glass. Watching her as she had a full-blown anxiety attack on her Aztec rug. The thought of that made her swallow down the ball of fear wedged in her throat and cross to the wood door where she knocked.

The dogs barked immediately but they didn't sound close. With every passing second, however, their barks grew louder. She snuck a look through the window in the door and saw them running toward her.

She spoke to them, unable to resist, expecting their excitement to cease at any moment with a command from Cam. But that didn't happen.

Is she not home?

She hadn't even thought to check for her vehicle before she'd come. Her stomach dropped, like she'd just plummeted down the steep hill of a rollercoaster. It wasn't a reaction she'd experienced before and it definitely didn't feel anything like relief in not having to face her. Which, if anything, she surmised, was what she should be feeling.

No, this was different. This was more like...

Disappointment.

But not just any ordinary sense of disappointment. This was stronger, deeper.

She felt it in her gut.

She turned to walk away, realizing just how badly she'd wanted to see her, to once again engage with her. She was confused by that and embarrassed. Embarrassed at her own feelings. She hadn't seen them clearly until now and that worried her. Another thing that worried her was her apparent inability to control them.

The dogs stopped barking behind her, but she assumed it was because she was leaving. She was just about to descend the steps when she heard the soft click of the door opening and a voice. A smooth, familiar voice.

CHAPTER TEN

"Not even going to stick around to get the last word in this time before you walk away?" the voice said.

Blake stiffened. Her heart froze mid-beat and flames shot to her face and scorched her skin.

She turned, ready to snap back at her, to bite into her good and hard, but she saw a grin on Cam's barely visible face. Not a snide grin, a playful one, and it knocked Blake off balance as she searched for an appropriate reply.

"I came for breakfast."

She inwardly cringed at her own statement and fought palming her forehead.

"For food, I mean—McKenna is hungry."

Can I sound any more pathetic?

Cam didn't respond right away. But she looked at her in a way that suggested she was doing more than just trying to make sense of her presence. After a few long seconds, she stepped back and eased the door open.

"Come on in," she said from behind the door.

Blake remained where she was, the invitation to enter her home completely unexpected. She'd been prepared for having to see her and speak to her. That however, was as far as she'd gone in her mind. She'd imagined Cam simply bringing the items she requested to her at the threshold.

This…she wasn't prepared.

She was barefoot and felt awkward. And the invitation felt too familiar. Like they were actually friends and she'd just stopped by unannounced to borrow some sugar.

The dogs came to her, tails fanning the air, ears back. They, too, were welcoming her, encouraging her to come inside.

"You coming?" Cam asked, peeking at her.

Blake followed the dogs and entered. She was almost completely caught up in the home's decor, as well as the exposed beams of the ceiling, when she glanced back at Cam as she closed the door behind them.

Blake was so struck by what she saw she felt both stupefied and electrified all at once. She hadn't thought being unable to see Cam fully from outside was anything to be concerned about.

She was wrong.

If she had seen her, there was no way she would've come in.

No freaking way.

Because Cam was…she was…

Wet.

Her hair, her skin. Probably every last inch of her. Even the little of her that was covered by a body-clinging, blue satin robe. And judging by the way she smelled, like she'd literally bathed in seduction itself, Blake guessed she'd just emerged from the shower.

"I didn't mean to disturb you," she said, heart flip-flopping in her chest like a fish out of water.

"You didn't." She breezed past her and Blake had the urge to close her eyes and stand there in her wake just inhaling the scent of her. "I had just finished when I heard the dogs."

Blake helplessly followed her farther in and she managed to tear her eyes away from her to take in the living room on the left. A huge stone fireplace on the far end drew her eye first. Walls painted a weathered coral color enclosed the rest of the room and they were adorned with more beautiful artwork. Some of it similar to the patina copper artwork she'd seen outside. A sizable leather sofa the color of dark chocolate faced the fireplace, and a matching chair was angled toward the hearth nearby. The tables in the room were bigger than the ones outside and the tobacco colored stain on the wood appeared to be hand rubbed, giving it the rustic look that seemed to be the theme of the house. The Navajo rug centered on the wood floor was beautiful and vibrant, the colors in it brought out by the coral painted walls, the artwork and the throw pillows on the couch.

A smaller adjacent room was to her right. It was painted a light yellow and housed similar rustic wood furniture. There was a bookshelf that spanned one wall, containing dozens of books and decorative knickknacks. There was a desk with an amber-shaded lamp and a leather chair the same color as the terra cotta pots outside sitting by the window. But her eyes were drawn back to the living room. She imagined sinking into the cushions of the couch, curling up with a glass of deliciously wonderful wine while basking in the hypnotizing heat of that fireplace. And possibly…basking in the heat of Cam's stare from the other side of the couch.

Stop it.

You can't do this.

Remember she's just a person.

A person who just happens to be a gorgeous, wet, and heavenly smelling woman, scantily clad in a rather revealing robe that only covers her to mid-thigh.

"Feel free to sit," Cam said. She'd bypassed the living room and was now at the brink of the kitchen. She'd turned to face Blake and appeared to have caught her staring longingly at the sofa.

"Oh, no thanks. I just came to get the food and I'll let you get back to your day." Blake's gaze fell to Cam's bare legs, the short length of the robe a cruel ruse. She didn't linger in her appraisal though, reminding herself that Cam was watching her and that she wouldn't cross that line with her, regardless of how divine her tanned, lean-muscled legs were. Even if they were still glistening with the moisture from her shower and probably as soft and as smooth as the very satin of her robe.

She trailed her eyes back up and found Cam looking at her as if she'd not only seen her visually devour her legs, but also had heard her thoughts about them as well. But she didn't acknowledge any of it and her expression changed to one which suggested she'd only been perceiving Blake as a moron.

"I can give you the food, no problem. It's just right behind me in the fridge." She stood still, as if waiting for Blake to say something.

"Okay," Blake said, drawing the word out to show her confusion. "That would be fine."

"It would be, under normal circumstances, yes. But…"

"But…" Blake said, searching her face for any sort of clue as to what she might be missing.

"Unless something has changed since the last I spoke to Sloane, then my giving you the food would be pointless."

"Pointless?"

What the hell is she getting at? And why won't she stop staring at me with those eyes that are as dark and dreamy as a moonless night sky?

"You don't have any way to cook the food."

Blake flushed so hard she almost grew dizzy from the heat.

McKenna. Fucking McKenna.

She sent me over here knowing that. But I was so busy trying to act like I didn't care about Cam that I didn't even think about it.

And now, I look like an idiot. Kenna got what she wanted, but I end up looking like a fool.

She's a dead woman.

D-E-A-D.

Blake's mind flew, desperate for a way, any way, to save face.

"We have the grill," she said.

Cam's eyebrow lifted.

Yeah. The grill. Good one.

"So, if you'll just kindly give me the food, I can be on my way."

Cam shrugged. "Okay then."

She opened the fridge and Blake heard her slide open a drawer as she purposely averted her gaze, knowing how dangerous it would be for her to see Cam bend over to retrieve the items from the fridge. She was already embarrassed, and she wasn't about to ogle the woman any further.

Cam turned, eggs, bacon, and orange juice in hand, and pushed the door closed with her hip. She put the goods in plastic grocery bags before carrying them over to Blake. She held them out with a sly smile.

"Enjoy your breakfast."

"Thank you." Blake gave her the biggest, fakest smile she could manage and walked back to the patio door. The view of the ocean through the large windows was spectacular and she lost her breath momentarily before regaining her composure, pushing yet another longing from her mind. This one had her curled up on the sofa in the evening, turned toward the window, taking in that vast view of the ocean as the colors of the sunset danced along the surface of the water. Only this time Cam wasn't sitting at the other end of the sofa. She was nestled behind her, holding her in her arms.

Blake was glad she didn't have to face Cam again as she left. She was certain she'd be able to see that longing in her eyes. The longing she hated to admit was there.

She left the dogs behind and hurried down the steps, through the sand back to Sloane's. When she entered the house, she found Sloane and McKenna locked in an embrace in the kitchen, kissing and laughing softly. They glanced over at her in surprise and McKenna's surprise seemed to double when she saw the bags.

"You got the food," she said.

Sloane looked confused and Blake guessed McKenna hadn't yet let her in on her little morning plot to get Blake and Cam alone together again.

"We can't cook it, B," Sloane said.

"I'm going to cook it on the grill." She felt pretty proud of herself. She'd found a solution and it was one in which McKenna couldn't claim total victory. Blake wasn't about to reveal how embarrassing and heart-stopping her visit to Cam's had been. Nuh-uh. She was just going to act peachy keen and cook breakfast on a pan on the grill.

Sloane pinched the bridge of her nose and the sigh she let out smashed Blake's redemptive mood to pieces.

"I don't think there's enough propane left to do that."

Blake's arms grew suddenly weak.

"There wasn't that much to begin with, and after dinner last night, and how long it took to light the grill and cook and everything, I'd be very surprised if there was any left at all."

"There's more, though. Right? In the garage? You have another tank."

"The guy who brings it comes on Tuesdays. I wasn't planning on having to need any before then."

"We should try though," Blake said. "I bet I can cook quickly enough." She started to walk into the kitchen, fiercely determined to make it work. Whatever it took.

"Blake, stop," Sloane said softly. "Don't waste food trying. We can make do with juice and granola bars for now. Cam's friend will be here soon to check on the electricity. Let's just wait and go from there."

"But I—"

"Just take the food back. Maybe we'll be able to cook it later. Have breakfast for lunch if you want."

Blake stammered. Blinked. All in an attempt to plead with her friends. But she could come up with nothing and they didn't seem to understand.

At last, she gave up and nodded. But there was one thing she wouldn't give in to. One thing she wouldn't do.

"You guys can take the food back. I'm going to go lie down."

"Okay," Sloane said, concern furrowing her brow. "We'll try to keep it down."

"No need," Blake said. "I'm not going to be in here." She grabbed a beach towel off one of the living room chairs and slid the back door open. She headed down to the beach where she was going to lie under the big, blue sky, close her eyes and let the sunshine and the hypnotic sound of the breaking waves take her away.

Chapter Eleven

T he woman?" Tomas asked, practicing his English as he often did with Cam while they finished up in Sloane's garage. They'd just reset the breaker for the fifth time after having gone back and forth from the house unplugging numerous appliances. "From the market?"

Cam nodded and he scratched his head as she explained.

"She's staying here with her friends. She's on vacation."

"Where is she?"

Cam shrugged. "I don't know. Maybe she's out on the beach." They hadn't seen Blake at all as they'd worked on Sloane's electrical problem. McKenna had also been absent.

"Is she...angry?"

Cam laughed. "Like she was yesterday? Not exactly. But she wouldn't have my vote for personality of the year."

He seemed confused by the statement but he moved on.

"But she is here? Next to you? Ay, Dios mío."

"Tell me about it." Cam closed the door to the breaker box and wiped the dust from her hands, hoping this was the last trip to the garage. Tomas had arrived at her house that morning thinking he was there to do a job for her. But he'd readily agreed to do what he could for Sloane as soon as Cam relayed the situation. He was one of those people who could fix just about anything having to do with construction or home repair. In fact, she'd learned most of what she knew from him. She kept encouraging him to start his own business, so he could give up having to fish with his brother during the season and focus on contract work full-time. But to date, he hadn't seemed to take her advice.

He patted her shoulder like he was offering condolences as they went back inside the house. Sloane met them just inside the door looking apprehensive.

"Give it a try," Cam said.

Sloane flipped the switch for the entryway light and beamed when it came on, and more importantly, stayed on. "It works!" She scurried to try the lights in the kitchen and living room. "Everything works!"

She returned to Tomas and pumped his hand vigorously. "You're a real lifesaver, my friend. How much do I owe you? Name your price. I'll give you just about anything. Money, kidney, anything."

He laughed and looked down as he shifted his feet. Cam could tell he was a little embarrassed at her enthusiastic gratitude, despite not understanding some of it.

"Nada," he said. He held up his palm. "Is not necessary."

Sloane looked at Cam.

"He just saved my entire stay and he doesn't want anything for it?"

"No," Tomas said, waving his hand. "No charge." He glanced at Cam and spoke to her in Spanish.

"You're my neighbor," she said to Sloane after he'd finished. "And my friend. So, he says there's no charge."

He touched Cam's arm and said something more, but she didn't want to repeat it.

Tomas slapped her arm with the back of his hand, demanding that she do so.

"What is it?" Sloane asked.

"He says he hopes it will make things right with your friend."

"My friend?"

Cam avoided her gaze. "Blake."

"Blake?"

"He—we—" Cam started. She took a moment to gather her thoughts.

She tried again. "Blake bought shrimp from him yesterday in town and she got upset because he didn't have any of the brown shrimp left. So, this is his way of trying to make things right with her."

Sloane seemed contemplative. "Yeah, Kenna finally filled me in on the fish market drama last night. We feel partly responsible. Blake was following Kenna's instructions and she's a very loyal friend who always does her very best to help. But sometimes she—she's a very determined woman and she doesn't like to disappoint. I apologize. For her, and for Kenna and me."

"Is okay. No problems," Tomas said.

"All right then. I'll be sure to let Blake know of your generosity."

"That's not really necessary," Cam interjected. She did not want the fish market can of worms reopened. "As long as you know why he—"

Tomas slapped her arm again. Hard.

She winced. "Okay, okay. Yes, please let her know if you would."

"You got it," Sloane said and she opened the back door for them, allowing Tomas to exit first. When Cam tried to leave, she stopped her with a soft hand to her forearm.

"What about you, Cam? Can you forgive her?"

"Pardon?" Cam tried to hide her stupor at being asked such a direct question.

"She's not a bad person," Sloane said. "Surely you've realized that by now."

"I don't really know her."

Yes, I do. She's stubborn and willful and prideful. She blushes profusely when she's angry or embarrassed.

And I do seem to know how to push her buttons.

"After some of the things we talked about last night, I'd say you know more than you think you do. Why don't you come over, spend some time with us, with Blake? I think you'll be pleasantly surprised."

Cam was so uncomfortable she was about to crawl out of her skin. She didn't like being cornered and put on the spot. And she didn't understand why Sloane was pushing Blake at her so hard. She'd mentioned that Blake was single when they'd gone to get the propane lamps the night before, and then more than insinuated her need for a girlfriend when Cam feigned polite interest to cover her surprise at the lack of concern over the fish market incident. Which Sloane never did bring up, choosing instead to ask Cam a few questions about herself. But Cam had passed that whole thing off as just an innocent attempt on Sloane's part to try to set her friend up.

Now, however, Cam could see that there was obviously something more to that attempt than she'd initially realized given what Sloane just said. Whatever it was, she wanted no part of it. "I'm pretty busy with my work."

Sloane dropped her hand from the door. "Not interested, huh? I had hoped the things I shared with you about Blake might cause you to feel differently. But, hey, if the magic isn't there, it isn't there, right?"

Magic? No, there's no magic. There's something there, I'll give you that, but it isn't magical or fantastical like some feel-good fairy tale. It's ardent and agonizing. Fervent and emphatic. To put it bluntly, it's maddening, and the things you said about her haven't helped with that in any way whatsoever.

Cam wanted to say it all aloud, but she was aware of the dichotomy of her feelings and any mention of the physical attraction she felt for Blake, maddening or not, would only encourage Sloane to keep pushing.

They stepped outside and Sloane once again focused on Tomas, offering him again some sort of payment for his help. But Tomas only smiled and politely declined. Then he and Cam turned to leave but were stopped abruptly by Blake as she tried to enter the patio.

Cam was jolted and immediately frustrated at her unexpected arrival. But those feelings quickly became trivial as Blake's appearance took precedence, rendering Cam speechless. She was wearing a bright yellow string bikini top, which left very little to the imagination due to her ample breasts, and a pair of very thin, very small, knit shorts. Her skin shimmered with coconut scented suntan lotion, which struck Cam considerably as she tried to control her breathing. Blake's fit body, particularly her muscles, only added to Cam's breathing troubles. They were so tight and carefully carved they rippled beneath her enticing skin at the slightest of movements.

Cam eased on her sunglasses to conceal the hunger she feared was apparent in her stare. Blake, however, did the opposite and pulled hers from her face. She looked at both her and Tomas in what could only be disbelief.

"Hola, miss," Tomas said. He sounded nervous and Cam waited to see how Blake would respond.

Blake's pink lips parted, and she seemed to be struggling in making sense of the scene before her. Tomas's presence was probably more confusing than it was shocking.

"Hello," she finally said to Tomas. "I—wasn't expecting to see you again—so soon."

McKenna walked up behind her, dressed similarly to Blake, only her bikini was red and she was covered in an open, light cotton robe that came to rest just below her hips.

"Hi, I'm McKenna. You must be the man we've been anxiously waiting for." She shook Tomas's hand.

"Tomas," he said.

Blake suddenly came to life and stuck out her own hand. "I'm so sorry, Tomas. I should've introduced myself. I'm Blake. It's nice to meet you."

Tomas shook her hand and Cam saw him begin to relax a little as he smiled. Cam searched for any sign that Blake was being disingenuous, but found nothing.

"Electricity's fixed!" Sloane said peeking between Cam and Tomas. "He fixed it. It was that old microwave your aunt gave us. It was faulty. All we had to do was unplug it. Can you believe it?"

McKenna shrieked and embraced Tomas, surprising him. But she didn't seem to notice or care. "Thank you! We were worried we were going to have to pack up and leave."

"He saved our asses," Sloane said. "And he did it for free. For Blake."

All eyes fell on Blake and hers widened.

"Me? Why?"

"He wants to make things right with you," Sloane said. "From your er…unfortunate encounter at the fish market."

"Oh." She touched her cheeks as if she were remembering what had transpired between them in town. "That's really very kind of you,

Tomas, but it isn't necessary. I—I'm the one who should apologize. I was out of line and I wasted so much of your time. I'm sorry I was such a cranky, crazy customer."

"Is good," Tomas said.

Blake smiled.

McKenna stepped away from the patio, allowing Tomas to exit. She palmed his cheek as she slipped past him. "If you won't let us pay you, why don't you two at least join us for lunch?"

"We still have some things to take care of over at my place," Cam said, eyeing Tomas, silently encouraging him to agree. She kept her gaze on him even after he complied, so she wouldn't look at Blake and see her piercing stare and her sun-pinked skin, which not only still shimmered, but smelled so good it had Cam obsessing over piña coladas, curious to know if one would taste anywhere near as good as she was sure Blake's skin would.

I need to get home and get busy and get away from this woman.

But will staying busy really keep the vision of her in that bikini out of my mind?

I'll have to work twenty-four seven.

"Another raincheck?" McKenna asked Cam as she wrapped her arm around Sloane and rested her head on her shoulder.

"Yes, another time." *And in another universe.*

They said their good-byes and Cam tried to exit the patio. But she did so at the same time as Blake tried to enter. They both paused, mumbled apologies, and tried again, but they did the same thing, mirroring each other's movements.

McKenna and Sloane laughed.

"You two ought to dance together," McKenna said. "You'd make quite the pair."

Cam tried to laugh to show her good humor but she couldn't. The best she could do was offer a strained smile.

"I don't dance," she said.

She took a huge sidestep and Blake edged past her, staring into her as if the sunglasses on her face didn't exist. "Me neither."

"Well, I hate to tell ya, but you just did," Sloane said. "And it looked pretty damn good."

Cam walked out into the sand without looking back, thinking about that old saying. About how looks can be deceiving. She now fully understood the meaning behind that phrase and she thoroughly agreed. Looks really *can* be deceiving. In more ways than one.

She joined Tomas who had stopped to wait for her. He grinned as they made their way back to her place.

"She's pretty, mi amiga. Very pretty."

"I hadn't noticed."

He threw his head back and laughed like that was the funniest thing he'd ever heard. Then he patted her shoulder again and said, "Okay, Santi, if you say so."

It seemed Tomas was coming to understand some old sayings himself.

Chapter Twelve

Cam set the glass of white wine on the table and then settled into her favorite patio chair. She kicked her feet up onto the ottoman and snuggled into her lightweight hoodie against the late evening breeze. She loved this time of year, when the evenings cooled and the beach grew quiet, as if it, like many of its seasonal inhabitants, was unwinding from a long hot summer.

The change in mood was in the air, for she too, had the inclination to rest with the oncoming of fall. She had to remind herself that she could appreciate it now, instead of dreading it like she had as a kid when she had to leave her aunt and uncle's house to return to school. She remembered how she used to cry in her bed at night those last few days in Mexico, not wanting to leave her aunt and uncle's warm home and the seaside town she'd come to love. She'd wanted more than anything to be able to call that place her home. But home for her had been a five-hour drive north to Phoenix, where she'd lived alone with her father. It hadn't been much of a home at all. There had been no warmth, no good, hearty humor and affectionate embraces like she experienced in Mexico. There had only been indifference. And sometimes, there hadn't even been that.

She sipped the cold wine and tried to swallow down the memories of her father, who had, according to him, been very decent in that he kept a roof over her head and food on the table and clothes on her back. According to him, she should've been grateful. She should've shown him more respect and thanked him for what he provided. Problem was, that even if she had felt like she owed him those things, he wasn't ever around to hear her express them. Their only source of communication most days had been hand-scribbled notes left for her on the kitchen table when she came out for breakfast before school. Notes that had informed her that he wouldn't be home for dinner, or sometimes even at all, and that food for sandwiches was in the fridge, or that she was to use the ten he had left to purchase the food herself on her way home from school.

He'd never left a location or a number where he could be reached or a number for her to call someone else should she need to.

He had just…left.

That had been his idea of decent parenting.

But she supposed she'd have rather lived with him than her mother. She'd seen Cam as more of an obligation, or honestly, just a big pain in her ass, as opposed to her child. Cam had interfered with her lifestyle, with her wandering, wild ways. And though she'd never been cruel or abusive, she'd never been deeply committed to the limited love and affection she did show her. The cruelty, that had been her stepfather's department. He, unlike her mother, did not hesitate to voice his resentment of her for dampening their parade. He'd wanted her mother all to himself and Cam had been a roadblock, a hindrance when it came to him carrying out those intentions. He did not want her there.

So he'd done what he could to make Cam miserable. The yelling and cursing had been bad, and so had the constant criticism and unjust punishments. But those hadn't bothered her like the pinching had. Every time he'd gotten upset with her, he'd pinched her. His favorite place had been the back of her arm where he'd squeeze her flesh and pull her around, yanking her along to wherever it was he wanted to take her while she cried in agony, her arms often so sore and tender she'd howl at the slightest touch. When the bruises would begin to appear, he'd go for her sides, just below her ribs. And he'd done it all right under her mother's nose. Granted, the both of them had usually been drunk or high, or more often than not, both, and Cam wondered, even back then, if either of them really knew what it was they were doing to her. Her stepfather would inflict his anger and cruelty, her mother would promptly ignore it, and then they'd either carry on in their daze until they either passed out in front of her or left to go party elsewhere.

Eventually, Cam's aunt Ginger, her mother's sister, took notice during a visit to Phoenix and she'd stepped in and taken Cam from her mother's residence. She'd wanted to raise Cam herself in Mexico, but Cam's father had refused. So, Cam had moved in with him in that quiet, cold house and her mother had moved to the Northwest somewhere with her stepfather. Cam would hear from her every couple of years when a postcard would arrive in the mail, letting her know which state or which country she was in at the time. But eventually, they'd stopped coming and Cam, by that point, had hardly noticed.

She drank more wine and stared off into the hazy, pink-and-orange-striped sky, the sun halfway submerged into the ocean as it bid her a good night. It never got old. Watching the sun rise and set. It had helped her get through the aching bright light of the long endless days and the painful deep darkness of the long endless nights. Without the promise of those beautifully painted skies, she wasn't sure if she would've made it, if she would've been able to continue. Sometimes she still wondered how she'd done it, how she'd made it through at all.

The dogs lifted their heads at her feet, ears at attention. Byron stood first and trotted to the edge of the stairs. He barked once. A single, loud alert. Then the other two joined him, giving short, raucous barks with their tails swinging boisterously.

Cam lowered her glass from her lips and followed their line of sight. A woman wearing a ball cap with a white sweater and gray leggings was walking along the water's edge, just to the left of the house, aiming for the sunset. Cam watched her for a moment, trying to see if she knew her, but the ball cap hid her hair and her features. Cam started to return her gaze to the setting sun, but the dogs went nuts, forcing her to take a closer look at the approaching figure.

The woman, who must've been alarmed by the barking of the dogs, glanced up the beach at Cam. Then she quickly refocused on the sand at her feet, pulling off her cap to thread her hand through her thick hair, smoothing it back from her face, before tugging the cap back on.

"Blake," Cam whispered. The hair, the face, the body, she recognized it all now, and apparently, so had the dogs. They yipped and whined, and just as Cam was commanding them to calm down, they took off toward the water, tearing through the sand, making a beeline for Blake.

"Shit." Cam scrambled from the chair and rushed down the steps in her bare feet. She whistled for the dogs, but they were already with Blake, already lapping up the jovial praise and affection she was bestowing. Cam didn't want to do this. She didn't want to see her. The image of her in that yellow bikini had been haunting her, forcing sleep away even when it did choose to come knocking on her door.

Cam called for the boys again, disbelieving what she was seeing. They'd never disobeyed before. Never chased someone down before either. Not until Blake.

What was so damn special about her?

The sense of betrayal from her beloved dogs was new territory and her heart felt like it was being dug out with a dull spoon.

"Boys, come," she said, her hurt now morphing into irritability as she stalked down to them. Blake straightened as she neared, but the dogs were still surrounding her, hopping around, tails wagging.

"Hi," she said, letting the dogs lick her hands.

"Boys," Cam said again, louder and firmer. They finally stilled and turned to look at her. She snapped her fingers and pointed to the sand at her side. Byron came to her and sat. But as for his brothers, Bo and Bingo, they just stared at her like they were clueless as to who she even was.

"They're okay," Blake said.

"No, they're not."

"They're just being friendly," Blake said. "There's nothing wrong with that."

Cam shot her a look. "There is something wrong with that. I didn't give them permission."

Blake reached down to pet the dogs while boring a stare into Cam. "They need your permission to be friendly to people? Is this a rule you expect them to follow for everyone, or just me?"

It felt like Blake had just stabbed her again with her words. Anger bloomed and burned beneath her skin. She'd left overpowering and irrational emotions like this far behind. And this woman, this... Blake, was somehow bringing them back, and Cam despised her for that more than she despised the anger itself.

Blake seemed unconcerned over Cam's reaction. She continued to shower the dogs with affection.

"Boys, come," Cam said, her voice raspy from a tightening throat. That, too, enraged her. Why was she getting so emotional? She spun on her heel, squeezed her hands into tight fists, and stormed up to the house. She hoped her dogs were right behind her because she couldn't turn to go after them again. If she did, and she laid eyes on Blake, all hell would break loose and she'd tear into her from stem to stern for being so rude, and for fucking making her feel all the shit she'd never wanted to feel again.

Why couldn't she just go back to Phoenix and leave her to her peace?

Cam made it to her patio and unclenched her hands. They were trembling. She swallowed down the jagged rock in her throat. Hot tears pooled in her eyes, as she waited quietly to see if her dogs had followed her.

Please, boys. Please. Don't do this to me.

She shook with relief as Byron hurried up the steps. Then, after seconds that felt like hours, the other two did the same.

They came. They listened. They still love me.

"Aren't you going to say anything?"

Cam bristled as a forceful wind carried Blake's voice to her, slamming into her from behind. She clenched her eyes just as she'd done her fists and willed herself to get control.

"Have a nice evening." The words came out on a whisper, her throat threatening to cave with something far more powerful than anger. She knew what that something was and its sudden reemergence was terrifying. It was roiling through her, spreading like a soul-eating disease, desperate to completely consume her and then break free for all the world to bear witness to the devastation it left behind.

If she tried to square off with Blake, she'd see it all.

And Cam would rather die than let her see that.

Blake made a noise that sounded dismissive and Cam was conscious of her rising emotions. They thickened the air and Cam wondered how weakly they were caged. Blake was probably just as irritated as Cam and probably very close to boiling over. But unlike Cam, she seemed to *want* that to happen and she was poking Cam with the sharp stick of her words and attitude *wanting* Cam to engage. And Cam's disarming, polite rebuttal must've felt like a slap to the face and a strong blow to her pride because when she laughed she sounded flippant.

"Uh, okay, you too, Cam. You have yourself a real nice evening."

Tiny pinpricks stung Cam's lower legs as Blake hurried away, kicking up sand. The dogs watched her go, whining as she went. Cam climbed the steps and tried to settle once again in her chair and enjoy the sunset. But there wasn't enough wine in her glass to effectively drown her inner turmoil and presumably not enough wine in existence to drink away the woman who was now disappearing into the deepening red and purple of the dying sun.

An unwelcome uneasiness descended on Cam. Soon she would be sitting with her empty glass in hand, encased by the draping darkness. It would settle all around her, smother her with its inky, weighted infiniteness. And she'd be vulnerable, swallowed up by it like the light of day was about to be by the sea.

It was already happening. Not just in the oncoming night, but from deep inside her, where that darkness was growing, contaminating, spreading the one thing she was truly helpless to fight again.

Pain.

CHAPTER THIRTEEN

Blake opened her eyes and squinted up at the pale blue sky. The crashing waves were louder than they'd been when she'd drifted off, letting her know the tide had come in. She sat up and inclined the back of her lounge chair. She shaded her brow as she glanced over at Sloane who was in a chair next to her.

"How long have I been asleep?"

Sloane didn't bother to look up from her paperback. "Couple of hours."

"Really?"

"Mm-hm."

Blake rubbed her arms, which were pleasantly warm from the sun, and she was relieved to see she wasn't burnt. But she still didn't like the fact that she'd lost part of her day to sleep. It was difficult enough for her to sit and do nothing and now she was napping on top of it?

"I wish you would've woken me," she said, slinging her legs over the side of the lounge to face Sloane. She brushed imaginary sand from her bare thighs, frustrated at both herself and her friend. Sloane knew she didn't like to take naps, but more importantly, she knew they had things they needed to accomplish while she was visiting. They'd wasted enough time as it was, but Sloane just kept insisting that she chill out and relax when they were supposed to be checking out some available real estate in a local village. Sloane's casual attitude about getting the ball rolling on bringing her dream to life was really starting to grind on her nerves. Not to mention that Sloane was supposed to be her partner in this venture. Blake had the skills and the medical know-how, and Sloane had the business sense. They were in this together. So what was the holdup?

Blake reached down and picked up the two books she'd been reading on nonprofit medical care. They were covered in sand and she shook them out, her frustration rising.

"You needed the rest," Sloane said, turning a page.

"It's been a week, Sloane. I've had plenty of rest."

"Must not've been enough because you were out like a light as soon as you started to read."

"It's the sun," Blake said. "It feels good. Relaxes me."

Sloane's lip lifted at the corner of her mouth. "That's kind of the point."

"I don't have time for naps." She slapped the books down on the small cooler between them. "There's too much to do and not much time to do it in."

"We've been here six days, B. Not an eternity. And you're exaggerating about the limited amount of time you have." She looked at her. "Or did you forget that Kenna and I were at your house helping you pack when your mother dropped by?" She lifted her chin as if searching the sky. "What was it she said again? Oh, right. She said you hadn't taken time off in years and that you should stay with Kenna and me for as long as you need to. That the practice would be just fine without you for a while."

"Right," Blake said. "I should stay for as long as I *need* to. That doesn't mean weeks. I don't need weeks. I'm ready to go back now if I want to."

Sloane laughed and returned to her book. "Good grief, woman. Have a couple of shots of tequila will ya? Or down a bottle of that expensive wine you brought. Or better yet, go get laid. A dozen orgasms or so will do you good."

"I don't need to do any of the above."

Sloane pulled off her sunglasses and looked at her like she was crazy. "I beg to differ, my dear doctor. In my opinion, you need *all* of the above. Preferably all in the same evening. Because we both know you'd never relax enough to let anyone touch you without the assistance of a little alcohol."

"That's not true. I've had sex plenty of times without having a drink first."

"Yeah, like ten years ago."

"Noo—"

Sloane grinned. "Yees."

"With Felicia I didn't drink."

"With Felicia you hardly had sex after the first few months."

"You don't know."

"You tell me everything, B. Or have you forgotten that as well?"

Blake stood, hating that she had nothing good to come back at Sloane with. The badgering was becoming frequent lately and she didn't understand why. Sloane would say it was because she was so high-strung and McKenna would say it was because of their neighbor. But they were both wrong as far as she was concerned.

She slipped on her white shorts and eyed Sloane, still hoping for a decent comeback. But movement down by the water garnered her attention. She blocked the sun from her brow and then felt her face draw with concern as a man dressed in jeans, cowboy boots, and a long-sleeve shirt, walked along the beach. He had a thick stack of folded blankets on one shoulder and several hard rectangular cases slung over the other. Blake could see the sweat reflecting off his face from where she was.

"Look at that guy," she said. "Look at all he's carrying and how he's dressed. He must be burning up."

Sloane looked down the beach and seemed to do her own assessment of the approaching man. "God, I wonder how long he's been walking."

"He's got to be exhausted." Blake waved at him and he nodded and came toward them.

Blake rummaged through the small cooler for a cold bottle of orange Fanta which she offered to him in greeting when he reached them. His smile was big and genuine, and he seemed eager to take the drink, but he didn't have a free hand. Sloane helped him set his blankets on her chair. The cases he set on the sand.

"Muchas gracias," he said, taking the drink. He hesitated though, when he saw the cap on the bottle. He tried to twist it off with his right hand, but he was using his palm rather than his fingers. He winced and his hand shook.

Blake saw the swelling around his knuckles.

"Here, let us help you," she said, gently taking the drink from him. She handed it to Sloane, who had the grip strength of an ax-wielding lumberjack, and she quickly opened the bottle and returned it to him. He thanked her and drank heartily. Blake tried to get a good look at his swollen hand, but she wasn't able to from her angle. She did examine the rest of him as he drank and he appeared to be well nourished, with a little bit of extra around the middle. He looked strong and well-built, though he wasn't much taller than she was. He had a thick head of black hair, deeply tanned skin, and his face and neck were shiny with sweat. She smiled at him and asked him how he was in her conversational Spanish. His answer was simple, short. He said he was good. But he seemed to be having trouble focusing on her, blinking his brown, weary eyes. She noticed his dry, cracked lips. He palmed his head as if he was in pain and then swayed a little.

This man was far from good.

The physician in Blake took over, and before the man could even blink again, she had him sitting on Sloane's chair. She drug her own lounge through the sand and sat facing him, her knees inches from his.

"May I see your hand?" She pointed.

He looked down at his hand as if bewildered, but then allowed her to take it in her own. She held it carefully, mindful to only touch his palm with her fingertips as she studied the back. She located the wound, which appeared to be a deep, one-inch cut that stemmed just below the base of his index and middle finger.

She spoke to Sloane who was paying close attention.

"Can you please get me my medical bag and a few of those bottled waters? Not the ones from the fridge. Get some that are room temperature. Those will be less shocking to him when I clean his wound."

"Anything else? Food maybe?"

"Not yet. I'm betting he doesn't feel much like eating right now."

Sloane left and Blake asked him in Spanish if he was hungry. He shook his head, which she'd suspected. Then she tried to ask him how long it had been since he'd last eaten, but she wasn't sure how and he didn't seem to understand.

She had a lot of questions for him that needed answers and she fussed at herself for not being able to recall more of the Spanish she'd learned during her summer volunteering in the region the year before.

She should've taken the time away from work to refresh and learn more Spanish before she'd come.

She asked him the one important question that she could. She asked him his name.

He said it was Alberto.

She told him hers and he seemed pleased even as he struggled to say it. He had trouble pronouncing the B and the L together. It made them both laugh.

Sloane returned with the water and the medical bag. Blake took his temperature and his pulse. She listened to his breathing and took a closer look at the swelling and redness around his wound, still mindful not to touch him yet. When she was satisfied with her examination, she cleaned and disinfected her hands with Sloane's assistance. Then she pulled on a pair of surgical gloves and prepared Alberto's hand, readying him for the thorough cleaning of his wound.

"This is going to hurt and I don't know how to tell him that," she said to Sloane as she was looking at her patient. McKenna joined them and as she took in the scene, her empathy was already apparent.

"What can we do?" she asked.

Blake pressed her lips together. "His wound appears to be infected. It's also quite deep so it's going to hurt when I clean it and stitch it up. I would like to be able to tell him that and make sure that this is something he wants me to do."

She tried again to speak to him in Spanish, but he answered her in broken English, saying he didn't understand.

Sloane said she'd be right back, but Blake hardly noticed. She was busy searching her brain for additional Spanish vocabulary, but she came up empty. McKenna transferred Alberto's blankets and cases to the patio and then returned and sat next to him. She spoke to him softly in English and held his free hand in an attempt to comfort him, something Blake had seen her do numerous times throughout the years when they'd come across someone needing assistance. He stared at both of them, spoke to them in Spanish and then stopped suddenly as he seemed to realize it was pointless. His eyes filled with tears, and Blake had never felt so helpless and frustrated in her life.

CHAPTER FOURTEEN

Blake heard someone approaching and Alberto's face lit up as he looked over her shoulder. Sloane rejoined them, a little breathless, and for a second, Blake couldn't figure out why Alberto was so happy to see her. But then someone came to stand at her other side, and Blake knew without having to look who it was. Her insides tightened at the sound of her voice.

"Hola, Alberto."

Blake looked up at Cam in surprise.

She knows him?

Of course she does. Cam lived there. She must see him all the time.

Alberto's sudden happiness now made sense.

He gave Cam a huge smile. "Hola, Santi. Como estas?"

Cam answered him in Spanish and the two of them briefly laughed. Then she looked at Blake and pointed at the space next to her on the lounge.

"May I?"

If you must.

But Blake merely shrugged, making sure to show the apathy she did not feel. "Sure."

Cam sat and Blake tensed slightly as Cam's body lightly pressed against hers. Ignoring her was the best and only option Blake had. The warmth of her bare skin, however, along with that tantalizing scent Blake recalled from that very first morning, made ignoring her an almost hysterical alternative to even consider.

The memory of her wearing that short, body-clinging satin robe soon added to the mix.

Cam spoke to her, breaking her thoughts. "Sloane said you need my help? To help Alberto?"

Blake analyzed her words expecting to have heard at least a hint of sarcasm. She felt oddly disappointed when she concluded there wasn't any.

"He has a bad cut on his hand, and I need to communicate with him in order to help him."

Cam studied her for a long moment, as if she, too, were doing her own analyzing. She focused on Blake's gloved hands as she responded.

"What do you need to know?"

"I need to know, number one, if he's okay with me helping him. If he's okay with me cleaning his wound."

Cam relayed the question and Alberto nodded. "Sí, por favor."

"He's okay with that. Very grateful."

"Great," Blake said, nodding back at Alberto.

Cam started to stand. "So, if that's all you need—"

"That's not all I need," Blake said quickly, agitated at her attempt to hastily exit. She didn't want Cam there either, but she needed her, and more importantly, Alberto needed her. How could she just up and walk away?

"He said he's fine with you tending to him," Cam said. "You can go ahead and bandage him up or whatever it is you're going to do with your first aid skills."

Blake blinked at her.

Huh?

"You obviously have a first aid kit or supplies of some sort."

Blake continued to stare, and her confusion must've been evident because Cam tried to explain further. "You have the gloves and stuff."

"Yes," Blake said.

"Then that's all you need."

She was searching Blake's face and Blake would've gladly offered her the answers she was seeking if she knew what the hell it was she was looking for in the first place.

"Oh, do you need more? I can go get mine if you need extra supplies."

"What, a first aid kit?"

"Yes," Cam said as if she hadn't been paying attention. "That's what you need, right? So, you can do your little first aid thing?"

Was Cam messing with her, trying to piss her off by undermining her skills as a physician? Blake opened her mouth to let her know just how it was she felt about that, but she thought of Alberto and steadied her anger. "He needs a lot more than simple first aid treatment. His wound is deep and infected and it needs to be thoroughly cleaned and sutured. And then he needs to be treated with antibiotics."

Panic, or something that appeared close to it, came over Cam's face. "Then he needs a doctor. I need to get him to town." She tried to stand again, but McKenna reached out and touched her arm.

"Cam, it's okay."

"It's not okay. He needs—"

"Blake can handle it," Sloane said.

Cam gave a short laugh. "No offense, but I don't think she can."

"What the hell is that supposed to mean?" Blake let out.

"Oh, my God." Sloane palmed her forehead.

McKenna stood, obviously worried about the escalating scenario. She grabbed Cam by the shoulders as she stood. "Cam, listen."

"No, I've heard enough. He needs a—"

"Cam—"

"Blake is a doctor," Sloane let out.

Cam froze. She looked first at Sloane and then back to McKenna. She swallowed. "What?"

"She can handle this. She can help your friend," McKenna said.

Blake then took her turn at looking at her two friends. "She didn't know? I thought you told her all about me?"

"A doctor?" Cam sounded as lost and confused as Alberto apparently was.

"Kenna?" Blake said.

She wouldn't meet her gaze. Kept staring at the ground.

"I may have left that part out of the conversation," Sloane said.

Cam spoke, her gaze fixed on Sloane. "You told me she was a workaholic. A high-strung overachiever. That she needed a vacation almost as badly as she needed a woman. You never said she was a doctor."

"What?" Blake felt her mouth fall open.

"Oh, my God," McKenna said again, rubbing her temple.

"Everyone just calm down," Sloane nearly shouted.

They fell silent and Sloane tried to control the situation by saying more, but Blake had had enough.

"Sloane, shush. You and Kenna go inside, please. Cam, you stay. Alberto is our main priority right now and we're supposed to be helping him. Not sitting here fighting like a bunch of lunatics." She looked at her friends. "Now. Get a move on. I have work to do."

Sloane and McKenna seemed reluctant to leave, but they slowly walked back to the house. Blake kicked things into an efficient high gear and asked Cam to sit and translate. She asked about his appetite. He said he hadn't wanted much since the day before, having very little to eat or drink. He felt weak and fatigued. He also had a headache. Blake explained that she thought he had the beginnings of an infection and therefore needed to clean his wound thoroughly and suture the cut. She told him it would hurt but that he needed to do his best to remain still. He gave his final approval without hesitation.

The procedure was painful and he cried out a couple of times and winced. But Cam, who'd moved to sit next to him, held fast to him, soothing him with her words. She seemed to be as kind and empathetic as McKenna, which surprised Blake a little. She was aware of the close bond Cam seemed to have with her friends by seeing her interact with Tomas, but she hadn't been privy to this nurturing side. It warmed her heart and she almost smiled. But then she reminded herself that Cam had been continuously rude to her. She couldn't excuse that just because she was kind to others. Could she? *Should* she?

She continued to question that as she finished cleaning the cut. By the time she was ready to stitch him up, the mood between the two of them had changed dramatically.

Cam was calm, soft-spoken, and thus far had been keenly interested in Blake's every move.

Blake, too, had calmed, but she was used to pushing her feelings aside to take charge and focus solely on what needed to be done during traumatic situations. Even so, she knew Cam's change in demeanor had influenced hers, more than she'd like to admit. Even Alberto seemed to have settled, though Blake suspected that was due to exhaustion. Whatever the reason, he sat quietly as she sutured him, only wincing and speaking a few times before she was finished.

He gave her a tired smile when she was done and Blake insisted he rest and recline back in the chair as she went inside to retrieve a vial of antibiotics from the fridge. An emergency supply of medication, along with her medical bag, were things she was sure to bring with her when appropriate. Given this trip and their rather rural location, she'd been sure to bring extra of everything.

"He's asleep," Cam said with a serene smile when Blake returned.

Blake touched his face with the back of her fingers. "He's beat." She looked back at Cam and found her staring at her. She realized she was still only wearing her bikini top and shorts. Any other time she would've blushed under such close scrutiny, but under the heaviness of Cam's stare she felt differently. She felt…a little thrill. A little rush of excitement at the notion that Cam might be admiring her.

"Can you open his shirt?" she asked Cam, breaking the moment. "So I can get to his upper arm?"

Cam knelt over him to unsnap his shirt. She then eased it away from his shoulder. His eyes fluttered open as Cam informed him of the coming injection. Blake pulled on a new pair of gloves, cleaned a small patch of skin and then gave him the shot. He smiled up at them, but his exhaustion was apparent and soon he was sleeping once again.

"Will he be okay?" Cam asked.

Blake sat next to her and peeled off her gloves. "His wound is infected, but not as badly as I feared. The swelling is probably from a combination of the infection and the way in which he sustained the injury. The redness is minimal and hasn't spread. But…"

"But?" Cam said, searching her face once again.

"He has a mild fever."

"That worries you?"

"A little, yes. His other symptoms could be due to the infection, but I don't believe they are. I think it's mostly dehydration and I'm hoping he will feel a lot better once he's properly hydrated. But to be safe, I'd like to keep an eye on him for the next few hours to be sure."

"He's been walking for hours in the heat without eating or drinking. With an infection brewing," Cam said, shaking her head, her sorrow for him obviously consuming her.

"As badly as he feels, I'm surprised he didn't stop for the day hours ago."

"He doesn't know any different," Cam said. "Walking beaches, selling his goods is what he does all day, every day. The thought of quitting probably never crossed his mind."

The lingering breeze came off the sea as the tide was pulling out once again. Blake shivered and rubbed her arms. Cam saw her hugging herself and she moved slightly, lifting her hand toward Blake as if she were going to draw her close but then stopped.

"You should go change into warmer clothes."

"I'm more concerned with him," Blake said, watching him sleep. "Does he live nearby? Do you think his family would mind if I stayed with him a while?"

"I'm not sure where he stays, but I know it's not close. He gets a ride in from somewhere near town and then, if he's lucky, finds a ride back. If not, he settles down in the dunes for the night."

Blake grew alarmed. "He sleeps in the sand?"

"Sometimes."

"And no one helps?"

"No one knows. The only reason I do is because I saw him walking through the dunes on my way home one evening. I tried to get him to come back to my place for some food and a roof over his head, but he declined, said he liked to sleep in the dunes. So, I gave him what I had with me in my Jeep and watched him walk away."

"What about tonight? Do you think he'll stay and let us help?"

"He's tired, so he won't be able to put up much of a fight." Cam knelt over him again and gently shook him. When he opened his eyes, she spoke to him and then helped him sit up and stand. She draped his good arm over her shoulder.

"What are you doing?" Blake asked.

"I'm taking him to my place, where he can rest. Whether he likes it or not."

Chapter Fifteen

Cam carried the glass of wine into the living room and handed it to Blake, who was sitting quietly on the sofa, her body turned to stare out at the dark beach through the window.

"Mm, thanks," she said as she took the refilled glass.

"Are you warm enough?" Cam asked, settling in on the other side of the sofa. The fire was putting off some good heat now. She hoped it was enough to keep both Blake and Alberto warm.

Blake sipped her drink. "Mm. This is so good. I had no idea you were into wine." She eyed the coffee mug Cam was drinking from. "Do you ever enjoy any or are you just a collector?"

Cam returned the mug to the table next to her. "I drink it. Otherwise I wouldn't bother chilling it." She nodded toward Blake's glass of chilled Chardonnay.

Cam expected her to snap back at her, offended.

She laughed. "Smart-ass." She took another sip and made another noise of approval. "What is this?"

"A Chardonnay."

"I know that."

"That's a 2017, Rombauer Chardonnay."

Blake seemed to be impressed. "A very nice, rather costly bottle of wine if I'm not mistaken."

Cam shrugged. "Cost isn't something I worry a great deal about."

"This is, what, a three-hundred-dollar bottle of wine? And that's not something you worry about? You must not drink very often."

"It wasn't quite three hundred and you're mistaken about how often I drink."

She laughed softly. "Dare I ask how often?"

Cam met her gaze. "Nightly."

She looked surprised. "You drink wine this expensive every night?"

"Like I said, I don't pay much mind to cost. What I do care about is whether or not it's good. But to answer your question more directly, yes, I have wine every evening, but no, I don't think about what it cost."

"If you enjoy it that much, then why aren't you having any tonight?"

Cam hadn't expected to be asked that and it took her a moment to figure out how to answer.

"I'm worried about Alberto. I want to keep a clear head." It was the truth, just not the complete truth. The real reason why she wanted to keep a clear head was sitting across from her on the couch, drinking her Chardonnay. She didn't want to risk doing or saying anything foolish.

Blake seemed to accept that explanation. She gazed down at Bo. He was draped next to her, his head in her lap while Bingo lay on the floor in front of her. That left Byron, Cam's ever faithful companion. He wasn't currently snuggled up to Blake, but that wasn't because he didn't want to be. He just couldn't seem to shove aside his brothers to get to her. He came up to Cam and rested his chin in her lap, pouting. She stroked his head.

"I don't feel sorry for you at all. I know the only reason you're here giving me those sad eyes is because you can't get to her. I know I'm now chopped liver."

"Does it really bother you?" Blake asked. "That the dogs like me so much?"

It was another unexpected question and Cam glanced over at her as she considered her response. The sight of her sitting on her couch, in a simple long-sleeved shirt and a pair of blue jeans, all cuddled up with her dogs, stirred Cam so powerfully she tried to make herself look away. But the firelight was breathing upon her face and setting off sparks in her eyes. The fact that her presence alone seemed to be threatening the tranquility of her home and the careful construction of her emotional ambivalence couldn't win against the way she looked at that moment.

To Cam it looked like, felt like…she belonged there.

"Maybe I shouldn't have asked."

Cam moved her gaze from Blake to Alberto, fearing Blake had seen too much in her eyes. Alberto was snoring softly in the chair by the fireplace, covered by one of his colorful hand-made blankets. But looking at him didn't help Cam much because she recalled the kind, gentle way Blake had been with him. Watching her with him made Cam realize that Blake had a heart after all. Another reason why her presence was a threat to the life Cam now knew.

Thank God I'm not drinking.

"Sure, it bothers me," Cam said, surprising Blake.

She had to say something to bring herself out of her thoughts.

"I adopted the three of them together when they were pups. I'm all they've ever had, ever known really. They've been my constant companions, my best friends, my family. And then in walks you," she said, looking over at her. "Someone they don't even know, and off they go, without giving me a second thought. So, I can't help but feel rejected in being so easily replaced." She stroked Byron and lifted his chin with her fingertips. "You little heathen. You're breaking my heart." He wagged his tail.

"You know they aren't rejecting you. Or replacing you. No one can do that. They're just excited at having someone new around. Someone…different. And based on their overzealousness with me, I'm guessing that having someone else around is a rare occurrence."

"That's not true. I take them everywhere I can. They're around all kinds of people all the time."

"But what about here, in their home?"

"Sometimes, yes. I have friends who come by."

"Who? Tomas?"

"Yes. And a couple of others."

"What about women?"

"What about them?"

She smiled. "There hasn't been any recently has there? Friend or otherwise?"

Cam averted her gaze again, but she could still feel Blake's eyes burning the side of her face. That was nothing compared to the burning in her gut. The questioning had now officially become too much to handle. Cam stared into the fire, wanting desperately to get up and run out the door, to tear across the sand and into the sea where she could wade out without looking back, until the cold water was deep enough to envelop her and carry her away.

But she couldn't take things that far. Not even in her mind. She couldn't go back to that dark place. And even if she moved to run at all, even to just escape out onto the patio where she could inhale large lungfuls of salty air, Blake would notice and she'd wonder why.

So, she sat, staring into the fire, petting her dog, hoping Blake would lose interest or move on to another topic.

"There hasn't been someone for a while has there?" The sharp edges of her voice had been sanded and smoothed throughout the evening, and this inquiry sounded like more of a quiet observation, one that she was careful in bringing up, rather than a probing question.

"No," Cam managed.

And you can't ask more.

Because I won't be able to answer.

Cam drew a deep breath and checked her watch for distraction. "Is it time to check him again?"

Blake was silent for a long moment, but Cam didn't dare turn to look at her.

"It's a little early yet," she finally said.

Another long silence stretched between them before Blake spoke again.

"So, what do you do, Cam? Do you go into work somewhere or have you left the mad world behind to retire here in this beautiful home on this beautiful beach?"

These were the very questions she usually made a point to avoid answering. She'd become somewhat of an expert at it, too. Skirting around the answers, giving as little information as she could and then leading people on to something else with distractions. Most accepted that or sensed her unwillingness to share the details of her life and let it be. Blake though? She was beginning to believe she wouldn't let anything go.

"I don't go into work." She didn't have to leave the house in order to do her job. "But I'm not retired, either," she said, sipping her coffee. *I haven't been producing the past few years, but I haven't retired. And with the way things are currently going with my newfound creative drive, I'm very hopeful I won't have to for a long, long while.*

"So you work from home? Or are you just independently wealthy?"

Cam wanted to return Blake's playful smile, her mouth even twitched in an attempt.

"No. I've earned my money."

"What do you do, then?"

I know she's seen me coming and going in dirty jeans and work boots, carrying my tool belt. So she must know more than she's letting on. Why the careful questioning?

"I mostly help friends and their families with the renovations on their homes or other projects."

She nodded and sipped her wine. "But that's not what you do for money." She set her glass on the end table and pinned Cam with her penetrating eyes. "You said you didn't have to leave home for work. So, that must mean the renovating you do, you do because you enjoy it and because you like helping people."

"Yes."

Blake waited, watching her closely. Cam didn't give her any more.

"You've done an amazing job on your home," she finally said, looking around. "Are you planning on selling and starting in on a new one?"

"No. I'm not going to sell. This is my home," Cam said sternly.

The logs in the fireplace crackled and sparked, as if they, too, felt the effect of Cam's tone. The largest piece of wood split, causing the others to shift and a wave of heat pressed into Cam's skin as if to exacerbate her agitation.

"Is that how you got injured?" Blake asked delicately, like she was well aware of the dangerous ground she was now walking on. "Doing renovating work like that?"

Cam lost her breath. Pain, icy cold and sharp, attacked everything in her, rendering her mute and unable to move. The only part of her that seemed to be functioning was her heart and it was thumping, thundering, crying out in sheer terror and torture as the pain sieged it.

Cam sat with a death grip on a throw pillow, her thinking and breathing bordering on panic. Deep inside she was screaming for help, for a way out. But no one could hear her. They weren't close enough, couldn't see that far inside her. Not because they didn't want to. But because she hadn't let them. Wouldn't let them.

She was alone.

Battling an unwinnable war alone.

Chapter Sixteen

"Cam?"

Cam heard Blake and the dogs rouse. Then, suddenly, she was at her side, hand on her shoulder, speaking softly.

"Are you all right?" She released a small sigh when Cam didn't answer. "I'm sorry. I guess I shouldn't have asked. I just—noticed that you'd been...hurt."

Cam felt the gentle caress of her fingertips as they skimmed over her scars. First near her hairline and then on her cheek, giving life to an inferno that passed from her fingertips into Cam's skin and then all throughout her body. The collision of that heat with the icy cold of the pain caused a cataclysm that literally made Cam shake, and she quickly stood, the instability and chaos inside making it impossible to remain sitting.

Blake rose alongside her and tried to touch her again, but Cam crossed to the hearth, grabbed the poker, and stabbed the popping logs. She was behaving erratically, and Blake was seeing it all, which was exactly what she hadn't wanted to have happen.

She kept attacking the logs, unsure what else she could do to avoid looking at Blake. She stabbed with the poker until she broke the wood into orange-glowing wedges. Blake was still watching her, and Cam knew she had to ease the tension she'd caused. But she wasn't sure how. So, she did what she knew.

She distracted.

"Fire's dying and I don't want Alberto to get cold." Cam snuck a look at her. Blake was still standing quietly by the couch. Her eyes, however, seemed to be doing so much more. Her penetrating gaze had a new and easily discernible empathy to it. The ripple of acceptance and understanding that came from it, along with the unspoken offer of more, was too overwhelming for Cam. Too tempting.

To keep from giving in to it, Cam had to look away and once again focus on the fire. Because Blake, unwittingly or not, had a clutching hold on her heart, like she was trying to pull it to her, for a closer examination.

"Are you cold? I'm feeling a little chilled," Cam said. Her skin had somehow chilled, despite the raging fire and despite the numerous raging fires now ablaze inside her.

"I'm actually very warm," Blake said, her voice so soft Cam had hardly heard her. She went to Alberto, pressed her hand to his forehead and face. Cam watched from her position by the fire, still putting on the terrible act of tending to the flames. Blake sifted through her bag and retrieved what she needed. She put on her stethoscope, which in itself was something that stirred Cam enough to acknowledge, and began going through the same routine Cam had seen her do a few times now. She was riveted nonetheless by her serious yet gentle manner, as well as her careful concern and thorough inspection.

With Alberto she seemed less guarded and she showed her empathy and concern for him easily. With Cam, those feelings seemed to have come from somewhere deeper, and Cam sensed that there had been some reluctance in letting them surface. Nevertheless, the feelings were there, Cam had seen them.

But those feelings were a lot like her beauty. They were in direct contradiction to the biting words and the fiery attitude Cam always seemed to be at the opposite end of.

Blake was fire and ice.

Like the collision currently wreaking havoc within Cam.

A collision, she realized, that Blake herself had initiated.

"Sloane tried to tell me you were a physician," Cam said as the quiet in the room began to weigh down on them.

Blake gave her a quick glance, then went back to her examination of Alberto. "It was my understanding that she told you I was an overworked, uptight, lonely professional who desperately needed to get laid."

"She didn't exactly put it like that."

"No? She had a nicer way of putting it?" She kept her focus on Alberto, even though the conversation was obviously somewhat distressing to her.

"I think she was expecting me to inquire further about you with the information she shared."

"But you didn't."

"No, I wasn't—"

Blake looked up at her. "Interested?"

"I—that's not—" *How can almost every attempt at conversation with this woman end up being fucked?*

"It's okay," Blake said with a snide laugh. "I wouldn't be interested in someone described like that either. And considering the very little you did know of me, I'm sure you assumed her description was more than accurate."

Is it?

"I didn't ask anything further because it wasn't any of my business. Nor did I think it was right for her to be sharing such personal information about you with me, a perfect stranger, regardless of how well meaning her intentions were. But she also said a lot of wonderful things about you. Things that, I now know, more than hinted at who you are. It shouldn't have surprised me to learn you were a physician. If I hadn't been so put off and just taken a moment to put two and two together…"

"Well, now you know. Cat's out of the bag."

"Yes, and it's impressive."

"Impressive? Is that what's prompted your change in attitude toward me? Because I'm a doctor? And that's a big deal?"

Cam pushed out a breath.

I can't say anything right. Not one thing.

"You had to work really hard to get where you are, do what you do. Sacrifice more than I probably even realize. But that's not what is impressive to me. It's you using all that skill and knowledge to help people, like Alberto, that's impressive. You're helping him, a man you don't even know, going out of your way to ensure he's okay. So, if my attitude has changed toward you, that's why."

Blake listened to Alberto's heart again and retook his temperature. Had she even heard her? Or was she buying time before she responded? Cam said nothing more and gave her the space and time she needed.

"His fever is coming down," she said, removing her stethoscope. "He should be feeling a lot better come morning." She put her things away, tucked her hair behind her ears. She turned to pet the dogs. "You're not heathens, are you? No. You're angels. Lovely little angels."

You're lovely.

Right now anyway.

Even though you're acting like you didn't hear me.

She glanced up as if Cam had said the words aloud. "I'm not sure what to do. Whether you're okay with my staying the rest of the night or not."

"I thought—" *You were staying. That was the plan. Now you're wanting to go? Or are you trying to get me to tell you that I want you to stay?*

"He is improving," she said quickly as she straightened. "Which is good. But if he happens to need me and I'm not here, you'll have to come get me. If I stay, that wouldn't be an issue and I'd sit up with him so you'd be able to get some sleep yourself."

A short, involuntary laugh came from Cam. "I won't be getting any sleep if you're—" The remaining words toppled to the floor unspoken. But Blake had heard enough to get the gist of what Cam was about to say.

Cam tried to speak, to explain, but Blake cut her off.

"I'll go then." She was already gathering her bag and her sweater. "Would you like me to leave the thermometer?"

She thinks I don't want her here.

"You don't have to go," Cam said. "I didn't mean—"

Fuck, what do I say?

Blake turned, bag slung over her shoulder. "I think maybe I should. He's doing fine and I'm sure you'd like to settle in and get some rest." She headed for the door, dogs on her heels.

"Blake," Cam said, as she watched her pull open the door.

Blake looked back at her.

Stay.

Talk with me.

I'll try to do better.

At the very least let me continue to watch the flickering flames kiss your beautiful face.

"Thank you." It was all Cam was able to say.

Blake seemed unable to process it, or maybe it was Cam having said it at all that was confusing to her. As if Cam thanking her was the very last thing she'd expected to hear.

"I just did what I do every day, Cam." She gave Alberto one last glance. "If he should leave before I get a chance to see him tomorrow, tell him...please tell him I wish him well and that if he needs anything, I'll be here. For a little while longer anyway." She whispered good night to the dogs, kissed their heads, and then stepped out into the night with Cam rooted to the floor, unable to do anything but watch her go.

CHAPTER SEVENTEEN

Blake was securing her wet hair into a small ponytail when she walked into the kitchen and found McKenna removing a large bowl from the refrigerator.

"There's my grill master," McKenna said as she caught sight of Blake. "Just in time to cook the chicken. I'm making your favorite."

Blake had just showered off the day's sweat, sand, and suntan lotion, but readily resigned herself to smelling like smoke the rest of the evening for her friends and for McKenna's Southwestern grilled chicken with peppers and onions recipe. It was McKenna's healthier take on fajitas and she loved it.

"And where is your preferred grill master?" Blake asked, referring to Sloane. She took the bowl of marinated chicken breasts from McKenna. She could smell the lime juice and soy sauce already.

"She's indisposed at the moment."

"Aw, don't tell me that," Blake said, making a face. "Now I know you guys got it on again while I was in the shower."

"Would you rather us get it on later while you're trying to sleep?"

"I have a choice? Because I could swear you do both."

McKenna waved her off and began washing some bell peppers. Blake was a little amused that she seemed to be so embarrassed.

"You know the walls are thin, Kenna. And I'm a light sleeper."

"Then I guess you'll just have to go for more of your runs, won't you?" She smirked.

So much for embarrassed.

Blake rolled her eyes. "Where's the lighter?"

McKenna tugged open a drawer and offered it to her. She didn't, however, release it when Blake took hold.

"Or you could say you're going for a run but instead sneak over to Cam's for a little midday roll in the hay yourself. Sloane and I would never know."

Blake yanked the lighter away. "Not going to happen."

"Why not? She's single, seems very nice and down to earth. Look at how she helped Alberto, how she helped us out. People seem to think very highly of her. And, of course," she said lightly, "there are those dark good looks of hers."

Blake looked up at the ceiling in exasperation. "Looks aren't everything, Kenna."

McKenna laughed. "Who are you trying to fool? You're attracted to her. Despite whatever went down between the two of you in town or what she's got going on underneath those looks. That may actually be what's drawing you to her more. The fact that she riles you up. Ruffles your tail feathers."

Blake laughed, incredulous. "Yeah. Sure. Okay."

McKenna went to the counter and began chopping the peppers and onions. She kept smiling over at her as she worked.

"What?" Blake said.

"She stood up to you, didn't she?"

Blake heated.

"Uh-huh. I thought as much. You argued with her and she didn't back down. That's why things got so tense at the fish market."

"She was rude," Blake said. "And insulting. She insinuated I was some sort of a—"

"Was she right?"

Blake blinked. "What?"

"Was she right?"

"No, she wasn't right. I'm not an ignorant, prejudiced jerk."

"No, you're not, but could you have possibly said something to come off that way to her?"

"No—of course not—I—"

She groaned.

"You're pissing me off, Kenna."

"I know and it's so much fun. After all, it's a rare moment when the great, brilliant Dr. Livingstone is wrong and she can't see it. And even better when I get to point it out to her. Little old me. The one without a college degree."

"You don't need a freaking degree," Blake said. "You're the most intuitive and perceptive person I know. And you're annoying as hell."

"And I'm proud of it." She finished with the peppers. "Why don't you go light the grill and get some fresh air? You look a little red. If you have any trouble, I hear there's a very handy woman next door who might be able to help you out."

She smirked again but Blake chose to ignore it. Arguing with Kenna when she was already flustered was pointless. The woman had x-ray vision when it came to emotions, she'd swear on it.

She walked out to the grill and lit it without issue, letting McKenna's teasing words slide off her back. She got lost in the repetition of the crashing waves as she waited for the grill to adequately heat. When it did she placed the marinated chicken on the grate and sat on a nearby chair as it sizzled.

She spotted one of McKenna's books on the small table next to her. Unlike Sloane, McKenna preferred romances to crime novels.

Maybe that's why their love life is still off the chart after eleven years together.

Blake picked it up and scanned the back blurb. It sounded interesting enough. For a romance.

She opened it and began reading, thinking that her curiosity would be satisfied after the first couple of pages. But, surprisingly, the more she read, the more curious she became. The two main characters were both highly successful professionals and they seemed to be in a battle of wills as well as in a battle over their underlying attraction. And the perceptible undercurrent of eroticism she found just a few pages in was something she hadn't been expecting.

Maybe these romances do rev up some passion. It's already got me going and I was skeptical.

"Looks like you've got the lighting of the grill conquered."

Blake looked up, startled. Cam was standing in the entryway of the patio, leaning on one of the wooden posts. The uncomfortable and avoidant woman Blake had seen last night appeared to be gone.

She looked more like her usual self, with her hands in her pockets, wearing a tilted grin, representing the word "casual" like a paid spokesmodel. With her perfectly tousled hair, rich sun-tanned skin, and laid-back, leisurely lean, the word "model" seemed more than fitting. And the long-sleeved T-shirt and loose-fitting jeans she had on were an appropriate addition to her overall relaxed demeanor.

How does she make easygoing look so damn good?

"I'm a fast learner," Blake said, unable to resist giving her a grin of her own. She'd seen her in passing earlier that morning, but only long enough for her to relay that Alberto had risen very early and set out on his way, insisting that he was feeling better. Blake had been disappointed in not being able to check on him and she would've liked to have said good-bye. Cam had tried to reassure her by telling her that he had promised to get some more rest.

"I bet you are," Cam said.

Was that...flirtation?

Blake waited for more, for some clarification that might prove her wrong, but Cam focused on the book in her hand. "That any good?"

Before she had time to even think of an answer, Blake was flushing and worried about whether or not Cam had seen the rather risqué cover. She quickly set it face down on the table.

"It's Kenna's," she found herself saying. She wasn't sure why but she didn't want Cam to know that a book like that had garnered her full attention.

Full attention? I was consumed.

"But you were reading it," Cam pointed out.

"I was just curious. Romances aren't really my thing."

"Really?" Her eyes glinted as if she were feeling roguish. "Judging by the look you had on your face when I first walked up, you seemed to be enjoying it."

Blake shook her head. "No, I—I only read the first few pages." She didn't understand her need to defend herself. Why did she care whether or not someone knew she was interested in a romance?

Because that particular book is an erotic romance.

And because the someone who is asking is Cam.

Cam came closer, slid her hand from her pocket, and pointed at the grill.

"You want me to check on what you've got cooking before I sit down?"

Blake stood, flustered by her choice of words and confused by her presence and nonchalance in making herself comfortable, as if she felt right at home and was intent on staying a while. It was such a drastic change from her usual reluctance to stick around that Blake couldn't help but wonder if it had anything to do with the previous evening and the complimentary things Cam had said to her.

Was it possible she had a romantic interest in her? Even though they seemed to clash at every attempt at normal conversation? Could Kenna be right?

"No, no, please, stay where you are," Cam said, holding out her hand to stop Blake from moving farther. "There's no need for you to get up when I'm right here."

Blake slowly sat and watched Cam from behind as she opened the grill and turned the chicken. Blake felt somewhat shameful in doing so, but she took advantage and studied her unabashedly. Her shirt got her attention right away. The bold, colorful letters on the back advertised a popular wax that surfers used on their boards.

Otherwise known as sex wax.

Blake couldn't believe how crazy the word "sex" was making her feel simply because it was on a shirt worn by Cam. It was just as perplexing to her as her embarrassment over the book.

Sex and Cam seemed to be a disruptive combination to her.

Can I be any more fifth grade?

Blake's eyes traveled downward to her jeans. They sat so seductively low on her hips that Blake knew she'd get an ample view of her smooth lower abdomen if she were to turn and lift her shirt. She might even get a peek at the planes of her pelvic region where she imagined her skin to be soft and pale. But as appealing as that sounded, the view from behind was just as tantalizing with the snug fit of the denim over the rounded top of her buttocks. McKenna had been more than correct when she'd said Cam had a cute butt. Not only was it very, very nice, it appeared to be the only thing holding the jeans in place.

Cam closed the grill and eased into the chair next to her. She reached for the book and paused as she lifted it, looking at Blake as if to ask her for permission to peruse it. When Blake didn't protest, she read the back cover and returned it to the table. She stared out at the sea.

"I can see why you were enjoying yourself."

"It's not even mine," Blake snapped. "It's Kenna's." She ran her hand through her hair, tucking errant strands back into her ponytail. When that didn't suffice, she pulled it loose and sighed, upset at how quickly and irrationally she'd reacted to Cam's teasing.

Cam looked at her and for an instant she appeared to be mesmerized by the fall of Blake's hair. That look however, was gone in a flash. "Why does that matter? And why can't you admit you might've been enjoying it?"

"Because I don't read romance."

"Why not?"

"Because I—they're—silly."

"Is there *anything* you enjoy?"

"Yes," Blake shot back. She'd done it again. Spoke without thinking. But the question had riled her up and she continued, unabated. "Is there anything *you* enjoy? Other than driving nails through wood and drinking expensive wine?"

Cam looked back at the ocean without showing any effect from Blake's words. That bothered Blake so she couldn't resist an additional snide comment.

"That's what I thought," she said.

Cam laughed softly and shook her head. "You're—"

Blake glared at her. "What? Uptight? Stubborn? Impossible? Come on, Cam, I'm sure you can come up with the appropriate adjective for me. So, go ahead. Tell me. What am I?"

"Scared."

Chapter Eighteen

Blake blinked and stared transfixed at the side of Cam's face. Her heart was beating so fast she almost couldn't feel it. Like how the wings of a hummingbird moved so quickly they blurred almost to invisibility. That's what her heart felt like. Like it was going to beat itself out of existence.

Blake swallowed against her dry throat. Forced herself to confront her.

"What am I scared of, Cam? Huh? Enlighten me."

Cam turned to look her directly in the eye. "You're scared of losing control."

What?

Blake felt her jaw slacken and she feared her chin might fall to the floor. Worse, she seemed unable to reel it back in order to speak.

"Hey, you two," McKenna said, sliding open the back door. "Chicken almost done?" She carried plates and silverware to the patio dining table and began setting a place for everyone. Blake counted four settings.

It seemed, unbeknownst to her, that Cam had been invited to dinner.

That was why she'd come over. It had nothing to do with Cam having a secret romantic interest in her.

Blake propped her elbow on the armrest of the chair and massaged her brow.

She felt sick. How could she have been so stupid to think that Cam had an interest in her? Just because she'd been polite to her for a few moments the day before?

How could I have made that leap? Why had I made that leap? And why is it upsetting me so much to realize that I'd been incorrect?

Blake sat motionless, caught up in the quicksand of her mind as she tried to make sense of her emotions. Sloane, McKenna, and Cam moved around her, preparing for dinner. She heard them talking, heard their lighthearted laughter, but she could only nod when McKenna came to her and asked about the chicken, which she then removed from the grill herself, correctly asserting, like she usually did when she sensed Blake's feelings, that Blake wasn't up for it.

She did, however, manage to lure Blake over to the table to join them. But Blake's silent stupor didn't begin to fade until near the end of their meal, which she'd done little more than pick at despite it being one of her favorites.

"Why are you so quiet, B? You feeling okay?" Sloane asked, sipping from her bottle of cold Modelo.

"Mm-hm." She gave a smile but knew it probably appeared as half-hearted as it felt. "Just have a lot on my mind." She took a bite of the chicken in an added effort to reassure them she was fine.

McKenna, who was watching her closely, seemed to be questioning her with her eyes.

"Have you come up with any more ideas for the clinic?" McKenna asked. She looked to Cam. "Blake wants to open a medical clinic down here."

Cam looked up at her, showing the slightest hint of surprise before she returned to her plate, once again appearing unaffected. "That sounds nice."

Nice?

Blake wasn't especially happy in McKenna bringing up the clinic. It had become more of a sore subject for her seeing as how Sloane, yet again today, made an excuse as to why she couldn't take her to check out possible places for the clinic. And she wasn't especially happy in having this conversation in front of Cam.

"No, no new ideas. I really need to see some things for myself before I can go any further with my plans. And since that seems to be an impossibility, I think I'm just going to go rent a car in town and check things out for myself."

Sloane cleared her throat. "That's not necessary, B."

"At this point, I think it is." She shoveled her food around with her fork.

"I said I would take you and I will. I just wanted you to take some time to relax before we started in on that."

"And I told you, I don't need any more time to relax. I have things I want to get done while I'm here. Important things. You have a home here now so you have all the time you need to explore. But I don't have either of those."

"I understand that you feel that way," Sloane replied evenly. "But I don't understand the big rush. You don't have to go back right away, and I don't know why you'd want to. You've talked nonstop about this venture for over a year. You've said time and again how you can't wait to leave the practice and start anew down here. So, why can't you just relax and enjoy yourself for a little while before we go traipsing around inspecting buildings and property and thinking about finances?"

Blake's fork clanged as she let it fall from her hand. "Despite your awareness of my vacation allowance, I don't necessarily want to take it. So, if you must know, I'm not planning on staying here much longer. In fact, I'd like to leave as soon as possible. As soon as you and I traipse around and I see what I need to. And as for relaxing and enjoying myself? I don't need any help in doing either, and I'm getting a little pissed at everyone, even those who don't even really know me, insinuating otherwise. You would think you all would be smart enough to realize that your suggesting that I'm incapable of relaxing or enjoying myself feels like an insult, like there's something wrong with me, and therefore, makes it more difficult for me to actually relax and enjoy myself."

The table grew quiet. Sloane and Cam stared at their plates while McKenna continued to look at Blake. Her eyes were big and brimming with obvious concern. "You're going to leave?" She sounded heartbroken but Blake didn't fall prey, regardless of how strongly McKenna's sadness was affecting her.

"As soon as I can, yes."

"But, why?"

Blake could no longer hold her all-knowing gaze. Cam's presence, no more than a few inches to her right, was also weighing on her. Its heavy press into her psyche the very answer McKenna was after. Though she knew her long-time friend would eventually discover that, if she wasn't already suspecting, Blake didn't want that discovery to come to light at the current moment.

"Because I've had enough—relaxation." If you can call the constant colliding with a rude, intruding neighbor relaxing. She'd be better off at home, sitting poolside with a book, even if her pool and walled in yard with a few palm trees didn't come anywhere close to comparing with this oceanside view. The peace of mind would be worth it.

McKenna clasped her hands together and attempted a smile. "Why don't we all go for a walk on the beach before the sun goes down?"

Sloane patted her stomach. "I'm all for it. I ate enough for three." She touched McKenna's hand and leaned in for a quick kiss. "Dinner was fabulous, honey. Thank you."

"Yes, thank you," Cam said. "It was wonderful."

"We loved having you," McKenna said. "You'll come again soon, won't you?"

Cam seemed to hesitate. She put off answering by drinking from her bottle of beer. "I'll do my best to try."

"She's busy, Kenna," Sloane said. "All that work she does on houses takes time. Her business must be thriving. That's why she's gone so much."

"I love what you've done to your place," McKenna said. "You can really tell that you put your heart into it. It must be nice being able to make a living doing what you love."

Cam took another drink from her beer. Blake noticed the bottle was empty.

She was apparently as uneasy and eager to escape as Blake was. The questions regarding what she did for a living obviously still an uncomfortable subject for her.

"How long have you been doing that kind of work?" McKenna asked.

Cam shifted and slowly turned the base of the bottle in increments on the tabletop. "I don't know. Three or four years or so."

"Is that all?" Sloane said.

"What did you do before that?" McKenna asked, resting her chin on her entwined hands.

"I've been self-employed."

Blake thought back to her evasiveness the night before when she'd asked her similar questions. She found it rather ironic how she seemed to be hesitant in sharing things about herself when she'd just called Blake on doing the same thing.

Sloane and Kenna seemed to sense the topic was off-limits and Blake knew they wouldn't press Cam for more than she was willing to offer up. Had it been her, they definitely would've continued to push. But they wouldn't do that to someone they didn't know well.

"How about that walk?" Sloane said, rising and stretching.

They all stood and Blake began clearing the table. "You guys go ahead, I'll clean up." She wanted to make up for her indifference at dinner and she needed a good excuse to avoid being around Cam.

McKenna grabbed what was left of the dinnerware and followed her inside. When they reached the sink and deposited the dishes, she touched Blake's arm.

"Come with us. These can wait."

"Kenna, it's the least I can do for all your effort with dinner."

"You mean the dinner you hardly touched?"

"I ate. Just not a lot." She turned on the faucet, but McKenna quickly shut it off.

She tugged on her. "You're coming."

Blake protested but McKenna drug her to the open door to where Sloane and Cam could hear. They turned, curious at the bickering. Blake stopped resisting, not wanting to cause a scene in front of Cam, who also seemed less than thrilled at the idea of a walk. But if McKenna and Sloane noticed, they didn't seem to be deterred because Sloane was already walking off with Cam, talking her ear off and McKenna held firm to Blake as they chased after them.

When they fell into step alongside them, and McKenna dropped Blake's hand to slide her arm around her waist as they aimed for the setting sun, Blake relented and accepted her fate.

Her evening with Cam was far from over.

Chapter Nineteen

They weren't five minutes into their walk before Cam concluded she'd made two big mistakes. The first was agreeing to accompany her new neighbors on an after-dinner walk, when she'd known good and well that she was only accepting the invitation because she was too big of a chicken to say no because she feared more probing questions. One of which would no doubt be why it was she didn't want to go. She couldn't very well tell them that she was uncomfortable, both by their questions and by Blake. The second mistake she'd made was hurrying to her house to get the dogs so they could join them on the walk. She'd hoped that having them with her would help to lesson her qualms, but she'd forgotten how they were around Blake. And true to form, they'd quickly dashed after her and McKenna. Cam had only called for them twice before giving up, already too embarrassed at being ignored.

"I know how you feel," Sloane said as their feet sank in the wet, pliable sand. She and Cam had been walking quietly up until then. Sloane with her hands in her pockets and Cam with her flip-flops dangling from her fingers. The sea was headed back out for the evening and the moist, dark sand was spread out before them for miles, marked by small tide pools reflecting the orange of the setting sun. It was a beautiful evening and Sloane sounded thoughtful, seeming to sense Cam's unease. Whatever she was about to say was bound to have some heartfelt meaning behind it.

"I was so excited for my nephews to meet Kenna when we first started getting serious. I just knew they'd adore her and she them. And that's exactly what happened. They fell in love with her immediately and I was so thrilled at how well they got on. But soon thereafter I noticed that they'd taken to her a little more than I'd anticipated. They'd all but forgotten about me, following Kenna around, wanting every second of her attention. And Kenna was just as smitten with them."

She laughed softly into the wind as it whipped her hair.

"But my jealousy was short-lived. Because as I watched them together I came to understand that my nephews were just seeing in Kenna what I did. She's an amazing human being with a heart that rivals the saints. How could I argue or interfere with that? Why would I want to? So, on our last evening together, I settled back on the couch and smiled as I watched them all bake cookies together in the kitchen. Kenna and my nephews. The people I love most. I'll never forget that day. And I'll never forget those cookies. They were the best damn cookies I'd ever had. Because they were made with so much love."

Sloane glanced over at her. "There's a reason why your dogs are drawn to her, Cam. They sense how special she is. How good her heart is."

"I get what you're saying," Cam said. "And I can understand why they may like her. But my situation is a little different than yours was with McKenna. I'm not in love with Blake. I don't feel about her the way you do McKenna or the way my dogs obviously do."

Cam saw her smile out of the corner of her eye but she didn't acknowledge it. She just kept staring ahead, trying to stay solely focused on her dogs, even though her eyes kept creeping back to Blake. She couldn't get over how incredible her ass and thighs looked in those black leggings.

"Have your dogs ever been wrong about anyone?" Sloane asked.

"I know what you're getting at," Cam said, wishing she'd drop it.

"So, that's a no?" She looked ahead to McKenna and Blake, but Cam could see that the smile remained on her face. "Don't you think it's possible that they may know something you don't? That they may see something you've yet to see, or maybe don't want to see?"

"She can be a good person, Sloane. And I'm...sure she probably is. But that doesn't mean I've fallen for her or that I should fall for her. And besides, she's not a big fan of me either. We just don't click. I don't get the person you guys get or the person my dogs see. I get the angry, stubborn, and defiant Blake."

"Blake can be very stubborn, there's no doubt about that. She's a very passionate woman and she puts her all into everything she does and sometimes everything she feels. You've got her number, Cam. I've never seen anyone get to her the way that you seem to. It's freaking her out. She's fighting it. That's the part of her you're seeing."

"I'm not buying it. But regardless of the reason, the part I get is not very appealing."

"It can be."

Cam looked at her, sure she'd misheard.

"Nothing incites and feeds a passion better than a mutual resistance to attraction. And the longer that resistance plays out and the more insistent the denial, the more powerful that passion becomes. Until eventually, it can no longer be contained and the resistance, no matter how strong, falters, and that passion is finally released and, well, when it's released like that after being held in for so long…it makes for some seriously hot sex."

Cam refocused on the beach ahead of her, disconcerted at where Sloane had taken the discussion. Her body, however, was reacting, on its own. Blake and her beautifully muscled body directly in her line of sight didn't help matters any. Cam had to stare down at the sand so her mind wouldn't jump on board with her body.

"You know," Sloane said. "The kind of sex where you can't seem to get at each other fast enough. And when you do you attack each other in a frenzy, desperate to get as much of them as you can, because you've waited so long, denied your feelings for so long, you feel like you're going to die—"

"I get the picture," Cam said, the image of Blake and her fused together at the mouth, kissing and devouring while tearing at each other's clothes now playing out on a very large screen in her mind. *Sweet Jesus.*

She felt woozy, overloaded by Sloane's compelling suggestion.

"I'm going to turn back. I have some things I need to do at home."

Sloane nodded, saying nothing more. She yelled for McKenna and motioned for her and Blake to return to them. When Blake and McKenna reached them, along with the dogs, who seemed irritatingly happy, Sloane grabbed McKenna's hand and headed off with her back toward the house, leaving Cam and Blake alone. Cam started to protest but clenched her jaw in frustration as she realized it would be a waste of breath. She whistled for the dogs and walked away from Blake, following Sloane and McKenna. The dogs, however, didn't budge. She looked over her shoulder and sighed.

"Damn it, boys, come on."

They remained at Blake's side as she walked toward Cam. Cam begrudgingly fell in line next to her, knowing that was the only way she was going to get her dogs home.

"Maybe if you would calm down and relax a little they'd respond to you better," Blake said without bothering to look at her.

Cam, however, looked at her in complete disbelief. "*You're* giving *me* advice on relaxing? And on how to handle *my* dogs?"

"They're choosing to walk with me for a reason," she said matter-of-factly, reminding Cam of Sloane's insight. "You should probably take some time to figure out what that reason is. Who knows? Maybe you'll come to realize that I'm not as uptight and bitchy as you think. That maybe it's you who needs an attitude adjustment."

Cam felt her face contort in anger. "You're delusional, woman."

"Shall I walk ahead so you can see, once again, your dogs leaving you behind? Because it's not a delusion. And while you're busy doing your inner reflecting, you might want to take a look at your considerable need for privacy, which, by the way, is more than obvious. Especially since you seemed to have had no trouble in chiding me on my hesitance to disclose my personal thoughts and feelings to you about something as ridiculous as a romance novel. And should I mention how you also made yet another grand assumption about me? About my inability to enjoy anything?"

"It wasn't an assumption. It was an observation." Cam was nearly speaking through clenched teeth she was trying so hard to hold her anger back. She couldn't believe the nerve of this woman.

"An observation? You've known me for what, a couple of weeks? Spent all of a few hours with me and you think you've made an accurate observation?"

"I know I've only seen you enjoy one thing since you've arrived. Wine. If there's been something else, I must've missed it. And from what I heard tonight, it sounds like Sloane and McKenna must've missed it too. It sounds to me like, not only do you not enjoy much of anything, but you don't even really want to. Why else would you be so eager to leave? Sloane has told me how much you love the beach. So why aren't you enjoying it?"

Blake stopped and turned to Cam with her hands on her hips.

"You want to know why I want to leave and why I'm not enjoying myself here?"

Cam saw the fierceness in the set of her jaw and the hurricane that had blown in to cloud the Caribbean Sea of her eyes. She knew what she was about to say and it made her mad as hell.

"You're blaming me? I'm the sole reason why you're so unhappy?" She shook her head and laughed in disbelief. "Well, here's a newsflash, Blake. The feeling is mutual. So, if you want to use me as an excuse to go back home, then go right ahead. You won't get any objection from me."

It will be a relief and I'm already anticipating it. I just hope you don't keep reappearing if you do happen to succeed in opening your clinic.

Byron jumped up on Cam then, his muddy paws resting on her hip. Bo and Bingo were next to him, ears back, stepping in place. Bo whined and Byron yipped at her. They were distressed by the heated arguing. She stroked Byron's head and reached down to pet the other two. She felt terrible. They'd never seen her lose control like this.

"Let's just get back to the house," Cam said, softening her voice for the benefit of the dogs. "Think you can manage to hold your tongue that long?"

They started walking again and Blake gave her a very obvious forced smile and spoke with a sugary sweet voice. "I don't know, Cam, can I? You tell me. Since you claim to be so insightful when it comes to me."

"I'd say it's highly doubtful."

Blake laughed again. "I've said it once and I'll say it again. You don't know me."

"And I'll repeat what I said in response to that statement back at the fish market. I don't think I want to know you."

Blake looked stung.

"It's no wonder these dogs are so starved for attention from a woman. There probably hasn't been a single one who was willing to give you the time of day, even if they were initially lured in by your looks. As soon as they saw through that exterior, that was all she wrote. That's why there hasn't been anyone. That's why you're alone."

Cam balled her fists and trembled. An excruciating ache tightened her chest and it hurt to breathe. Her eyes began to water and she tore her gaze from Blake and stormed away. She didn't pay attention to whether or not her dogs followed and she didn't pay any attention to Sloane and McKenna when she passed them by, leaving their questions of concern unanswered. She just kept walking, head held low, body stiff and rigid from the pent-up pain that was just about killing her as it tried to claw its way out.

She kept walking until she came to her patio. She rushed up the steps, crashed into the house, and headed straight for her bedroom. Once there, she grabbed the framed photo she'd had at her bedside for the past four years. She smoothed her hand over the photograph, curled into a ball on her bed and burst into tears, holding Lexi tightly to her heart as the pain finally bled out.

CHAPTER TWENTY

Blake sat in the sand hugging her knees, watching the ocean's rhythmic churning. Her pulse and her breathing were beginning to slow from her run, but she was mostly mindless to her physical state. The strands of wind-whipped hair stinging her face were also ignored. Her stare soon went beyond the vastness of the sea and her thoughts grew equally as distant. But they, unlike her stare, had a focal point. Cam. Regardless of how hard she tried, her mind wouldn't veer from what had happened on that after-dinner walk two days before.

She couldn't shake what was said, how she'd been hurt by Cam's words and how Cam had seemed terribly hurt by hers. And she couldn't shake what had happened when she'd followed Cam to her house, worried about the pain-riddled look that had come over her just before she'd hurried away, leaving her beloved dogs behind without even looking back. She'd rushed up her patio steps and into her house without another word, slamming the door closed behind her.

Blake had been so perturbed that she'd dismissed McKenna's and Sloane's questions as she and the dogs hurried after her.

Blake could still recall how cool the steps had felt on her bare feet as she and the dogs hurried up them. She remembered how quiet everything seemed to be, save for the waves and the blowing wind. She'd knocked softly on the door as the dogs pawed at it, staring up at her in confusion. She'd waited. And waited. Then knocked again. But Cam hadn't answered and Blake's concern had grown. The anguish that had come over Cam and the way she'd taken off, had differed greatly from her usual calm manner. And what had come over her face instead was more than the avoidance and distress Blake had witnessed in her the night they'd been with Alberto. Something was seriously wrong, and the dogs seemed to have sensed it as well, and they'd started whining in addition to scratching at the door.

Blake had known she couldn't leave them outside. That's what she'd told herself when she'd knocked again and then carefully eased open the unlocked door. She'd called for Cam, though not outrageously loud for fear of startling her, as she'd stepped inside. The dogs had bolted ahead, searching for her, and they'd disappeared into a room beyond the kitchen. There had been no further movement and no answer to her second call. She'd stood near the kitchen, debating what to do while looking at the dark entryway to the quiet room. Her anxiety had escalated as she'd whispered for the boys, hoping at the very least that they would respond and give her some sort of sign that things were okay. But they hadn't come.

She'd taken a step, then changed her mind and turned to leave. But there had been something in her that wouldn't allow her to go. The need to know that Cam was okay had won out and she'd crossed to that room and had just about announced herself again when she'd heard it. She'd froze, the sound instantly recognizable and so heartbreaking, Blake had gone limp with heavy sorrow and she'd covered her mouth to stifle her own tears. She'd heard Cam crying, sobbing, and Blake had turned and left, feeling responsible and like she'd intruded on a very private moment.

She hadn't seen Cam since and she knew Cam had spent most of those subsequent days away from home. She knew because she'd been checking for her Jeep, hoping for the chance to go offer an apology, to see, at the very least, if they could somehow call a truce. But the few times Blake had seen her Jeep it had been late at night and Cam hadn't been out on her patio at dawn when Blake had gone for her runs. So, she'd stayed away and told herself it was out of respect, but deep down she knew it was also because she feared rejection and feared that she'd only cause more trouble.

And now she'd just finished another run, her second of the day. Her inability to sleep and to sit still were unnerving, and she was caught between an agitating restlessness and extended periods of mindlessness. McKenna and Sloane were worried. She hadn't yet filled them in on the situation with Cam, so when she couldn't sleep, she slipped outside and sat seaside, looking up at a night sky so completely covered in stars she often stared until her neck began to ache. When she grew restless during the day, she went for runs or long walks, going until she was too far away or too tired to continue. But the distractions were only temporary, and Cam always quickly returned to her thoughts.

She sunk her hand into the thick, warm sand. She knew she needed to clue McKenna and Sloane in. She couldn't avoid them forever and they'd only keep worrying. She lifted a handful of sand and then spread her fingers, watching as the sand filtered through. She repeated the motion again and again, finding it strangely soothing. She became so engrossed she nearly jumped out of her skin when someone approached.

"Did you run this far?" Sloane asked as she eased down next to her. She didn't seem to realize she'd startled her.

"Uh-huh."

What is she doing here?

"I almost gave up looking for you a half a mile back. Didn't think you were running this far down the beach."

"I like it here. It's really quiet. No people."

"Yeah, I guess the lack of homes here kind of assures that." She glanced over her shoulder at the dunes behind them. The row of houses came to an end close to a mile back. "Probably won't be this way for long. I'm sure they'll continue to develop eventually."

Blake clasped her hands together around her knees again and returned her attention to the water. She was surprised to see Sloane, or anyone for that matter, and she was a little alarmed. "You didn't walk here did you?" She'd seemed to appear from an angle from behind, like she'd come from the road that paralleled the houses rather than the beach.

"I started to, but Kenna suggested I drive after reminding me of your abilities as a marathon runner. So, I drove and kept an eye out for you as best I could. Good thing I didn't give up."

"Has something happened?" Blake asked. "That you needed to find me?"

"I thought you might like to take that ride to look at real estate you've been so keen on."

Blake was slow to respond. Sloane's offer to finally take her to explore possible locations for the clinic was the last thing she'd expected to hear. And the urge she'd had to do that very thing had been, believe it or not, the last thing on her mind. She hadn't thought about the clinic since her last encounter with Cam. In the past, she had always, always carried on with the pursuance of her goals no matter what obstacle she came up against. So, why had she been derailed now? If anything, she should've been more determined than ever to do her exploring so she could leave the beach and never have to think about Cam again.

"Okay, what's going on?" Sloane asked. "You've been an insomniatic space cadet since that walk with Cam. I know something went down between you two, and I respect that you haven't wanted to talk about it. But I thought for sure that offering to go for that drive would have you racing for the car."

"That's fine," Blake said softly. "We can go." She stood, careful to brush off the sand away from Sloane. Sloane stood too and they headed through the short batch of dunes to the SUV.

"Do you want to talk about it?" Sloane asked as they drove toward town.

"Not especially." Her arm was resting on the windowsill, the wind flying through her raised fingers. It was early afternoon and balmy with the temperature in the seventies. McKenna and Sloane were right. The fall months were absolutely beautiful here.

They rode in silence for most of the trip and only made small talk when they did speak. Sloane was respecting her need for space and she was grateful. She wanted to wait until after this excursion before she brought up Cam.

About fifteen miles before town, they turned to head south and then drove for another forty minutes until they pulled into Pueblo de Consuelo, the small village Blake had visited the previous summer. She'd worked in the area as a volunteer physician and had fallen in love with this particular village.

Excitement began to build. She was back. Finally. She crossed her fingers, hoping they could somehow make things work here. Sloane, too, had said she really liked it here. She and McKenna had come to see the village on their last trip down from Phoenix. Everything was moving along seamlessly.

That was good, right?

Then why am I getting so nervous?

She closed her eyes and took a deep breath. They'd already developed a business plan. She and Sloane were doing most of the financing but also had a few charitable donations lined up. Blake had already made arrangements with a volunteer organization to recruit medical staff and others who wished to donate a few weeks of their time to come serve others. She actually already knew seven physicians and a handful of medical assistants who were anxious to be her first volunteers. They were friends and they were almost as excited as she was about this venture.

A lot of the hard work had already been done.

And now she and Sloane were about to embark on the next step. That step, which was finding and purchasing a location to set up shop, would be the biggest one to date.

That was why she was nervous.

This was really happening.

She opened her eyes, determined to get on with it.

It was time to put this dream into serious motion.

Chapter Twenty-one

B lake and Sloane walked on one of the cobblestone streets through the village, taking in the surroundings. The village itself was only about four blocks long and two blocks wide. Most of the old buildings populating it were made of stone and painted in varied shades of pastel colors like pale yellows, oranges, pinks, and blues. Signs in Spanish in the windows beckoned customers inside, and some shop owners were standing in their doorways, talking to passersby, one woman sweeping her front entrance. A few kids rode by on bicycles and Blake stopped to pet a friendly, roaming dog. She did the same to a gentle burro being led by a quiet but friendly man and woman with hauls that looked equally as heavy as the one the burro carried.

The others they saw eyed them with curiosity and eagerly returned their smiles. Some waved, and one man tried his best to lure them to his cart to buy hot corn on the cob. It smelled delicious, as did a café they passed, but they politely declined, promising to return another time.

After they passed through the center of the village, they came upon the small, faded white building for sale Sloane had previously discovered. Blake was relieved to see it was still available. Just as she was trying to read the information on the flier in the window, someone called out. Sloane tapped her shoulder to get Blake to turn and look. A woman, along with two children, was waving at them from across the street. Blake grabbed Sloane's wrist as recognition took hold.

"I know them," she said, completely surprised. "That's Marta." She waved back, and Marta and the children crossed the street toward them. Blake was thrilled to see them and after jovial embraces she introduced them to Sloane in her limited Spanish. Thankfully, Marta could speak a little more English than Blake could Spanish. After they managed some pleasantries, Marta asked about their visit. Blake pointed at the building and asked if she knew anything about it. Marta nodded and spoke to her son, Marco. He and his sister, Isabel, ran off, and Blake spent the next few minutes doing her best to find out how Marta was fairing.

She was a young mother in her early twenties with long, dark hair and bright, friendly eyes. She'd traveled to the nearby church where the temporary medical clinic Blake had been volunteering at was. Blake had treated her and the kids, and she'd developed a strong fondness for them. And Marta, to show her gratitude, had invited Blake and some of the other volunteers to her village. They'd readily accepted and come for a visit, where they'd met Marta's friends and loved ones as well as other villagers. It was then that Blake had heard firsthand about their great need for medical care and she'd begun thinking about opening her own clinic.

Unbeknownst to Marta, her friendly invitation had led Blake to the biggest dream of her life. And as soon as Blake was able to tell her that, in the Spanish she was now very intent on learning, she was going to.

Blake listened as Marta relayed how she was feeling, using both English and Spanish. Blake was elated to hear that she was doing well, and reportedly so were her children. When they returned, they had a middle-aged man with dark, sun-weathered skin and a crown of receding, silver hair with them. He greeted Blake and Sloane with the same friendliness exuded by Marta. His name was Javier and though his English wasn't as good as Marta's, he was still very willing to show them the building.

He unlocked the door, and Blake and Sloane entered the dimly lit space. The front room was wide and open but otherwise sparse. There was no flooring, or counters or cabinetry. But the walls seemed to be intact and they found the same to be true in the three small adjoining rooms. The ceiling, however, needed repair in four places and two new windows were also needed. As for the rest, they'd have someone else come in to assess that. But otherwise Blake couldn't help but feel a rush of enthusiasm at what she'd seen. It was the perfect size for a clinic and the location couldn't be better.

She thanked Javier and asked him for a phone number. He held up a finger and spoke to Marta, who then took Blake by the hand and led them down the street. Blake shrugged at Sloane, who was now holding the children's hands, and followed Marta to the café they'd passed earlier. Javier waved and continued on while they entered the establishment with Marta and her children. The café was really a bakery of sorts, with the heavenly scents of freshly baked food filling the air. A counter ran along the back, with a glass display of said food. Blake looked longingly at the pastries and breads, and their delicious smells quickly lured the kids over to peer through the display. Blake smiled at their excitement and turned to take in the rest of the café.

It was small, but not uncomfortably so. Four round tables set for two were positioned in front of the windows. Marta urged Blake and Sloane to sit before she disappeared behind the counter. She returned a few moments later with another woman, who Marta introduced as Sofia. She appeared to be older than Marta, with her dark hair wound into a bun and a well-worn apron covering the front of her stout figure. She gave them each a plate of small shell-shaped goodies and then nodded to Marta, who gave them both mugs of what looked to be hot chocolate.

Blake knew better than to try to politely decline their generosity. So she and Sloane thanked them and the women disappeared behind the counter, this time taking the children with them.

"So are we supposed to wait here for Javier?" Sloane asked.

"I think so." Blake picked up a warm, doughy shell. "I really need to work on my Spanish." She took a bite of the pastry. "I hate not being able to talk to people, and if I'm going to live and work here, I can't expect everyone to speak English as well as Marta can." She chewed and savored the flavor of cinnamon bursting in her mouth. "Oh, my God, these are good."

"You're not doing so bad," Sloane said, laughing a little, probably at her reaction over the food.

"Yeah, but I need to do more than just get by. I need to be fluent."

"You know more than I do."

"That's not saying much." She took another bite, thoroughly enjoying the treat. "What are these? They're so good they're almost sinful."

"Now this I do know," Sloane said. "They're called conchas. Mexican sweet bread. And you're right, they are killer good. These are the best ones I've had so far."

Sloane chewed and then sipped her hot chocolate. "Kenna and I are going to order one of those language programs. It'll probably be one of those older ones with the cassette tapes since we can't do it online at the beach house. This living for weeks at a time without internet thing we're embarking on is already hurting me. Kenna loves it, though. She's going all Little House on the Prairie on me. The electricity fiasco didn't really bother her. She snuggled up to me all night long talking about how romantic it could be if we lived without it and used candles instead."

"But she was so grateful to Tomas, so thrilled that he was able to fix it."

"She was glad we didn't have to pack up and go back to Phoenix. That was what she was worried about. She'd be fine living without power if we were prepared. She sure did her best trying to convince me that I'd like it to."

Blake grimaced. "Spare me the details, please."

"What? All I was going to say was that she was right about the candles. It was romantic." She sipped her cocoa and gave a crooked grin.

Blake gave her her usual rolling of the eyes and took the last bite of a concha. Her eyes rolled again, this time in sheer delight. "I have got to learn how to make these."

"Yes, you do. That way you can make some for me, too." Sloane chewed a bite and swallowed. "I get why you like it here," she said. "Why you want to help so badly. This little village is so quaint and colorful. The people are so friendly and generous."

"Thank you." She touched Sloane's hand, but then looked away. "I'll never be able to express just how much your help in this means to me."

"I've got a pretty good idea."

Blake smiled at her graciously and then her mind went to the one concerning obstacle blocking her dream. "I just wish my parents could be as understanding."

"When are you going to tell them?"

"When I'm sure we can really make this happen."

"And you don't think they'll be supportive? Maybe even want to help?"

"I don't think so. They barely tolerate my being gay. That's enough of a difference for them. Anything more would be unheard of. And the plan has always been for me to take over the family practice."

"Whose plan? Yours or theirs?"

"You know how it is with them. They are the all-knowing, all-powerful parents and I'm—well, I've always been the good girl. The ever-obedient daughter. My coming out was the one and only time I've ever risked disappointing them. And that was years ago."

She drank her cocoa before continuing.

"I love being a doctor and working at the practice, so I haven't been miserable or anything. But after volunteering, I realized that I want more. I want to do more. And I want to do it here, where I can hopefully make a really big difference. Whether they understand that or not, I can't let that stop me."

Sloane squeezed her forearm. "I'm so freaking proud of you." Her eyes teared. "You can do this. *We* can do this. And you know, no matter what, you've got Kenna and me standing right by your side."

Blake felt her own tears threatening. "Thanks."

The door to the café opened and three men entered. One was Javier, and one was a man Blake had never met before, and the other...the other was Tomas.

She was so shocked to see him again she nearly swallowed her food wrong. She immediately stood, dumbfounded.

"Tomas." She blinked. "Hello."

"Hola, miss."

The man Blake didn't know offered his hand. "Hi, I'm Alejandro. You're the ones interested in Javier's building?"

"Yes. I'm Blake and this is my good friend, Sloane."

He shook Sloane's hand. "Javier is my tio. Uncle. And Tomas is my cousin."

"Oh."

"You and Tomas know each other?" he asked.

"Yes, we do. We've—met before."

"He fixed my electricity," Sloane said. "I live next to his friend Cam."

Alejandro looked puzzled, but Tomas said something and he laughed, nodded, and looked at Blake with what she perceived to be some sort of secret, knowing smile. She dismissed it, though, when he focused on Sloane.

"Ah, Santi, okay. So, you moved into that house next to her?"

"A few weeks ago."

"That's going to be quite a little gem once you chip away the rough edges."

"That's what I'm hoping."

"I'm sure Santi will be a big help. And Tomas, well, there's no one better. And I've worked with a lot of contractors in my day so I know what I'm talking about."

"I'm sorry, Santi? Who is that?" Blake asked, the name sounding vaguely familiar. She knew she'd heard it before but couldn't place it.

"Santi is Cam. Her last name is Santiago, so everyone calls her Santi."

"Oh."

"She hasn't told you that?"

Blake shook her head. "She—no, she hasn't." But now that she thought about it, she had heard Alberto call her that.

"Give her time. She'll come out of her shell once she gets to know you."

"I'm not sure that's ever going to happen," Blake said with sadness. "She—seems very private." *And she seems to hate my guts.*

"She can be at first. It took her a while to open up to people here when she first moved down after her accident. She didn't hardly speak to anyone for months."

"Accident?" Sloane asked. "Like a car accident?"

He nodded solemnly.

"The scars," Blake whispered. "She was injured."

"Yes," he said. "She was lucky she survived. But she has, and probably still, would argue that."

"Why?" Sloane asked.

Alejandro looked at both of them. "Because she doesn't feel lucky at all. She feels guilty for surviving when her wife didn't."

The café seemed to tunnel in around Blake. "Her *wife?*"

Alejandro nodded, and when he spoke again he seemed regretful.

"I probably shouldn't have said anything." He scratched his temple. "Santi...she means a great deal to a lot of people around here and...we hate to see her so alone. She holes up in that house, sometimes behind that laptop with her work and...it would be nice if she could meet other women. Women like her."

"You mean lesbians?"

"Well, yes."

"We've been trying," Sloane said. She looked at Blake.

Blake's mind was racing and she struggled to speak, her brain and mouth disconnected. "Work? I thought—doesn't she work on houses?"

He pressed his lips together and suddenly appeared very uneasy. "She does. But let's talk about Javier's building. Will you be in the area for a while? We could do another walk-through and I could work you up an estimate and answer any questions you have about repairs and renovation."

She just blinked, unable to process quickly enough. The words "wife" and "didn't survive" just kept echoing in her head.

"She's not planning on staying for very much longer," Sloane said for her. "But we are interested."

"Great." He dug his wallet from his jeans and pinched out two business cards. He handed them over. "Here's my number. I'm here for another week, then I'll be back in Tucson. But feel free to call me anytime. I'm happy to translate for Javier. And if you need to reach Tomas for any reason, such as further renovation questions from someone local, your best bet is to ask Santi. She knows where he is more often than we do."

He shook their hands, and after they said their good-byes, they left.

Blake was staring at her cocoa mug so hard it blurred. When she felt Sloane's hand on her arm again, she looked up and tried to focus on her through pooling tears.

"Would you like to talk about it now?" she asked gently.

Blake swallowed and stifled back more tears. She nodded. "Yes."

CHAPTER TWENTY-TWO

It was just before noon and the sunlight was weak and pale, mostly hiding behind the thin wisps of drifting clouds. Cam felt a kinship to it, knowing she too, looked weak and pale from days of hiding away and eating very little. It was why she was debating whether or not to remove her sunglasses. Normally, she would under cloudy conditions like these, but today her physical appearance took precedence over the shyness of the sun. Maybe her aunt and uncle wouldn't notice her wearing them despite the lack of sunshine.

She checked her phone for the time. It was ten past noon and her aunt and uncle were fashionably late like always. If they ever did show up to anything on time, she'd wonder if it was really them or if it was some sort of alien being disguised as them.

They'd agreed to meet at Juanita's, a popular restaurant in town they'd been frequenting since Cam's move to Mexico. The crowd on the outdoor patio was thin today, and she was grateful. She had an oceanside view from her table, and if it weren't for the overzealousness of the seagulls and the occasional shriek from the diners at the table next to her every time a bird came near them, she'd be enjoying a pretty peaceful afternoon.

One of the waitresses hurried to the shriekers table and chased the birds away. It made Cam laugh because she and the waitress both knew her success would be short-lived. The gulls were always a problem on the patio. Most people just accepted them as part of the experience, part of the decor.

Cam watched the gulls return, this time landing closer to her, where they seemed to feel safer. She looked back to the neighboring table to see if they'd start to freak out again, but instead saw Aunt Ginger and Uncle Tony weaving through tables. They were smiling broadly, walking hand in hand in their typical beachwear, most of which consisted of airy, light cotton or linen clothing. Today, however, was significantly cooler, especially when the breeze kicked up, and it was the first real indication that summer had indeed finally bid them farewell. Which, from what Cam could see, still meant shorts for the two of them, but they did have on sweatshirts instead of short sleeves. They still wore their sandals, however, which didn't surprise her. They would, after all, only pay so much credence to the change in season.

"Hey, look, honey," Uncle Tony said. "It's the beach bum." He hugged Cam firmly enough to lift her off the ground and continued his teasing. "We heard you live on the beach now. That must be why we never see you anymore." He set her down and drew back to look at her. "You're too good for us now. You're a sand-snob."

She could tell by the grin beneath his long white beard and the sparkle of his lively, olive green eyes, that he was in an unusually playful mood, and Cam found herself laughing, his happiness already wearing off on her.

She needed it too.

The depressing mood she'd been plagued with had worn out its welcome but had yet to leave.

"A sand-snob? Is this a new term? Am I supposed to be offended?" She turned to hug Aunt Ginger, careful to mind her straw hat.

"Don't listen to him," Aunt Ginger said, "He's already had some tequila so he's feeling himself." Her embrace was as light as a feather compared to his. But then again, so was her build. Uncle Tony was a big guy, standing over six foot four and weighing over three hundred pounds. He had been a rowdy biker in his younger days and his tattooed arms and intimidating frame were enough to make some people wary. Aunt Ginger, on the other hand, was a slight woman, who stood just short of Cam's five foot six. She shared Cam's dark looks and Hispanic roots and people often mistook them as mother and daughter. Some people also made the mistake of assuming that she was, due to her slight build, a timid, passive woman. That, however, couldn't be further from the truth. And Uncle Tony, despite his intimidating physicality, wore his heart on his sleeve. He even cried over heart-tugging commercials.

The three of them sat at the round white table and the waitress that had chased the birds took their drink orders and left them to their conversation.

They were quiet for a moment and Aunt Ginger was smiling at Cam in the way she often did when she was trying to read her. Her close study was interrupted though, when she had to grab hold of her hat to prevent the breeze from carrying it off.

"Something's changed," she said to Cam when the wind died down. "What's going on?"

"I have no idea what you mean," Cam said. It was an evasive response and for her, not at all unusual with most people. But her aunt and uncle weren't most people. Cam removed her sunglasses to rub her eye.

"You look like shit," Uncle Tony let out. "And we haven't seen you in weeks."

"Tony," Aunt Ginger chided. "What he means, and what I mean, is that we're a little worried about you. We thought maybe you were just busy and that's why you've been putting off our weekly lunches. But now that you're here, we can see that it's obviously something more."

"Like what?" Cam asked. She'd never lied to them and she'd never had reason to. But she didn't want to get into what was going on. Just thinking about discussing it was already causing her stomach to plummet.

"We don't know," Uncle Tony said. "But we got eyes, Cammie. And you don't look good. You look like you did when you first came down."

Though his words could sound harsh, Cam knew they weren't intended that way. He just happened to be a little rough around the edges and sometimes the love and good intentions he had in that big heart of his came out with a serrated surface, like the filter his words had to pass through to reach his mouth was old and in need of an update because it couldn't smooth and polish like it should.

As Cam thought about that and felt the abundant warmth of his familiar sincerity, something unexpected popped into her mind.

Could Blake be the same way?

Could she be like Uncle Tony?

Could she possibly be as loving and well-meaning as he was but just have a fucked-up filter?

A million things came at her mind then in support of her hypothesis. But she pushed them away. It wasn't the time or place to think about something that involved. And if the answer to the mystery of Blake was that simple, then how could she have missed it when she'd been loved and protected by someone similar since her childhood?

"So, you gonna tell us?" Uncle Tony asked.

"I've been a little down," Cam finally said with a shrug like it was no big deal. She instinctively turned to look at the sea so they wouldn't see the emotion in her eyes. She put her sunglasses back on, but the protective lenses didn't feel like enough of a barrier.

"What's got you down, Cammie?" Uncle Tony asked, the big teddy bear sensitivity coming out a little more polished this time.

"You were doing so well lately," Aunt Ginger said. "Getting out of the house, spending time with your friends. You almost seemed content."

Cam had made a lot of friends once she'd finally begun to socialize after her move down. Meeting Tomas and a few others had led her to her interest in renovation, and she'd spent a lot of time remodeling her house with her new friends. Eventually, she'd become skilled enough to help her friends out with their projects. But up until a few months ago, she'd still felt alone. She'd only let people in so far and she'd only spend so much time with them. Most of the time, preferring to hovel up with the dogs and confess her feelings to the whispering sea when she went for walks. But slowly, that, too, had begun to change. She'd been out a lot more, helping more than just her friends, and sometimes, she'd even met up with her friends just to socialize.

Now, however, she seemed to have taken a hundred steps back. And she couldn't even bring herself to confide in the sea.

"I—" She sighed and rested her head in her hand. Then ran her palm over her hair as she tried to find a way around having to share the truth.

Aw, fuck it.

Keeping this inside was eating her alive.

She had to tell them, for her own sanity.

Surely, they'd understand.

They'd see that Blake was the root of all her troubles.

Chapter Twenty-three

Cam took a deep breath and composed herself, hoping to control the tide of emotions that were threatening to come. "There's a woman staying in the house next to me and—"

"A woman?" Aunt Ginger said. She shook her head quickly. "Sorry, go on."

"Her name is Blake and we don't get along. We—we *really* don't get along. We butt heads every time we see each other. Which, up until a few days ago, was pretty frequently because she's right next door and the women she's staying with, the actual homeowners, who are a couple, are really nice and we have become friends. This couple, Sloane and McKenna, have been trying to get Blake and me together. And that hasn't exactly turned out like they'd hoped. All it's really done is cause a lot of problems between Blake and me."

"So you two got together?" Uncle Tony asked, his shock very apparent on his face. "You and Blake? And it didn't work out?"

"No, Uncle Tony, no. I don't have an interest, obviously. You both know the main reason why. But even beyond my grief over Lexi, I don't have an interest. Nor does Blake. We, upon occasion, have tried to humor Sloane and McKenna, by spending time together and attempting to be civil. But it always ends in disaster."

"Can you stop trying to humor your new friends and just stay away?" Aunt Ginger asked.

"I have," she said softly, staring off toward the water. "That's what I've been doing."

"But Blake's still bothering you," Uncle Tony said.

The waitress brought their drinks along with a large bowl of tortilla chips and three kinds of salsa. Uncle Tony dipped a chip into the salsa verde, crunched a bite, and slid the bowls toward Cam. She waved them away, not even having a desire to drink her beer.

"She's not coming around," Cam said.

"But you're still bothered by her," Uncle Tony said.

"I don't know what I'm feeling. I just know it's not good."

"Are you anxious for her to leave?" Aunt Ginger asked.

Cam let out a laugh. "Well, yeah. That will solve everything."

"How so?"

"Because she'd be gone," Cam said, appalled that she'd even have to explain. Neither of them seemed to get it. "Because then I wouldn't have to worry about avoiding her or worry about what's going to happen if we do run into each other."

"So, this is something that's always on your mind, even though you aren't around her anymore," her aunt said.

"Yes."

"So, you're thinking about her a lot."

Cam looked at her. "Not in the way you're implying."

"I didn't imply anything," she said. "I just stated the obvious." She squinted at her. "Are you sure her leaving is what you really want?"

Cam groaned. "Christ, you sound like Sloane and McKenna. Yes, I'm sure." She banged her fist on the armrest of her chair.

Uncle Tony chuckled and sipped his salt rimmed margarita. "She must be something," he said. "To have you so strung out."

"I'm not strung out. I'm pissed. I'm angry. She's said a lot of nasty things."

"Like what?" Aunt Ginger asked.

"Like—telling me that I'm alone because no one can stand to be around me once they get past my looks."

"Ohhh," Uncle Tony said, dipping a chip into the salsa rojo. "So, she thinks you're hot stuff."

Cam shook her head. "That's not what she meant—"

"That's what she said, though, right?" Aunt Ginger asked.

Cam sat back and sighed. "You're missing the whole point. And I told you, we do not like each other. I mean, she hates me."

"I don't think she does," Aunt Ginger said. "And you don't hate her either."

"I don't like her," Cam said. "And I want her to leave."

Her aunt and uncle exchanged a look. They both smiled.

"What was that?" Cam pointed from one to the other. "You two aren't seriously thinking there's anything going on between this woman and me, are you? Because you'd be dead wrong."

"Maybe not physically," Aunt Ginger said, indulging in a chip. "Not yet, anyway."

"I mean at all," Cam said, feeling her face burn. She had both hands clenched into fists.

"Okay," Aunt Ginger said.

Cam leaned forward, her impatience and frustration now irritation. "Didn't you hear me? Hear what it was she said to me about why I'm alone?"

"She doesn't know about Lexi," Uncle Tony said. "I'm assuming she doesn't because you don't tell anyone anything that personal until you know them very well."

"I haven't told her but that doesn't matter."

"It does, Cammie," Aunt Ginger said. "She might not've said something like that had she known."

"How do you know? You don't know this woman."

"No, but it doesn't sound like you know her very well, either."

Cam closed her mouth. "No, and I don't want to."

"You sure about that?"

"Yes!" She turned away from them. "And I've told her so."

"So you've said some unkind things to her too," Uncle Tony said.

Cam directed the glare she had for him out at the sea.

He chuckled again and the sound of it was like nails on a chalkboard to her.

"You're awful upset there, Cammie," he said. "For someone who doesn't let shit get to her anymore."

"Is she pretty?" Aunt Ginger asked.

"I'm not even going to dignify that with an answer," Cam said. "Because it has nothing to do with anything I'm saying."

"Then she must be," Uncle Tony said.

This time Cam directed her glare at him regardless of the fact that he couldn't see it through her shades.

"I'd even go so far as to say that you're very attracted to her, seeing as how fired up you are. My niece who doesn't do 'upset.'"

"Forget it," Cam said. If getting up and storming off wouldn't help prove them correct, she would've done it in a heartbeat. But as it was, she sat there and stewed in her anger. "Just forget I said anything." She grabbed her beer and took two big swallows.

"All right, Cammie," Aunt Ginger said, rubbing her shoulder. "We'll drop it. But we do understand how you suddenly finding yourself attracted to someone must be scary. Lexi was your world. But she's gone, hon. She's been gone a while now. You've been through enough, punished yourself for something that wasn't your fault. Don't continue to do that because you've met someone you're attracted to."

Cam swallowed down the painful tears with more beer. She was too close to crying to respond. And even if she'd been able, the fight she'd put up would've been weak. She was too exhausted. A prizefighter stepping into the ring to battle after already having gone through ten harrowing rounds with an undefeated opponent.

"Here," Uncle Tony said, once again sliding the chips and salsa her way. "Relax. Kick your feet up." He gave her his best goofy grin.

"And stay a while?" Cam finally said, trying to sound unimpressed by his attempt at humor. "I'm not hungry."

"Well, you better get hungry," Aunt Ginger said. "Because you're not leaving here until you eat something." She slowly shook Cam's shoulder back and forth. "So you might as well tuck in that pouty lip and enjoy your lunch with us. You know you want to."

"Not especially," Cam said, taking a deep breath that shook in her chest. Her body was clear, the heavy emotion gone. Breathing, though shaky, felt really good again.

"Everything we've said to you today was said in love."

Cam laughed. "Then I'd hate to see how you are when you're mad at me."

"If you don't eat something, you'll get to see that here real quick."

Cam sipped her drink. They did love her. If there was anything left on this planet she was still sure of, it was that. They'd been there for her her entire life. Been the parents her own mother and father refused to be.

"Okay, fine," she said. "But you guys are buying. And with that in mind, I suddenly just became very hungry." She held up her beer. "And very thirsty, too."

CHAPTER TWENTY-FOUR

Blake slipped out the back door quietly and hugged herself against the cool, late night breeze. The sand that swallowed her feet was just as cool, and she thought about going back inside to pull on a thicker sweater. As she came to her favorite stargazing spot however, she stole a glance next door, just as she'd done since the day she'd heard Alejandro's revelation, and was surprised to actually see Cam's shadowed form sitting in her patio chair. The woman had been incognito for days.

Blake gathered her nerves, fearing this might be her one and only chance to talk to her, and walked quietly to her house. She'd just reached the outer edge of the patio when the dogs barked and scrambled down the steps to greet her. She knelt and gave them love but then straightened right away when she saw Cam rise and head for the door.

"Wait," she said, hurrying to the bottom of the steps. "Cam, please."

Cam stilled but didn't face her.

"I would like to talk to you for a minute. It won't take long, and I promise, if you don't want me to, I'll never bother you again."

Cam didn't move and she didn't respond.

"Please, Cam. I didn't come to fight. I don't want to cause you any more pain."

Cam's rigid posture softened and her hand fell from the doorknob.

Blake walked up two steps, hopeful.

"Is it okay if I come up? I won't sit, I'll just stay here by the steps."

Cam finally turned and Blake tried not to gasp at the drawn, gaunt look of her face. Blake wanted to believe that it was just the shadows playing tricks, that the light filtering out from inside the house wasn't adequate enough to see her clearly on the unlit patio. But Blake worried that what she was seeing was reality and that Cam truly did look like she was lost and defeated.

Blake cleared the last step, yearning to cross to her to take her in her arms and hold her until all the regret and apologies she had inside passed through to Cam, filling her with some sort of peace and comfort. She couldn't take that risk though, too afraid that Cam would run again. So, she remained where she was, tentative, like she was approaching an injured bird who had no idea she only wanted to help.

"I wanted to apologize," Blake said. "I've said some really hurtful things to you. Things I never should've said and had no right to say." She hugged herself again as she shuddered from the breeze. She felt as fragile as Cam looked, and when the wind penetrated again she felt as if her bones might snap. "I know I've hurt you, Cam, and I'm so sorry." She couldn't tell her that she'd heard her sobbing uncontrollably, and that she knew about the accident and the tragic loss of her wife. She could only tell her how sorry she was and try, probably for the rest of her life, not to think about the awful things she'd said to her about her being alone. Things that she'd never forgive herself for, regardless if Cam ever did or not.

"You're cold," Cam said.

Blake shook again, surprised she'd said anything at all. "It's a little cooler tonight than I'd anticipated." Bo came to her and she actually debated whether or not to remove her hand from the warm place beneath her arm to pet him. But she couldn't resist his sweet face and the other two then came wanting her affection. She grew a little sad as she realized that this might be the last time she'd ever see them. And when she looked back to Cam, that sadness rose to nip at her throat, as she thought the same about her.

"How are you doing? Are you feeling okay?" Blake asked. The physician in her wanted to know because of the way she looked, but she knew it was her heart that had really spurred the questions.

"I'll be all right," she said.

"If you need anything—I'm—don't hesitate to ask. I'll be around for another couple of weeks or so. I've decided—I'm going to stay a while longer." She and Sloane were looking further into buying Javier's building. She hoped Cam wouldn't be unsettled by her decision to stay. If she was, she wasn't showing it.

"I should get going," Blake said. "I...I wish you nothing but the best." She started to walk away, but Cam spoke again, halting her.

"Tomas told me he saw you."

Blake faced her again and nodded. "Believe it or not we ran into each other again. I'm beginning to think that living here is a lot like living in a small town. Everyone seems to know each other."

"Sometimes," Cam said. She crossed her arms over her chest, but Blake didn't get the impression that she was cold. Was it a subconscious indication of protection or discomfort?

My words have really hurt her.

"He said you're interested in Javier's building."

"It looks promising." *Does she know what Alejandro told me?*

Another chill swept through and Blake squeezed herself tighter.

"You're planning on living here, then? In Mexico?"

"Yes. But not here," she said quickly. "Not—on this beach." She looked back toward her favorite stargazing spot, wistful, knowing she was going to miss it. "You wouldn't have to worry," she said softly.

She brought her focus back to the patio. "I really should get back. I can't feel my feet anymore." She laughed a little, unnerved with the silence.

"Would you like to come in?"

Blake wasn't sure if she was serious. Her eyes were full and dark, like the surface of a lake at night. A lake that had depths one couldn't even begin to fathom. She seemed to be offering Blake a chance to explore those depths a little further, and for a very long, tumultuous moment, Blake considered accepting the invitation to dip her toe in the water.

Would things between us be any different this time if I did? Or would we enjoy each other's company for a little while only to end up arguing again?

Cam already looked distraught enough. Another round of hurtful words and assumptions wouldn't be good for either of them. Especially Cam.

"That's very nice of you, Cam, but I—I should go." She said good-bye to the dogs and gave Cam a soft, sincere smile. "Good night."

She heard Cam wish her the same as she hurried down the steps. The dogs followed her a little ways, but then stopped when she neared the edge of the house.

She walked back to Sloane's and entered with the intention of grabbing another sweater and possibly a blanket. But when her skin tingled from the warmth of the house and the tension she'd been carrying for days over Cam began to dissipate, she was suddenly so tired she could barely make it to her bed. She left the light off and didn't even bother with changing her clothes. She just pulled back the covers, slipped inside, and cozied up, feeling relaxed, truly relaxed, for the first time since she'd arrived in Mexico.

The next morning, she was jarred from sleep by loud singing and the bouncing of her mattress. She opened her eyes and saw first the wall moving up and down, then the ceiling moving, and finally, the hovering faces of her friends, Rylee and Sage, who were carefully balanced on either side of her.

She'd totally forgotten they were coming. And that's even after Sloane reminded her yesterday over breakfast.

Where has my head gone?

She immediately thought of Cam and had her answer.

"Morning, Dr. Livingstone," Rylee said, her mischievous eyes twinkling. Her closely cropped blond hair was the same shade as her older cousin Sloane's. That and her affluent tom-boyishness, were where the similarities between her and Sloane stopped. Rylee, however, had always idolized Sloane, and she'd been tagging along behind her for as long as Blake had known them.

"Your nurses have arrived," Sage added in an equally seductive tone from the edge of the bed. Her face crinkled all the way up to her eyes with her devilish grin. Her oversized, purple tortoise-shell eyeglasses didn't stand a chance at hiding their ominous intentions. Blake had only known Sage for a couple of years, but that had been plenty of time to get to know her inside and out. She and Rylee were tight, kind of like Blake and Sloane.

"Oh, God help me." Blake covered her eyes with her arm.

"What would you have us do first?" Rylee asked. "A thorough examination? A sponge bath?"

"Think she's naked?" Sage said and Blake felt the covers pull away from her body.

"Hey!" She quickly grabbed the blankets and yanked them back up.

Sage shook her head at Rylee. "No-go. She's fully dressed."

"Go away, you pervs," Blake said, unable to stifle her own grin. "I'm tired." She hadn't seen either of them in months, and their ridiculous antics reassured her that they were just the same as ever.

Rylee bounced the bed again. "It's after eleven, Blakey B. The day's a wasting."

Blake sat up on her elbows. "After eleven? That can't be right."

Sage showed her the time with a flick of her wrist. "We've been here over an hour already. We couldn't resist harassing you any longer." She poked at her stomach.

"As you know, patience is not our strong point," Rylee said.

Blake knew that was true. They were ten years younger and their boundless energy often made her feel ancient.

Blake eased Sage aside and stumbled from the bed, still confused as to how it could be nearing noon. "I never sleep this late," she said, pulling the shade aside to look outside. The sun was bright and high overhead. Morning seemed to be long gone.

"Kenna said you needed to rest," Rylee said, sliding from the mattress. "Said you haven't been sleeping much."

Blake ran her hand through her hair. "Yeah, but still. This is just not like me. I haven't slept this late since high school, and even then it didn't happen very often."

Sage stood and slipped an arm around her waist. She was shorter than Blake and thick with curves and muscle. "So, you needed to sleep? It's not a crime, you know."

Blake opened her mouth to disagree or to explain her concern, but as she looked at them with their happy, glowing faces, already dressed for a day in the sand, she realized they were right.

"You're right," she said, squeezing Sage tight. "Who cares?"

They walked from the bedroom toward the living room.

"That must've been some sleep," Rylee said. "I've never heard those words come from you before."

"Me neither," Sage said.

"Yeah," Blake said as she looked out the back window and saw Sloane and McKenna rubbing suntan lotion on each other in the near distance. "I feel good. Really good."

"Fantastic," Rylee said. "Because we've got an adventure planned."

Blake continued to watch as Sloane and McKenna finished with the lotion and then eased on their sunglasses. McKenna handed a helmet to Sloane, and then pulled another one onto her own head. Sloane moved away from McKenna, and Blake saw what the adventure Rylee spoke of was all about.

"Ready for some serious fun?" Rylee asked, wiggling her eyebrows.

Blake slowly nodded.

"Know what? I think I am."

CHAPTER TWENTY-FIVE

B lake and her friends sat at the patio table enjoying their late evening dinner of grilled fish tacos with a delicious spicy coleslaw Kenna had concocted and icy cold beer. They were pleasantly sun-soaked and fatigued from an eventful afternoon riding Rylee's quad runners down to the estuary, where they'd fished and snacked and collected dozens of beautiful seashells before riding back.

It had been a wonderful day full of laughter and good fun and Blake felt so content she was sure her friends would have to peel her from her chair because she'd happily melted into it like a long burning candle.

"You look just like you did after that crazy costume party in college," Sloane said, looking at Blake.

Blake was surprised at Sloane for bringing up such an old memory. She hadn't thought about that night in many years. "I do not."

"Um, yeah, you do."

"What party?" Sage asked, being her extremely curious self.

"Tell us," McKenna said, placing an encouraging hand on Sloane's forearm. She knew damn well Blake wouldn't spill the beans.

"Okay," Sloane said, taking a swig of beer. "It was our junior year of college, during rush, and one of our friends threw a party at her house off campus for all the people who weren't trying for a sorority or fraternity. Tons of people came, and her house was so full I thought it might literally pop. So, anyway, I had to just about force

Blake to go with me, because as we all know, parties were too much of a distraction from studying for Miss Goody-goody over there."

The others voiced their agreement and Blake leaned back and crossed her arms over her chest, somewhat amused, wondering as to what all Sloane was about to share.

"I had to bribe her with the promise that I'd wear my headphones from then on when listening to music if she was in the room studying, but I got her to go."

"You guys were roommates?" Sage asked.

"Oh, yes," McKenna said. "And they've been as thick as thieves ever since."

Sloane continued.

"So, this party was a costume party and we didn't have anything to wear, so we went across the quad to some friends of ours dorm and they tricked us out in disco outfits, complete with wigs, platform shoes, everything. They were theater majors and these guys always had all kinds of crazy stuff. Well, there just happened to be a woman at their place, who was also a theater major, who we had never met before, who took a very big interest in Blake. And she ended up coming with us to the party."

Sloane held up her palm.

"Now, I can't say for sure what happened at the party between the two of them, but I do know that Blake got drunk, like silly, happy kind of drunk, and she got very demonstrative with me and her new friend. At some point they disappeared together, and the next time I saw Blake was hours later when she finally made her way back to our room. She stumbled in the door, wig in hand, hair and makeup askew, and plopped down on the beanbag chair. She had this big, sloppy grin on her face, and this totally relaxed devil-may-care look to her eyes that I'd never seen before."

She motioned toward Blake. "Very similar to the way she looks right now."

Sloane took a drink.

"Only one thing is missing." She raised an eyebrow at Blake. "You have any idea what that may be?"

"No, not a clue," Blake said.

Sloane grinned. "Hickeys."

They burst out laughing, McKenna clapping her hands.

"She had three on her neck and from what I could see, at least that many on her chest." She tipped her beer at her. "Remember now?"

Blake was blushing, but she wasn't really embarrassed. She was remembering, what, up until that point, had been the best damn night of her life.

"You're exaggerating a bit, but yes, I remember."

"Remember how we had to go back to the same theater guys to have them cover your hickeys with makeup the following week when your parents came to visit?"

Blake grimaced and sipped her beer. "Ugh, yes. I was so worried I still wore a turtleneck on top of the makeup."

"So, what happened with the woman that night?" Sage asked.

"She got laid," Sloane said. "At least that's what I always thought."

They all looked at her, as if waiting for confirmation.

Blake threw up her hands. "All right, fine. I got laid."

They laughed and cheered, and Blake rolled her eyes at their silliness.

"Your first time, huh?" Sloane asked. "I knew it."

Blake didn't bother to answer. Sloane knew her too well.

"And you kept seeing her for a while, didn't you? Those nights when you thought I was asleep and you snuck off and returned a few hours later. You were hooking up."

"Maybe," Blake said, her own grin tugging at the corner of her mouth.

"Why didn't you just tell her?" Rylee asked. "I thought you two told each other everything?"

"Not always," McKenna said. "Blake doesn't usually like to kiss and tell. Especially if it's a new relationship or she really likes the woman."

"Seriously?" Rylee asked.

Blake shrugged. "It's no one's business."

"But weren't you dying to tell someone?" Sage asked.

Blake thought for a moment. "No, it was exciting enough on its own. And keeping it just between the two of us made it even more so. It was ours and ours alone."

"It must've been good because you mysteriously disappeared a lot that semester," Sloane said.

Blake laughed and lifted a shoulder. "It was…definitely an experience."

"Whatever it was, it was good for you," Sloane said. "And it's nice to see you look like you did then. Like you're happy."

"I'm getting there."

McKenna suddenly leaned forward, eyes wide. "Oh, my God, did you get laid? Is that why—"

"No!" Blake said. "God, Kenna."

"You can't blame me for thinking that. The way you've been sneaking off at night recently. And Cam…"

Blake massaged her brow. "Kenna, nothing has happened."

"You did say you were wanting to go over there to apologize," Sloane said. "Maybe you did and maybe you two did a little making up."

"Nothing happened," Blake said. "Nothing."

"Did you go over there?"

"Yes, but—"

"Who's Cam?" Sage asked.

"Our neighbor," McKenna said.

"Is that her?" Rylee asked, her gaze somewhere beyond Sloane who turned to look along with McKenna.

"Yes, that's her."

Blake shifted for a better view and saw Cam coming around the side of her house carrying some two-by-fours. She had on what Blake now knew were her renovating clothes. Worn jeans, work boots, a tank top, and an old Billabong cap. And dear God did it make Blake's heart race.

"Damn," Rylee said.

"Double damn," Sage added.

Blake felt the burning churn of jealousy and she tried to drown it with beer.

"Cam!" McKenna called.

Oh, God, Kenna no. Please, no.

Cam glanced over at them and McKenna waved her over. Cam crossed through the sand.

"We want you to meet our new additions," McKenna said. "Cam, this is Rylee, Sloane's younger cousin, and this is her good friend, Sage. Guys, this is our neighbor, Cam."

"Hi," Cam said with a polite smile.

"Hiya, hiya," Sage said, making her approval of Cam well-known.

"Ditto," Rylee said.

Blake didn't like the blatant lust her friends had for Cam. They were ogling her and she wanted them to stop. She wanted Cam to go, so they would have to. But what she really wanted to stop, was the fucking jealousy gnawing at her insides.

"How have you been, Cam?" Sloane asked. "Haven't seen you much."

"Oh, I've been busy."

"Come, sit down and eat," McKenna said. "We have plenty and you look like you need a good meal."

"Thanks, but I can't." She tugged off her cap and scratched her head. She had, as Blake had suspected when she'd seen her in the shadows the night before, lost some of her color, and she was noticeably thinner. But she was still absolutely gorgeous. Unfortunately for Blake, she was not the only one who seemed to think so.

"You can have my chair," Rylee said, standing.

"No, please," Cam said, tugging on her cap. "That's not necessary."

"How about joining us around the beach fire tonight?" McKenna tried.

"Maybe another time," Cam said.

"You better come back around again soon," McKenna said. "Or I'll hunt you down. You know I will."

Cam laughed. "I don't doubt it."

"Have we met somewhere before?" Sage asked Cam, surprising everyone.

Cam studied her briefly. "I don't think so."

"You look familiar. I could swear I've seen you somewhere before."

"You got me," Cam said. "I gotta run. You guys enjoy your dinner." She gave Blake a look that lingered just a little bit longer than the one she gave the others. It seemed to be a silent message that what had happened between them the night before had resonated with her and that it had meant something. Cam was gone, though, before Blake had been fully able to comprehend.

"Whoa," McKenna said.

"She is *fine*." Rylee added.

"That's not what I meant," McKenna said. She looked at Sloane. "Did you see that?"

"Mm-hm."

McKenna looked at Blake. "Something happened between you two. Don't even try to deny it. I saw the look, so did Sloane."

"Kenna," Blake sighed.

"Are you two an item?" Rylee asked. "Because if you are or you want to be, I'll back off."

Sloane again raised her eyebrow at her. "Well?"

"Nothing is going on," Blake said. "Nothing has happened. Besides, you know I don't kiss and tell, so I wouldn't tell you if it had."

"Exactly," McKenna said. "Which is why we're grilling you."

"Do you *want* something to happen?" Sloane asked.

Blake stood and gathered her plate and beer. She didn't want to answer and she shouldn't have to answer. Her feelings were her business even if she didn't understand them or think them possible.

"B?" Sloane said.

Blake looked at her, frustrated that she was pushing, but knowing damn well it was because she cared and because she and McKenna seemed to think that she and Cam would be good together. Why and how they'd come to that conclusion was still a mystery to her.

"I'm going to go for a walk," she said. "Kenna, dinner was amazing. Thank you."

"Blake—I won't—" Rylee stammered, still standing in front of her chair.

"Do whatever you like, Rylee. Whatever makes you happy." She said it with sincerity and meant it. She had no claim to Cam, no intention of pursuing anything further with her, despite the way her heart was bleeding out in her chest in protest. Despite how saying those words aloud went against every fiber of her being.

She tried to reassure them all with a smile, but it didn't seem to have the effect she was hoping for. They remained quiet, their concern evident. She sensed that they were unsure what to say or even what to believe. She walked inside, fearing that maybe they could somehow see the bleeding of her heart and how it was filling up her chest so thoroughly that she would soon begin to drown.

She hurried to the sink, already feeling like she couldn't breathe, and washed up her dishes. She then slid into a soft jacket and headed back out onto the beach, rushing past her friends and their questioning stares, not giving anyone a chance to stop her.

Chapter Twenty-six

The bright, white glow of the computer screen blurred, along with the dozens of typed black letters. Cam sat back in her chair and rubbed her tired eyes. She glanced at the clock in her cozy den, noted it was after midnight, and yawned.

She'd been writing for six hours straight and if it wasn't for her eyes, which were now burning, she would've put on a pot of coffee and continued. But she'd been at it for three days, working for extended periods, completely engrossed in her newly created world, until either the dogs yipped at her for a bathroom break, or her own body protested for one. She was tired, bordering on exhausted, but man, did it feel good to be back in the zone.

She rolled away from her desk, leaned forward, and jostled the dogs' jowls affectionately when they came to her with wagging tails. Then she stood for a long, bone-popping stretch.

"What do you say we call it a night, guys?" They ran to the door in agreement.

"Go on," she said as they stepped outside. The dogs hurried down to the sand, eager for the freedom to explore and run around. She watched them from the edge of the patio, hands resting on the waist-high wall. The moon was luminous and its reflection rippled in tiny lights along the surface of the inky ocean and lit up the milky white sand for miles. Cam inhaled, thankful for the moment, thankful for the return of her imagination and the drive to put it to paper. She almost felt like her old self, the writer who worked long hours when the mood struck and constantly thought about the story when it didn't.

She almost felt like she had before the accident.

Like her long empty glass was filling from the bottom up with water she'd been dying for, water she was so incredibly grateful to have. But as needed and as wonderful as it was, the water came to a stop, filling less than halfway, only providing enough to wet her parched mouth and give her throat and body a tease of what was really needed to quench her thirst.

Nevertheless, that small amount of water had reawakened her and moved her to action, to sit at her desk and begin. And the more she worked, the more she began to relax, reassured that her creativity seemed to be here to stay.

She no longer worried about losing it to that dark abyss that loomed in the back corner of her mind.

She closed her eyes against the breeze and listened to the gentle crashing of the waves. Her glass was finally refilling and she was relieved. She knew though, why it was only filling to a certain point. Lexi was gone and she was never coming back. She'd been the main reason why her glass had been so full. Without her, there was a void, an emptiness that she doubted would ever be filled. The return to her writing and the truce she seemed to have with Blake, however, made her feel hopeful about possibly regaining some of the person she'd been when Lexi was alive.

She opened her eyes and wiped away the tear that had slipped down her cheek. She wasn't ever going to be exactly the same as she was then. She knew that and she didn't expect it. She could even see the difference in her writing. It was deeper now, more human, more emotional. Love, loss, and pain were all explored and a huge part of her characters' journeys. Her previous work had been driven by action, setting, and the struggle to exist. This new story was character-driven and all about the inner journey and the inner struggle to survive the love and loss that every human endures. Love and loss that she knew all too well.

The dogs came back from the west side of the house. Bo froze, ears up and then back. His tail started going and he took off through the sand with the other two close behind. Cam walked down the steps and followed them, wondering if she should call for them, but hoping she wouldn't have to since it was so late.

She didn't have to go far to see what they were after. Or rather, whom they were after.

Blake was sitting in the sand.

The dogs interrupted her solitude but she didn't seem to mind. She greeted them as she always did, with love and affection.

Cam shook her head as she smiled.

Blake sure did love her dogs. And they definitely loved her.

Maybe that does mean something.

"I would apologize for their intrusion, but something tells me you wouldn't accept it," Cam said as she approached Blake, who was all smiles, loving on the dogs.

"You would be right. They are always welcome by me."

"It's a good thing, because I'm too exhausted to continue to fight that battle." She eased her hands into the pockets of her thick athletic pants. She felt the wind toying with her hair and with her T-shirt, but the chill felt good, refreshing.

"You're not cold?" Blake asked. She was bundled up in a soft hooded jacket, jeans, and thick-looking socks. The blanket she had wrapped around her shoulders was an additional layer.

"Not at the moment," Cam said. "You look a little warmer than you did the other night."

"You would think, right? I'm afraid that's not the case. I'm still cold."

"Don't be too hard on yourself. You're from Phoenix. Phoenicians don't do cold. Or anything below seventy degrees." Cam looked up at the sky. "The view is just too good to miss, though, isn't it?"

"It is. It's one of those things I know I'll miss when I'm gone. One of those things I'll never forget and will always want to see again and again." She laughed a little and began playing with the sand. "That sounds sappy, I know."

"It's beautiful," Cam said. "And I know exactly what you mean."

Blake looked up at her curiously.

Cam chuckled. "Don't look so shocked." She nodded toward the sand. "Mind if I sit?"

"Please," Blake said.

Cam sat and leaned back on her hands.

"And I wasn't shocked," Blake said. "Not at you understanding what I mean, anyway."

"Then what were you shocked at?"

"The fact that you shared that with me."

They both looked out at the sea and the dogs left them to explore the area nearby.

"You're usually rather reluctant to share personal things about yourself."

"That's funny because I find the same to be true about you."

Blake looked at her like she expected to find Cam upset. But Cam smiled and crossed her ankles.

"Why are we like that?" Blake asked, gazing back toward the sea as if it might have the answers.

"I know why I'm like that," Cam said. "Why are you?"

Blake made a noise. "I don't know, obviously, or I wouldn't have questioned it. Why are you so private?"

"I have my reasons."

Blake laughed. "But you're not going to share them."

"No."

Blake shook her head.

"How's your book?" Cam asked.

"Book?"

"Your romance."

Blake tossed some sand at Cam's legs. "Are you *trying* to start something with me?"

"I'm just curious." She couldn't help but grin. "It's good, isn't it?"

"I wouldn't know."

"That's a big fat lie."

Blake turned and almost completely faced her. "You don't know," she said. But the raised pitch to her voice and her overly adamant denial were enough proof to Cam that she was right.

"I do know," Cam said, looking directly at her. "But that's okay if you still don't want to tell me. I'm sure you have your reasons. It is a good book, though. Very steamy."

Blake was quiet, her eyes appearing to be on a very serious mission to suss Cam out.

"I've shocked you again."

"Frankly, yes."

"Because I read romances like that?"

"Because you read at all."

Cam cracked up. "For someone who isn't fond of assumptions, you sure make a lot of them."

"I feel the same about you." She smirked. "I'm just giving you a hard time. I already knew you liked to read. I saw you reading on your patio one day. It did surprise me though."

You saw me reading?

What else do you know about me, that you haven't shared?

CHAPTER TWENTY-SEVEN

Cam sat up, the chill of the night air starting to get to her. Or was it Blake all snuggled up in that blanket that was causing her to feel cold?

She hugged her knees and smiled over at her, thinking about the confession she'd just made admitting that she was surprised that Cam read.

"It's strange but I'm not getting upset at you right now. I'm actually kind of finding this whole conversation funny." She shrugged.

"I'm not upset either," Blake said softly. "I'm not sure why because you're definitely getting under my skin again. Maybe I'm just getting used to you being a pain in the ass."

"I can live with that," Cam said. "As long as you can live with my thinking you're a seriously stubborn one."

Blake tossed more sand at her. "Deal. But don't push it."

"I'll try not to."

"That's a big fat lie."

Cam laughed. "You're really funny for someone so uptight."

"And you're really deep for someone who doesn't seem to give a fuck."

They both laughed and Cam tried to curl up tighter against the breeze. Blake scooted closer and held open her blanket.

"Wanna share?"

Cam saw nothing but kindness and sincerity in her eyes, but that did very little to reassure her considering all those crazy feelings of desire she'd experienced when she'd first met Blake were returning. Cam wasn't sure if she could handle trying to wrangle them up again.

What was worse was wondering if she ever had really gotten them under control the first time.

"Since we haven't seemed to be able to share anything else between us, including polite conversation, I thought at the very least we could manage to share a blanket," Blake said.

The image of Blake sitting there in the sand with her arm outstretched to her, offering her warmth and solace, was irresistible, and Cam edged closer, until their bodies were lightly touching and allowed Blake to drape the blanket around her shoulders.

"Better?"

Cam nodded. "Much. Thanks."

They sat in silence and Cam was very still, aware of Blake's warmth, her scent, and her breathing. The suntan lotion Cam usually smelled on her was gone, replaced by something sweeter. Cam wasn't sure if it was a perfume or what exactly. She just knew that she was reacting to it much stronger than she had the suntan lotion. And that reaction had been powerful in itself.

Especially when she was in that yellow bikini.

"You really read that book?" Blake asked.

"I did. A long time ago. I believe I finished it in a day."

"It must be good then."

"Have you really *not* read it?"

"I really haven't."

"Should I ask why? Or would that get me ousted from the cover of the blanket?"

Blake smiled and rubbed her palm over her knee. "I don't know. They seem silly to me, I guess. Overly dramatic and fantastical. No one really wants someone else that badly. Or feels that strongly for someone else. It's just not reality."

"Those are the very reasons why people like them. It's an escape, a fantasy, and even though it's made up, it represents something that they may want or wish they could experience. That's what books do. They take us to places we can't necessarily go to, and enable us to experience things we otherwise may not be able to."

"I understand. I love to read for those reasons too," Blake said. "Just not those particular books."

"Too much emotion?"

"Could be."

"People really can feel that strongly for another person," Cam said. "That does happen."

"Maybe for some."

"But not for you?"

"The uncontrollable love and desire, willing to sacrifice anything for it kind of thing? No." She laughed.

"I'm sorry to hear that," Cam said softly. "Maybe that's why you've had trouble relating to romances. You haven't ever felt that way."

Blake was quiet.

"Or maybe you don't want to read about something you've never had because deep down it is something you want. And reading about it might make your longing for it worse and more difficult to ignore." Cam glanced at her, hoping with having said the words gently, that they wouldn't upset her. "That wasn't meant as an insult or to start anything with you."

"Then why did you say it?" She met Cam's gaze and her tone was as soft as Cam's had been.

"Because I understand. For a while I avoided reading them for similar reasons. I didn't want to read about what I no longer had."

"Did you think you'd never have it again?"

"Yes."

"But now you're reading them again?"

"Yes. I started reading them again a little over a year ago."

"Does that mean you've changed your mind about ever having that kind of love again?"

I don't know.

The thought came out of nowhere and Cam was stunned, her answer always so perfectly clear before. For years, she'd believed that she'd never have those feelings for anyone else for as long as she lived. Lexi was her one true love, the only person she'd ever loved, desired, and cherished so deeply. Losing her had very nearly killed her, her heart torn from her chest and then torn to bits right in front of her eyes, over and over again for four years. Until she no longer felt the pain of her chest being plunged into by that vicious hand and no longer felt the ripping of her heart as that hand tore it out.

About a year ago, that had changed. The scene of her heart being torn out of her chest had still played out for her, but she'd no longer felt the pain that had always accompanied it. Mercy was what she'd called it. And although she'd been gifted that, one thing had stayed the same. Her firm belief that she'd never feel for another like that again.

So, why was she unsure about that now?

Her attraction to Blake was new and surprising, but it couldn't cause her to doubt what she'd been so certain of. They didn't even get along and Cam hadn't been with a woman since Lexi, so her desire for Blake was probably more of a natural, strictly physical occurrence. Her body crying out for touch and affection.

Crying out.

Like right now.

The way Blake was looking at her, with such deep empathy and understanding, was pulling her in and Cam wanted to lean in and kiss her beautiful lips to see if they held the same emotion as her eyes. She wanted to know, wanted that connection, wanted to feel in the physical what Blake was showing her in her gaze.

Cam's eyes brimmed with tears. She was overcome by Blake and her willingness to show her such emotion. And she was overcome by the way she wanted to respond.

Blake's face clouded and she rested her hand on Cam's forearm. Cam startled at the unexpected touch and Blake retreated.

"I'm sorry," she said quickly.

Cam wiped a fallen tear and focused on the ocean. "It's okay," she said.

"I should've asked before I touched you and my hand is probably freezing."

Cam managed to laugh a little. "It is a little cold, but it wasn't awful."

"I—you are so sad. I just wanted to comfort you."

"I'm okay," she said.

"You're crying. So, I think you're the grand prize winner of the big fat liar contest for tonight."

Cam wiped her cheek again as she laughed. "For tonight, maybe. But I'm sure you'll give me another run for my money."

Blake nudged her playfully. "You can count on it."

The dogs chased each other at the water's edge and Cam wondered if she'd ever be that lighthearted and carefree again.

Blake spoke, interrupting the thought. "It isn't my place to say, and I know you're already hurting...but, Cam, I hope you don't continue to believe that you'll never have love again."

"I hope the same for you." She smiled, deeply moved by her words. The tears threatened again so she decided to lighten things up once more. "So you should go back inside tonight and give that book another chance."

Blake shoved her. "God, you and that book!"

"I know you'll do it. There's no way you won't read it now. You just probably won't tell anyone."

Byron trotted up to Cam and kissed her. Cam smooched his face and hugged him. "Someone's ready for bed."

Cam shrugged out from under the blanket and stood. "I better go tuck these guys in." Bo and Bingo joined them, kissing on Blake, who thoroughly enjoyed it. "Are you ready to call it a night?" Cam asked her.

"Mm, I don't know. I might." She stared up at the moon. "Or I might stay out here a while longer and soak this in."

"Stay warm, then. And thanks for sharing your blanket."

"You're welcome. You...stay warm too."

They looked at each other for a few seconds and Cam realized that she didn't want to leave her. She wanted to be back under that blanket snuggled up next to her, staring up at the sky.

"Good night," Cam said.

"Good night."

Cam walked away, but the yearning she had to stay with Blake was so strong it felt like there was a rope between them that was tightening with every step she took toward her house. She couldn't go back though, no matter how badly she wanted to. Because she knew if she did and she got that close to Blake again, she'd end up wanting to do far more than just snuggle. And that was something she still didn't quite understand.

Chapter Twenty-eight

Cam killed the engine to her Jeep and climbed out slowly, the dogs right behind her. They bounded toward the side of the house as she paused and stretched her back. She'd spent the latter half of the day helping her friends with some home repairs and she'd grown stiff on the ride home. A nice hot shower was calling her and though she actually had a healthy appetite for the first time in days, she was willing to put off dinner until she had that shower.

She tucked her leather work gloves in her back pocket and followed the path the dogs had taken. Varying shades of midnight blue were creeping in on the twilight, making it easy to see the stark orange of a beach fire not far from the edge of her property. She should've gone in the front door, but she'd wanted to let the boys run and play a bit first.

Laughter rang out and became louder as she got closer. She recognized McKenna's voice and Sloane's laugh and she was glad that they seemed to be having a good time, but she hoped to slip inside unnoticed. If she didn't, they'd probably insist she join them, and a long evening of socializing with people she didn't know very well was the last thing she wanted for her evening after hours of physical labor.

She searched for the dogs as she neared the back of the house, but she'd lost sight of them. When she finally found them, she felt her body deflate.

"Shit."

The five women from next door were sitting around a sizable fire with her three dogs right there with them, happily eating up some ample attention. She considered leaving them be, to let them hang out with Blake while she showered and made dinner. That seemed to be a solution that had worked lately when Blake went for her morning runs and asked if the boys could tag along. But Cam couldn't assume it was okay even though Blake had been more than happy to let the dogs join her on her morning excursions. There were others with Blake now and Cam didn't want to risk the dogs interfering with their fun.

She pulled off her cap and slapped it against her leg as she headed toward the group.

"Cam!" McKenna said. "Just in time." She stood and hurried to her, clutching her arm and escorting her to the fire. Sloane crawled to a cooler and dug out a beer. She twisted it open and offered it to Cam.

"You look like you could use one of these," she said.

"You *look* positively yummy," Rylee said and Sage laughed and agreed.

Cam gave a quick laugh and awkwardly fingered her dirty tank top, unsure as to why her current appearance seemed so appealing. The new additions to the group, Rylee and Sage, had expressed their avid appraisal of her quite a few times since their arrival, and Cam had mostly shaken it off with a laugh or a wave as she walked by. But tonight she felt differently about their flirtation. Blake was sitting next to them and she had the same look Cam had seen on her when she'd met Rylee and Sage for the first time.

When she met Cam's gaze, she held it for a long, intense moment as the women chatted around them. There was something that looked familiar to Cam in her eyes, something that looked a lot like pain. Blake turned toward the sea, seeming to prefer to focus on the hypnotic waves rather than Cam or her friends. Her silent but obvious discomfort made Cam feel even more awkward about Rylee's and Sage's attention, though she wasn't totally sure why.

"You sit down right there next to Sloane and I'll go get you some dinner. You must be starved." McKenna took off toward the house as Cam was trying to protest.

"Don't even try," Sloane said, handing her the beer. "Trust me. I know of what I speak." She patted the sand next to her.

"I don't want her to go to any trouble over me," Cam said, hesitating a second before sinking into the sand.

"She's a mama bear," Sloane said. "It's just who she is. Makes her happy to care for others. And she's not in there making a gourmet meal for you or anything. She's fixing you a burrito. Leftovers from our dinner. But had there not been any leftovers, she definitely would be in there cooking for you."

Cam sipped her beer and relished the iciness of it sliding down and soothing her dry throat. She really had been in need of a cold beer.

"I can't stay long," Cam said, noting Rylee's and Sage's continued focus on her. But more unsettling was Blake's lack of interest at all. She was still lost somewhere out beyond the sea.

"Were you working on a house today?" Rylee asked. She was a petite woman with short, messy, blond hair and a playful smile. She seemed to be buzzing with energy twenty-four seven and Cam wondered if she ever closed her lively eyes to rest. She had her arms around her knees and her ankles crossed, but she didn't seem to be as bothered by the night air as her friend Sage. Sage was dressed in head-to-toe sweats, complete with socks and shoes as well as a hooded jacket. Completely opposite of Rylee who had on a pair of long cargo shorts and a T-shirt.

"Yes," Cam said. "I was helping a friend with some repairs."

"That the house you were telling me about yesterday?" Sloane asked.

Cam pulled the beer from her lips. "No, that's another friend. He lives closer to town. We'll be starting work on his roof soon."

"You work on roofs?" Blake said, tearing her gaze away from the ocean.

"Sometimes."

"That's dangerous—" She stopped just as suddenly as she started.

"I'm careful," Cam said.

"You're thinking about Susan?" Sloane asked, looking at Blake. Blake nodded.

"One of our friends took a bad fall last year while she was repairing her roof. She got hurt pretty bad. Broken back, head injury. She's just now getting back to her old self again."

"That's terrible," Cam said.

"So, Blake's a little uneasy about roof work. What happened to Susan scared us all."

"It's not just Susan," Blake said. "I've seen more injuries than I'd like from falls like that. Even…a death."

"Ugh," Sage said. "Where, in the ER?"

Blake began explaining and Sloane gave Cam a soft nudge. "She cares about you," she whispered. "She's worried for you."

Cam wasn't sure what to say. But Sloane just nudged her again and winked. She looked up at McKenna as she came to sit on Cam's other side.

"Here you are. One nice big chicken and bean burrito. With all the trimmings." She handed Cam the plate and set a couple of napkins in her lap.

"McKenna, this is too much," Cam said, examining the big burrito.

"You can take what you don't eat home." She held up a large storage bag with rolled aluminum foil inside, all set for Cam's leftovers. She placed that on a towel and placed a fork on Cam's plate. "Just in case you don't want to eat it with your hands." She touched Cam's shoulder as if to reassure her. "Just eat what you can. You look so thin."

Cam thanked her and took a bite. It was a wonderful mix of shredded chicken, refried beans, pico de gallo, and a bit of guacamole. Cam nodded her approval and took another bite as McKenna smiled.

They talked for a while, mostly about old times, laughing as they recalled shared memories. Cam soon relaxed and became rather amused as they relayed stories about Blake. Apparently, she'd had her first lesbian experience at college and they kept bringing up the hickeys she'd been left with.

"It gets less and less funny the more you guys bring it up," Blake said.

"Not to us," Sage said.

Sloane looked at Cam. "Blake's embarrassed. She doesn't like to kiss and tell and now she's pissed because I did it for her."

"I'm not pissed," Blake said. She shoved her hands into the front center pocket of her hoodie. "And I'm not embarrassed. You guys are just being ridiculous over it now. It's old news."

"Not to Cam," Rylee said. "I'm sure she'd like to hear the whole story so she can laugh too."

"Cam...she's probably tired," Blake said. "And she wouldn't be interested."

"Just tell us what it was like," Sage said. "And where you guys went to get it on. Or did it happen at the party?"

"Why would you want to know that?"

"Why *wouldn't* we want to know that?" Rylee asked. "Those are the juicy details, the cream filling of the donut."

"And it's you, Blake," McKenna said. "No one ever gets to hear your juicy details. Well, other than Sloane, and you don't always tell her everything."

"Yeah, so spill it," Sage said. "Give us some excitement."

Sloane drank from her beer. "Face it, B. You're the crème de la crème of donuts and everyone's dying to squeeze out your filling."

The women laughed, and Blake made a face showing just how crazy she thought they were being.

"I think even Cam would agree with me on that. I bet she wants to know just as badly as the rest of us do," Sloane said.

Cam swallowed a bite and felt all eyes on her. Blake was staring at her intensely, and Cam couldn't tell if she wanted her to agree or disagree. If she disagreed, Blake might not share any more details and it would probably be very difficult to get any of them out of her later. And Cam had to admit, she wanted to hear those details.

"I wouldn't mind hearing," Cam said.

The women cheered and Blake's mouth fell open. Cam gave her a helpless shrug and grinned.

CHAPTER TWENTY-NINE

O kay, so tell us," Sage said. "What happened at the party?"

"If I tell you, do you all promise to leave it alone from now on?"

"No," Sloane said. "I'll tease you about it until the end of days. You know that."

Blake sighed. "Damn, Sloane, come on."

"We'll tease you about it," McKenna said. "But we won't ask you for any more details. How's that?"

"You won't ask me anything about it at all," Blake added.

"Fine," McKenna said.

Blake stared into the fire and cleared her throat. "Her name was Penny. She was a year ahead of me and we met at our mutual friend's dorm that night as you know. I noticed she was staring at me, but I wasn't sure what to think about it if anything. I had kissed a couple of girls before, but not anything more, so I was a bit of a novice. Eventually, she started talking to me and she helped me with my costume and she smiled the whole time and seemed to only be interested in talking to me. I was flattered, and she was, you know, really cute."

"What did she look like?" McKenna asked.

"She was about my height, slender, with short, dark red hair. Her haircut was kind of similar to Halle Berry's. Her eyes were a really deep green and she was as outgoing as I was introverted. And she was, I don't know, kind of a rebel. Well, compared to me anyway. She was extroverted, wanted to teach drama and direct plays, and she wore whatever the hell she wanted. I remember that night she had on ripped jeans, purple Doc Martens, and a Rage Against the Machine T-shirt that she'd cut into a sleeveless crop top. And I couldn't stop staring at her belly ring."

She laughed.

"Sloane, at some point, gave me a look letting me know that this girl was really into me, and when Penny said she wanted to come to the party with me, that pretty much confirmed it. So, we went and I proceeded to get very drunk on Jaeger shots, which I still can no longer stand the smell of, and I totally relaxed and started dancing with her. We were surrounded by people, crammed in with them, but all I could see was her, and the way she looked at me and the way she moved against me. I don't know how long we danced before she pulled me tighter, whispered in my ear that she wanted me, and started grinding against my thigh. I just know I dug my fingers into her back at how incredible her mouth felt against my ear and soon my neck. And then the next thing I knew, we were on the move, hurrying from the house."

She paused, seemed to be lost in the fire.

"She led me by the hand and kept smiling back at me telling me to hurry. It wasn't long before we were back on campus and she was tugging me down the hallway of her dorm. And then we were in her room, her tiny little room that she lived in alone because she was an RA. She grabbed me and kissed me as soon as she closed the door. Well, I had never been kissed like that before and I was just completely helpless at how turned on I was, and she pushed me down on the bed and had me undressed before I could even contemplate what was happening."

She paused again, and Cam set aside her burrito, lost in her story, lost in her. She could see it all in her mind, like a movie, and she was hanging on every word, desperate for more, wishing like hell she had been Penny and had been the one to take her to that place for the very first time.

"What happened next?" Rylee asked, breathless. They all seemed to be hanging on edge.

"I—" She shook her head.

"Blake!" Sage said. "Jesus, don't stop now. You're killing us."

"You don't want to share anymore?" McKenna asked gently.

"Can you give us just a little?" Rylee asked. "Just a smidge? So we don't tear our hair out?"

Blake's eyes sparked with the reflection of the fire.

"I remember I felt like I should stop her, like I should get up and leave. But…that wasn't what I really wanted. I didn't want her to stop. I didn't want to leave. And as soon as she put her mouth on my body, there was no fucking way I was going to stop her or was going to leave. I didn't care about being the good girl, the one who always did right and whatever it was my parents expected. I didn't care. And it felt so God damned good, that did. Not as good as her mouth did, but pretty close."

The others laughed, but Cam was quiet, riveted, her body burning hotter than the fire right in front of her. What she would've given to be the one in that room with her that night. She was in disbelief at how intense this longing was. And she expected guilt and shame and fear to find their way in to kill it. But they didn't and she could think of nothing else. Only Blake. In that bed, totally nude, her body being awakened for the first time.

"I had my first taste of freedom that night," Blake said softly. "Penny set me free."

"How many times?" Rylee asked.

Blake smiled. "I lost count."

"Did you stay with her all night?" Sage asked.

"Yes. Well, most of the night. I stumbled back to my dorm close to dawn. Penny had said if I didn't leave she'd hold me captive forever."

"That sounds like a punishment I'd gladly accept," Sage said.

"It was true," Blake said. "We had a hard time parting every time we got together. It was a very fiery affair. And it made studying all the more difficult to say the least. She was on my mind constantly. It was…life changing."

"Why did it end?" McKenna asked.

"She left. Well, she moved. Off campus, miles away. I saw her a few times at her new place, but she had roommates and we were rarely alone. Things just kind of fizzled."

"That sucks," Rylee said.

Blake laughed. "It did, but on the other hand, I might not have graduated had it continued."

"It was that intense, huh?" Rylee asked.

Blake met her gaze. "Yes."

"That explains so much," Sloane said. "I wish I'd known at least some of it, maybe I could've helped or been more supportive. Or given you guys some time alone in our room."

"It was pretty good the way it was," Blake said. "I don't have a single regret."

"That was better than some of my books," McKenna said.

The others agreed and, after a long silence, Sage looked at Cam with huge eyes and pointed.

"Oh, my God, that's it! That's how I know you!"

Cam stiffened. *Oh, fuck.*

"You're her." She snapped her fingers at her. "Oh my God, you're Camille Cruz."

"Camille Cruz?" Rylee asked.

"You know," Sage said, looking at Rylee with excitement. "The book series I love. The dystopian ones. She's—she's—you're her, aren't you?"

Cam couldn't breathe. Her cover was totally blown. She couldn't deny it. It would be pointless and she didn't like lying. People had recognized her before when she'd lived in the States, but she'd hoped no one would stumble upon her here, in her private beach haven.

Fuck.

"Yes," she said simply.

She felt McKenna touch her arm, heard Sloane and McKenna both say things, heard the same from Rylee as Sage continued to carry on with excitement about her books. But Blake didn't say anything. Not a word. She just looked at her with a blank expression, as if she hadn't really heard or made sense of what Sage had said.

"I need to get home," Cam said, standing.

They all protested, all except Blake. Sage asked her about autographs, McKenna had questions, though they were kind and more concerned with how she was feeling. Sloane asked her to stay, to hang out, obviously sensing her discomfort. She even said they wouldn't bother her about the books if she did.

Cam thanked them, for the food and the kindness. But she said she was tired and needed to call it a day. She bid them good night and headed home, the dogs finally doing her a solid and giving in to follow her right away. As if they somehow knew that tonight, she wasn't up for trying to corral them home.

As if they somehow knew that tonight, everything had changed.

CHAPTER THIRTY

I thought you'd be more excited," Sloane said as she and Blake walked through the village to meet Alejandro and Javier. They were going to do a walk-through of the building and get the estimated costs of repairs. Alejandro had said that he'd asked Tomas to come to give his opinion as well.

Sloane seemed ready to close the deal, even before knowing what all needed to be done. Her excitement had done nothing but grow.

Blake's, however, had given way to her mind, which had been solely on Cam since the night of the beach fire. She still had a hard time believing that what she'd heard about her was true. She'd considered that there might be more to Cam than meets the eye, but she never could've imagined something like this.

Cam, a writer?

A popular fiction writer?

"Hellooo?" Sloane said, bumping her. "I'm looking for my friend, Blake. Is she in there?"

"I am, excited," Blake said, snapping out of her trance as they walked down the street. "It's just that now that things are really happening, I'm anxious."

"That's understandable. This will be a big move for you, B. Anyone doing something like this would be anxious, especially for the first time."

"You aren't worried at all? Even though you've done this before?" Blake asked.

Sloane threw her arm around her shoulders and pulled her close. "You know why I think those risks I took turned out so well? Because I invested in the people behind them. I knew them. Believed in them. I'm doing the same thing here. I'm investing in you, in your dream. You are the backbone. And I have more faith in you than I do anyone."

Sloane pulled her closer and kissed her temple.

"We'll make it, B. Have faith."

They walked past the café and heard something.

Two men were running down the street, waving their arms and yelling. It was Alejandro and Javier and they looked frantic.

"Help!" Alejandro shouted.

Blake took off toward them. She sprinted down the street and heard Sloane follow. They met the men in the middle of the road and the guys were so frantic and breathless they could hardly speak.

"He's hurt. He fell," Alejandro said. Blake touched his shoulder.

Javier, who was struggling to breathe, rattled off something in Spanish, his eyes wide with fear.

She didn't understand him, but she knew it must be bad. "Where?"

He pointed back down the street and said something more. But Blake couldn't make out what he was saying.

She grabbed Alejandro by his shoulders. "Alejandro, take some deep breaths and tell me where this person is."

"The building. Javier's," he managed.

Blake took off again and outran Sloane. She came to the building and hurried along the side to the back. She stopped cold in her tracks as she tried to make sense of the two figures before her.

There was a man, on his side, on the ground. She could see his legs.

There was someone squatting next to him, rocking back and forth, mumbling.

Blake came closer, her heart pounding as she realized she recognized the person squatting.

"Cam?"

Cam jerked and inched closer to the man on the ground. "Get away from him! Don't touch him!"

She huddled over the man and her back shook with sobs.

"Cam—"

"Go away!" She waved Blake away but she'd yet to look at her. She continued to rock and sob.

Blake came closer, spoke very softly. "Cam, it's me, Blake. I'm here to help. I'm a doctor, remember?"

Cam was quiet for a few seconds as Blake's words seemed to sink in.

"He's hurt," Cam said. Blake could see that she was holding the man's hand.

"I'm going to come closer now, so I can help him, okay?"

Cam didn't respond and Blake approached and knelt on the other side of the man. He was breathing but lying in a twisted heap. Blood covered his head and face. Other than a laceration to his scalp, which was where the blood was coming from, there appeared to be no other external injuries to his head. She quickly scanned the rest of him. She didn't see any blood or injury to his chest or torso. But there was a significant injury to his leg. A piece of rebar had pierced through and lodged.

"Cam?" She didn't answer. "Cam, look at me," Blake said louder. Cam looked up at her from beneath her Billabong ball cap and blinked rapidly as if she were just now registering her presence. Her face was ashen, her eyes wide and glossy. She was in shock. Blake quickly scanned what she could of her. Her hands were covered in blood and she had some smudges on her face, but otherwise she appeared to be uninjured.

"I'm not going to move him," Blake said, as she reached out to take his pulse. "We're not going to move him, okay? We need to keep him still."

She returned her focus to the man. She looked into his eyes, which he was struggling to keep open. Her heart sank. The man was Tomas.

"Tomas, can you hear me?" His bleary eyes shifted ever so slightly toward her. His pupils weren't dilated, but his pulse was rapid and his breathing was shallow.

"Miss," he said weakly.

"Yes," she said, smiling softly at him. "It's Blake. I'm going to help you, okay?"

She shouldered out of her linen button-down shirt and pressed it to the wound on his head.

"Cam, can you hold this for me?" Cam kept hold of Tomas's hand while she held Blake's shirt to his head with her free hand. "Keep some pressure on it." Blake then eyed the rebar. Removing it would be dangerous and he'd bleed more, so she left it alone and slipped off her belt and secured it carefully above the wound. Not too tight, just enough to help with the bleeding. Then, she opened his shirt and did a more thorough check for wounds. To her relief, she saw none. But that didn't reassure her as far as internal injuries.

Sloane skidded to a stop with her cell phone gripped tightly in her hand. "Oh, Jesus."

"Did you call for help?" Blake asked, realizing that in her rush to get there, she hadn't told anyone to call. She had every faith that Sloane already had done so, though.

Sloane nodded, staring at Tomas.

"Is that…Tomas?"

Blake nodded.

"Is he going to be…?"

Blake looked at her and shifted her gaze toward Cam. Sloane got the message. Her face clouded.

"The woman I spoke to said if the injuries are serious or life threatening it would be faster if we transport him ourselves."

Blake sighed, not surprised at hearing that news. "Call them back. Tell her he needs to go to the best hospital equipped for traumatic injuries. Find out where that is and go get your SUV and back it in here."

"Okay."

Blake caught sight of Alejandro lingering behind Sloane. She waved him over.

"Do you have anything we can use to transport him with? Like a board? It needs to be hard and flat."

"I'll see what I can find."

Blake checked Tomas's vitals again. There wasn't much change.

"How are you doing, Tomas? Try to stay awake, okay? Stay with us." She lightly stroked his brow.

Cam then spoke to him in Spanish. Blake understood enough to know she was relaying what she'd said.

"You doing all right, Cam?" she asked softly. She was relieved to see that she'd stopped rocking. She gently touched her forearm.

"He—couldn't breathe at first," she said, her voice strained. "Then he—said he hurt."

Blake looked at the building. "He fell from the roof?"

"I told him not to go up there. Told him it wasn't necessary yet. But he wanted to see what had caused the damage to the ceiling." She grew quiet. "He always wants to do the best job he can." She met Blake's gaze. "He got tangled up in something, lost his footing and fell." She swallowed and closed her eyes like it was painful. "He hit hard, first on the edge of this." She motioned toward a large stack of cinder blocks. "That's where he hit the rebar. Then he landed on the ground here." She choked back sobs. "I can still hear the way it sounded."

"Take some deep breaths," Blake said gently. "Nice and slow."

Cam did, though her body shook as she inhaled and exhaled.

Blake gave her something else to do.

"Cam, can you untie your flannel shirt from around your waist and cover him?"

Cam hesitantly released his hand and stood to untie the shirt. Then she carefully covered his upper body.

"Thank you, that will help keep him warm." Cam really needed something warm covering her, but there was no way she'd use that shirt for herself when Tomas was lying there in need of it. Blake knew that without a shadow of a doubt.

Tomas said something and Cam covered her eyes with her hand. Blake tried to console her.

"What did he say?"

"He wants his wife."

"Does she…know what's happened?"

"No. Not unless someone else has called her."

"We will make sure she's notified as soon as we find out where we're taking him."

Cam didn't seem comforted. "She should be here. They should be together. In case…" She started to tremble.

"Do you want to go call her now?"

Cam shook her head and wiped her cheek. "I'm not leaving him." She dug her phone out of her back pocket. She pressed some buttons and held the phone to her ear. She spoke to someone in Spanish and fought back more tears. Then she held the phone to Tomas and Blake could hear a woman's voice. Blake could hear the turmoil and pain.

Tomas's eyes pooled with tears and he managed to say something.

Blake motioned for Cam to end the call. She didn't want Tomas overly stressed. Cam said something more to the woman on the phone and then hung up. She wiped her face again as more tears came.

She looked up as Alejandro returned. Two teenage boys ran up behind him. One had a surfboard under his arm. Alejandro took it and stood it upright.

"Will this work?"

"It's perfect."

Blake sent Alejandro for men to help move him and something to strap him down with. A moment later, Sloane was backing the SUV in. A few minutes after that, Alejandro returned with the supplies and a few of his friends. They set to work on transferring Tomas to the board, following Blake's instructions carefully. Once they had him secured, they lifted him and carried him to Sloane's SUV. Blake and Cam climbed in and eased him into position.

Sloane closed them in and climbed behind the wheel.

"The hospital we're going to is in town," Sloane said as they pulled away.

"Puerto Tranquilo only has trauma one facilities." Blake said, alarmed.

"They're going to assess him and hopefully have transport waiting there."

Blake started to protest and ask for more information, but she saw Sloane eyeing her in the rearview mirror. Whatever she had to say, it wasn't good, and she was silently asking Blake if she should share with Cam there. The kind of hospital he needed must not be anywhere close. If that was the case, it definitely was not good news.

"You're right," Cam said as if she suddenly came to life. Her eyes were no longer wide with fear. She looked certain, determined. "The clinic in town won't be able to help him like he needs. I've been there, I know." She turned toward the front and spoke to Sloane. "We can't take him there. It will be a waste of time."

"They're going to have transport waiting," Sloane said.

"Yeah, that means an ambulance from Cruz Roja. They're great, but Tomas needs help now. He can't wait another two hours for an ambulance to drive him into the city."

"I'm sorry, Cam, they said that's the best they can do for now. Unless…"

"Unless, what?" Blake asked.

"They mentioned air transport."

"They have that?" Blake asked.

"They said it's an option, but that people don't use it very often because of cost."

Cam looked back at Blake. "Call them. Tell them you're a physician and that we want the air transport waiting and ready."

"Cam, they said it cost thousands of dollars," Sloane said. "Thousands."

"I don't care." She stared at Blake. "Tell them I'll pay whatever it costs."

Chapter Thirty-one

Blake hurried back to the waiting room after reporting what she knew about the accident and Tomas's condition to the doctors at the awaiting hospital. She'd just seen Tomas off in the air transport a few moments before. Now Cam was foremost on her mind. Blake had left her in the waiting room with Sloane as she went with the staff to stabilize him and ready him for transport.

Blake rounded the corner and found Sloane standing by the window biting her nails and Cam sitting on a chair, looking lost and frail. Cam didn't seem to notice Blake until she was kneeling in front of her and taking hold of her hands. Sloane came to stand next to them.

"How is he?" she asked.

"He's on his way," Blake said. She squeezed Cam's hands to get her to look at her. "They'll take good care of him."

She nodded, the news apparently not giving her much comfort. It was going to be a long day and a long evening.

"Should we go back to the house?" Sloane asked.

"No!" Cam said with a sudden jerk. "I'm not going anywhere unless it's to that hospital."

Blake spoke to Sloane. "Why don't you go on back? I'll keep you updated and maybe you could," she glanced at Cam "take care of the dogs?" Blake touched Cam's shoulder. "Would you be okay with that? With the dogs staying with Sloane and Kenna?"

Cam looked at Sloane. "That would be really nice. If you don't mind?"

"Not at all," Sloane said.

"There's a spare key under the potted rubber tree by the garage," Cam said. "Thank you. And please, give McKenna my gratitude as well."

"Will do." Sloane kissed Blake's cheek and set off.

Blake looked at Cam, concerned. Her dark eyes were glazed. Smudged streaks of blood marked her jaw.

"Let's go get cleaned up." She encouraged Cam to stand but she resisted.

"I want to go to Tomas," she said.

"Cam, I think it's best if we stay here for now. Wait until we get word from the hospital before we decide what to do next."

"Why?" She shook her head. "I want to go. I should be there."

"You called his wife?" Blake asked. "Told her where he was going?"

"Yes, she said she was leaving right away. She'd already called someone to take her."

"That's good, he'll have someone there. We can stay here."

"But—"

"Cam, we aren't family. We won't be able to be with him tonight. And you—"

"What about me?"

You need to rest. You need a break.

"We aren't going to leave here, I promise. We're just going around the corner." She lightly tugged on her again and Cam relented and stood. Blake led them to a woman sitting behind a counter.

"Dr. Gomez said we could use a room to clean up?"

The woman nodded and pointed to an open door behind them. Blake thanked her and took Cam inside and closed the door. They stood at the sink and Blake began washing, first their hands and then, with gentle strokes, Cam's face. She worked slowly, paying attention to the slope of her jaw and the softness of her skin. When she finished, she led them to two chairs against the wall. She eased Cam down and then sat next to her.

"Let's relax in here for a while. Where it's quiet."

Cam kept glancing at the door, obviously still uneasy.

"What's wrong?"

"We should be out there. What if they call with word on Tomas and we aren't out there? What if they call from the chopper even?"

"Cam, I've already made sure that we will be kept up to speed on everything. Okay? If someone calls, they will find us. This place isn't very big."

She didn't seem comforted.

"We should go. Drive to that hospital now."

"Cam—"

"His condition could change. At any second. He could flatline." Her breath hitched and Blake could see the emotion threatening to overtake her. "And we wouldn't be there and we wouldn't—" Blake held her hand.

"Wouldn't what?"

"Wouldn't get—to say good-bye." She crumpled, overcome with sobs. Blake held her as she cried, suspecting this wasn't just about Tomas. She held her and soothed her until the sobs stopped racking her body and her breathing became steady. Blake brought her a box of tissues and Cam wiped her face, sniffling.

"I'm sorry," she said.

"There's no need to apologize."

"I just cried all over you."

"You needed to," Blake said.

"I've never done that before. Lost it like that in front of someone."

"You've been through a lot today. Seen things you're not used to seeing. That can do a lot to a person."

She took a deep breath. "It can, yes."

"You sound like you speak from experience."

She threw away her tissue and set the box on the small counter next to them.

"I've...been through something similar before."

Blake reached out and offered her hand. Cam took it and held tightly.

"Would you like to talk about it?"

She leaned back and breathed deeply as if readying herself for something monumental. "I don't like talking about it. Haven't really talked about it."

"You don't have to if you don't want to. But it might help."

Cam stared straight ahead. Took another breath. After another firm squeeze of Blake's hand, she spoke.

"Four years ago, my wife and I were T-boned going through an intersection. I have no memory of the impact. Only what happened shortly before and then after, when I came to as I was being taken from the car. We—she—Lexi, her name, my wife. She was slumped in her seat and the impact had shoved her door against her and she was close to me, too close, and she was at an odd angle. But I couldn't make sense of any of that at the time. I was so confused, I fought the fireman trying to help me and I clung to her, trying to get her to respond to me. But she was cold. Limp, like a doll, like she had no bones. And there was blood. So much blood. On her head and face."

She covered her mouth and clenched her eyes.

"Like Tomas." Her eyes opened and they were glossy with tears. "The firemen were pulling me away from her and I—was screaming. At Lexi, at them. I didn't want to let her go. I didn't want to let her go. Because I knew, I knew I'd never get to touch her again. I knew she was gone."

She started crying again, her chin at her chest. Blake held her close and let her cry.

"I'm so sorry, Cam," she said, wiping away her own tears.

"I didn't want to live," she said. "I didn't deserve to live."

"Cam, that's not true."

"It is true." She pegged her with a pain-filled look. "It's my fault she's gone."

Blake shook her head. "How is it your fault?"

"Because I was arguing with her and I wasn't paying attention like I should've been. If I'd been paying more attention, I would've seen that other driver run the light, I could've swerved or—"

"No, Cam," Blake said. "It wasn't your fault."

Cam started to argue, but Blake held her face. "Listen to me. It wasn't your fault. It was an accident and you had no control over any of it. Do you understand?"

Cam swallowed and more tears trailed down her cheeks. Blake swiped them with her thumbs.

"You have to forgive yourself, Cam. To let go of this self-blame. Your wife…would she want you to do this to yourself? To live like this?"

"No. She'd kick my ass."

Blake smiled. "I think I would've liked her then."

They were quiet, Blake gently cupping her face and Cam staring into her with her deep, dark eyes. Her gaze was softer than it had ever been and it seemed to be taking Blake completely in. Like Cam was allowing herself to really see her for the first time.

And then Cam leaned toward her. An inch, only an inch, but her intention was clear. Blake wanted to meet her halfway, started to do so, wanting to kiss her just as badly as Cam seemed to want to kiss her. But Blake stopped, pulled back. Cam blinked and then straightened quickly, causing Blake's hands to fall away.

"Tomas," Cam said, standing. "I want to get back in case they call."

Blake stood alongside her and opened the door. Cam walked through and Blake watched as she walked ahead of her back toward the waiting room.

Tomas wasn't the only one healing this evening.

Cam was too.

And Blake knew it had been a long time coming.

CHAPTER THIRTY-TWO

Cam sat on the couch and leaned forward, elbows on knees, to run her hands through her damp hair. The hot shower she'd just taken had finally chased off the shakes she'd had for good. Yet she was still cold. Unusually so. She massaged her head and eyed the dim fireplace. She was dressed warmly, in thick, soft athletic pants and matching long-sleeved shirt. A fire seemed to be what she needed, but even just thinking about getting up to start one felt overwhelming.

What is wrong with me?

Her back door eased open and the dogs ambled in, trotting to her with welcome home greetings, though not with their usual exuberance. They seemed to be sensitive to her sadness, like they'd been after her big argument with Blake on the beach. They'd stayed in bed by her side all night long as she'd cried.

"Hello, my boys." She stroked their heads and buried her face in their fur.

"How are you feeling?"

Blake had stepped inside and crossed the room quietly. She'd gone back to Sloane's to clean up and to get the dogs after seeing Cam home safely from the emergency clinic. Cam had paid for a cab rather than having Sloane come get them. She hadn't wanted to come home at all at first and she'd fought Blake on it all evening, until Blake's reasoning finally penetrated her haze of fear and reached her.

Cam was grateful for her, for everything. And she couldn't help but smile weakly as Blake came to the couch. She appeared to have showered, like Cam, her hair damp and hanging loose along her face. She, too, was also dressed for warmth, wearing similar pants to Cam's and a cable knit sweater. Cam could smell the sweet scent she'd noticed on her days before. And it still, despite everything she'd been through that day, jump-started her heart.

"What time is it?"

Blake checked her watch. "After ten."

"Do you think he's still all right?" It had been hours since they'd gotten word that Tomas was stable and resting for the night. Blake had even spoken to one of the doctors personally, and Cam still had had a hard time letting go and trusting that Tomas was going to be okay.

"He's been stable for hours and none of his injuries are life threatening."

"That could change," Cam said. "Anything could happen."

Blake knelt before her and made a move to touch her hand, but stopped. "It's not likely, Cam. The surgery on his leg went well, he doesn't have any major damage. There aren't any signs of traumatic brain injury or spinal injuries. He's hurt badly, but his broken wrist will heal, along with his bumps and bruises. His prognosis is good. And considering that fall, and that rebar, this is good news. He was very lucky."

Again, she started to reach out to her and stopped. "Please, try to relax now."

Blake was being so thoughtful and kind and she'd already done so much for Tomas and for her. She'd even sat and held her when she'd completely broken down and told her about Lexi and the accident. And now she was with her again, after spending hours with her at the clinic, waiting for word on Tomas. She was there checking on her when she should be in bed herself.

"He was lucky you were there," Cam said. She glanced down at Blake's hand. Blake had been careful not to touch her since their time together in the room at the clinic.

When I tried to kiss her.

She felt a fool and wanted to blame it on the emotion of the moment. But there was more to it than that. So much more.

"Thank you, Blake." She choked up a little, her gratitude sincere. She managed to smile, and Blake slowly raised her hand and this time followed through and skimmed her cheek with her fingertips. Cam inhaled quickly, her touch like lightning. Blake stood, as if she'd been struck too.

"How about a fire?" She was already at the fireplace tossing in logs. She got it lit and going strong before she faced Cam again. "Are you hungry?"

Cam shook her head. "I'm good."

Blake didn't seem to like that answer and for a moment she seemed at a loss as to what to do.

"Are you sure you don't want something hot to eat? You've got to be starved."

"Blake, no. You've done...so much. I had a peanut butter sandwich. I'm okay."

She finally came and sat next to Cam. "What I've done doesn't matter. I'm not keeping score."

Her eyes were like sea glass being shone upon by the sun.

"If you need something more, I'll get it. Don't hesitate to tell me. Okay? It's been a rough day for you. Tomas's fall, your memories of the car accident, you've got to be exhausted."

"I am."

"Then we should get you to bed."

Cam straightened, the words taking on a different meaning to her than they obviously had to Blake.

"No."

"Why not?"

"I can't. Not with you here."

Blake's face fell and Cam hurried to explain. She gripped her leg when she tried to move and Blake stilled, obviously startled by her touch.

"You're taking that wrong," Cam said. "Just like you did the night we helped Alberto."

Blake glanced down at her leg where Cam held her.

"If you can't sleep with me here then I should go."

"I don't want you to go."

"You need to sleep."

"I don't want to sleep."

"I don't understand. What do you want?"

Cam couldn't answer. She didn't have the words or the courage to say anything. She just didn't want her to leave. She didn't want to stop looking at her or smelling her or having her so close to her she could almost feel the heat of her body.

"Cam?" Her breathing had quickened and her gaze was more alert and seeking than it was concerned.

"Don't go." She had the urge to kiss her again, lured by her parted lips, those beautiful bow-shaped lips. She began to lean in, drawn, pulled to her mouth.

"Cam," Blake breathed.

"Do you want to go?" Cam asked, pausing. She saw Blake swallow. "No."

And before Cam could move again, Blake's eyes hazed over and she came at her, pressing Cam back into the couch. She slid her hand along the side of Cam's face and singed her lips into Cam's, branding her with aggressive, hungry kisses that framed and tugged and sucked, like Cam was the best thing she'd ever tasted.

Cam relented, helpless, shocked, and so overwhelmed it took her a few seconds to catch up. When she did, she groaned at the feel of her plump, ripe mouth and the mind-spinning nectar of her taste. Cam pulled on her leg, urging her closer and Blake stopped suddenly and stared into her.

"I can't do this. You're so vulnerable right now, Cam. I'm concerned—worried that—Oh, God." Her eyes widened and then narrowed as Cam lifted her hand and began kissing her fingertips. Slowly, delicately, deliberately awakening each and every nerve.

"I'm okay," Cam said, trailing down to her inner wrist, kissing and breathing upon her skin. Taking in that new sweet scent of hers.

"You're—"

"I'm fine." She was better than fine. A sudden surge of energy was coursing through her now, fueled by desire. She extended her tongue, traced her way up into her palm. "Stay."

Blake shuddered, and with a fiery look that burned into Cam, she pushed her back again and crawled on top of her. But instead of kissing her, she reversed the hold Cam had on her and brought Cam's hand to her mouth where she began kissing her fingers just as Cam had done hers.

A hot shockwave rushed between her legs. She lost the ability to breathe and actually struggled, as if she'd never taken in air before.

Blake was watching her, grinning ever so slightly as she continued to tease her fingers with breath, lips, and tongue.

"Is this making you as wet as it did me?"

Her words hit Cam as powerfully as her touch, sending another shockwave through her, only this time it not only settled between her legs, it pulsed. "Yes."

"Good," she said and kissed Cam with lips that somehow seemed to burn hotter than her gaze and Cam felt the piercing of all those tiny arrows she'd imagined Blake's kiss to bring. Every single one was laced with Blake's own sweet elixir and Cam could feel it pushing through her veins like heavy, potent venom.

Cam had to touch her, had to have her just as vehemently as Blake was having her.

She slid her hand into Blake's hair and returned her kiss, using her tongue to hungrily devour her. Blake moaned as if she approved and straddled her legs. And Cam, desperate to feel her, fumbled with her sweater, finally finding the hem to shove it up over her breasts.

They were bare and the warmth of them skimming her hands as she tried to remove the sweater sent Cam into overdrive. And when Blake tore away from her and pulled off her sweater and looked at Cam with a flushed face and a wildly aggressive need, Cam knew that what Sloane had said about resisting an attraction was true.

This was their long denied desire coming to light and Cam knew it was going to be an explosion.

CHAPTER THIRTY-THREE

Touch me," Blake said, taking Cam's hands and placing them on her sumptuous breasts. Cam cupped them, almost closing her eyes at how wonderful they felt, so soft and full. But she kept her eyes open and watched Blake's face as she began grazing her nipples with her thumbs. Blake pressed her lips together, made small noises and began to move her hips. She was searching for connection, trying to rub herself against Cam's thigh. But Cam was too turned on to assist her by moving her leg. Too turned on to have to watch in sweet agony as Blake ground herself against her thigh.

Cam wanted to feel her now. She quickly lowered her hand and gave Blake what she was after. She pressed her hand directly between her legs and found the heat of her through her sweats.

"Cam, oh—yes." She gripped her wrist and gyrated slowly, but then, like Cam, seemed to lose all patience and control. She began to move faster, trying to control Cam's hand.

"You want more?" Cam moved up to her waistband.

"Yes," she breathed. "Hurry." She tried to push Cam in she was so desperate.

Cam was just as desperate to appease her and she hurriedly dipped her hand inside her pants and found her heat once again. Her blessedly hot, silky heat. They both cried out as she slid her fingers into her flesh and began to stroke her along her shaft.

"Oh, Christ you feel good," Cam rasped.

"Mm, Cam. So do you. God, so do you."

Cam fell into rhythm with her, giving as Blake eagerly took, gliding and groaning. Cam continued to tease her nipples, awakening the rosy centers, loving how they bunched and hardened, demanding more.

Blake seemed to love it too, calling out twice as she jerked her hips harder and faster, looking at Cam like she was going to eat her alive.

"Don't stop," she said. "Just—keep going." She grabbed fistfuls of Cam's shirt and lifted it only enough to get at the waistband of her pants. "I can't come without feeling you. And I'm really close to coming. Oh—God. Jesus. Cam, can I touch you?" Her fingers were teasing her skin just inside her pants.

Cam swallowed, her own flesh beating as hard as her heart.

"Please? Oh, God, Cam, please let me. I want to feel you."

"Yes," Cam said.

"You want me to?"

"Yes, touch me."

Blake slipped farther into her pants and Cam opened her legs a little, anticipating as she felt her fingers blaze a trail down to her center. And when she found her, when her miraculously warm fingers found her, Cam rocked back.

"Oh, God!"

"Yes," Blake said, eyes narrowing again. Deviously. "You are— so wet. Dear God, yes." She leaned forward as she began to rub her, quickly locating her most sensitive spot and plying it with heavy attention.

"Fuck," Cam said, easing down farther on the couch, opening herself more, feeling like she absolutely, could not possibly, get enough.

"Do you want me to stop?" Blake asked, grinning, voice heavy with seduction.

Cam felt her own pleasure come over her and she answered with a voice that rivaled Blake's. "You know I don't."

Blake laughed.

Cam watched her beautiful body dance against her hand, so fucking hot and slick, and she watched her beautiful face as it succumbed to the pleasure she was both giving and receiving. Cam looked down to where Blake's arm disappeared into her pants and watched the movement of her hand beneath her sweats, touching her, pleasing her, getting her off.

Cam bit her lower lip, it was all so fucking good she wanted to get completely lost in it forever.

"Do you want to come?" Blake asked, her eyes heavy lidded but wild. Cam had never seen anything sexier in her life.

"Fuck, yes, I want to come."

"You don't want to wait? To—go slow?"

Cam shuddered and her hips jerked. "No fucking way. Do you?"

"Nuh-uh."

Cam moved her hand from her breast and cradled her face. "Then come here." She urged her closer and stared into her.

"Hurry, Cam. I'm—close."

"You want to come?"

"Oh, Jesus, yes."

"Then kiss me. Kiss me while you come."

She tugged her to her and Blake's mouth met hers in a fierce collision of hunger and need. Cam plunged her tongue into her and Blake answered with her own and they stroked and danced there just as their hands did between their legs.

Their kiss fueled their fire and they both began to quiver as they moved and gave harder and faster. They moaned and made small cries, all of them muffled by their feeding mouths. They were fused in pleasure, refusing to part until they were satiated, until they had gotten what they so desperately needed.

And it happened for Cam first, a sudden, deep groan, and a melting of bones as her entire body opened up and allowed the pleasure to flood in. Blake jerked, made her own cry, and joined Cam in absorbing all the ecstasy they could, before the gate closed and the pleasure was suddenly too much, sending them into spasms that were, first reacting to sensitivities, and then, a split second later, hungry for more. Causing them to tear away from their kiss and attack each other's neck instead, like vampires thirsty for a vein, while their bodies convulsed, saturated and chaotic with the onslaught of pleasure.

"Blake," Cam said, unable to get enough of her skin in her mouth. She dug her fingers into her back and lowered her head to go after her breast. Blake grabbed her hair and called her name as Cam sucked, taking as much as she could of her into her mouth.

"Cam!" More spasms shot through them both, rocking them, insisting they take it all in fits of throaty cries and hungry, last second attempts to devour each other with mouths and hands. Until at last, they grew still, breathless, and wrapped together, Cam slowly massaging her nipple with her tongue, Blake grazing her nails through her scalp.

"I didn't think it was ever going to stop," Blake whispered. "So fucking incredible."

"I didn't want it to stop," Cam said, resting her cheek on the pillow of her breast. "And I don't want to move my hand."

"Mm, me neither."

"If I could walk around with my hand in your pants, I would."

Blake threw her head back and laughed.

"But someone might notice," Cam said.

"They might."

"Right now, I'm thinking I wouldn't care." She closed her eyes. She felt so warm, so relaxed, so right. She wanted to fall asleep in that position, her face resting against Blake's heartbeat, breathing in her sweet skin.

"Are you going to fall asleep on me, now?" Blake asked, touching her cheek.

"Mm."

She tilted Cam's chin and looked down at her. Cam could hardly keep her eyes open. Their lovemaking had used up every last bit of that energy surge. She was done for, and it felt so damn good.

The dogs barked.

"Shit!" Cam jerked awake and Blake jumped off of her and searched for her sweater.

"I bet it's them," she said, pulling it on.

"Who?"

"Who do you think? My nosy friends. McKenna, Rylee, and Sage weren't home when we arrived. They went somewhere for dinner and Sloane kept complaining about my not answering any of their texts."

"You didn't keep them updated?"

Cam adjusted her shirt and her pants.

"Of course I did. Just not to their liking. You know, meaning every five freaking minutes."

The dogs went crazy at the door. Someone was on the patio.

"Here," Blake said, tossing her a blanket. "Look," she shook her head. "Less…"

"Less?"

"I don't know."

"Satisfied? Spent? Satiated? Pleasantly fucked?"

"Pick one," Blake said, turning to look through the small window on the door.

"It's them," she whispered.

Cam sat back and attempted to look less like a woman who'd just climaxed so hard her mind had melted and her bones had shattered. But she didn't think she could pull it off.

A quick knock sounded and Blake answered.

"Hi," McKenna said, peeking around the door.

"Hey." Blake let her and Sage in and then ran a hand through her hair. She was obviously nervous and looking at Cam with wide eyes.

"How are you, Cam?" McKenna said.

"How's your friend?" Sage asked. "We've been so worried."

"They say he's going to be okay," Cam said. "And Blake has assured me of that."

"That's what she said," McKenna said.

Blake threw her hands up behind them, obviously frustrated that her update hadn't somehow been sufficient enough.

"And how about you?" McKenna asked.

"Tired," Cam said. She could hardly keep her eyes open.

Thanks to your good friend, Blake.

"You look…" she paused, confusion marking her brow. "Tired, but your color…your color is back. You look flushed."

Blake spoke quickly, crossing to sit next to her. "Must be all the stress from the day. She really needs to get to bed."

"I'm surprised she's not already in bed," McKenna said.

"She wanted to eat something first," Blake added. "We haven't been home very long." She tucked her hair, which was mussed, behind her ears.

She seemed to be so nervous she looked like she would've jumped sky high if someone were to clap. Cam would've laughed if she'd had the strength. But then again, if she'd had the strength, she would've been just as nervous as Blake. Neither of them, she knew, would want the others to know what had happened between them.

"Can I help with something?" Sage asked. Her gaze was mostly fixed on Cam and when it wasn't, she was openly taking in her home. "Do you need help settling in for the night?"

Blake stood and tucked her hair behind her ears. Again. "No, we're all set." She started herding them to the door.

"Are you—staying?" McKenna asked.

"Uh…"

"I need someone here," Cam said. She didn't want her to go. Especially now that she'd touched her and tasted her and knew for certain what that was like. She didn't care that she was so tired she could hardly form words. "Would like to have someone here."

"I can stay," Sage said. "Blake, you've got to be tired."

McKenna placed a hand on Blake's arm. "Why don't you go on home, Blake? I'll stay with her."

Cam watched their exchange. She could tell Blake was debating how to respond. If she protested again and insisted on staying, McKenna would know something was up. She was sharp. Cam had caught on to that quickly. But she was also very thoughtful and giving, and she was offering to stay so that Cam wouldn't be stuck with Sage.

Cam reminded herself to give McKenna a huge hug as soon as she was able.

"It's okay, Blake," Cam said, trying not to cringe at her own words. "McKenna can make sure I'm settled. You should go get some rest."

Blake nodded, her disappointment evident to Cam, though she'd tried to recover quickly. "Okay." She kissed McKenna on the cheek. "Thanks."

McKenna showed Blake and Sage out. Then she helped Cam stand.

"I think I'll be fine," Cam said as McKenna took her arm. "I was just a little nervous about being alone. So, you really don't have to stay."

McKenna was quiet as she walked with her to the bedroom.

"How are things with Blake?" she asked. "Better?"

Cam struggled through the cobwebs of fatigue to find an appropriate answer. "She—did a lot for my friend today. I don't think

I'll ever be able to thank her for that." She laughed a little. "This is in addition to what she did for Alberto. And me," Cam added softly.

They came to Cam's room and stopped.

"It was nice of her to offer to stay tonight. She obviously cares about you."

Cam glanced away from her penetrating eyes. "She's a doctor. It's what she does."

"Yes, but..." She shook her head as if something had come to her mind. "She didn't say good-bye."

"Sorry?"

"Blake. When she left just now. She had been adamant about staying...but she didn't even say good-bye to—you."

"I'm tired." Cam flicked on her light. "You really don't need to stay. I don't want to trouble you."

"I'd like to stay for a little while," she said, touching her arm. "To make sure you're okay. You're so out of it you're about to collapse and the day you've had...I'll sit by the fire for a bit and then go. Is that all right with you?"

"That would be fine." Cam wondered what all else McKenna had noticed. Blake's messy hair? Or what about her own hair?

Whatever McKenna had noticed, Cam couldn't do much about it now. The less she said, the better. She walked to her bed and pulled back the covers. The dogs jumped up to make themselves comfortable.

McKenna was looking at the photo of Lexi on the nightstand.

"She's lovely."

Cam's insides lurched, like the bottom had dropped out and everything was falling, a feeling she used to experience every time she woke and the reality of losing Lexi had hit her. She'd felt it every day for almost a year. Feeling it again, now, knocked the wind out of her.

"Yes," she managed to say.

She was.

"Thank you, McKenna. For your kindness."

McKenna wished her a good night and disappeared from the doorway.

Cam climbed into bed and took in Lexi's face just before she extinguished the bedside light. She reached out in the dark to touch the glass like she did every night before she closed her eyes. But she stopped herself as she realized she still had Blake on her skin.

Her insides dropped again and everything began to fall.

She closed her eyes and cried softly into her pillow.

❖

Cam sat cursing in her Jeep. She hit the steering wheel with the heel of her hand and then tried to start the engine again.

Nothing.

She climbed out, not even wanting to take the time to look under the hood. She was anxious to get to the hospital to be with Tomas. She didn't have time for this.

She stared at the garage door in front of her. There was another vehicle inside, one she was sure would start because she'd just started it up to keep the battery charged. But she didn't drive it often. It was just too hard. But she also couldn't bring herself to sell it.

"Hi."

Cam turned her head. Blake was walking through the sand in denim capris and a burnt orange Henley style shirt that fit her snug enough to show the hard curve of her muscles and the prominent swell of her breasts. It was a more androgynous look for her, and Cam did a double take and then looked away as she realized just how much she liked it.

"Hi." Cam couldn't hide the defeat in her voice and Blake picked up on it.

"Everything okay?"

Cam stared at the garage. "Jeep won't start."

"Oh. Were you—going somewhere?"

"I want to see Tomas."

"Have you heard something from the hospital?"

"Cell phones don't always work out here."

"Right. You were worried about that when we left the clinic last night. So, you were going to drive the two hours to the hospital?"

"That was the plan. I was going to spend the day."

Blake kicked the sand at the edge of Cam's driveway. "What about the dogs? Do you need someone to look after them?"

"I asked a friend to come check on them. He's in a house just down the beach. Says he doesn't mind."

"Oh." She slid her hands into her pockets. "Do you need a ride, then?"

"I have one." She motioned toward the garage. "In there. I just don't want to drive it."

Blake came closer. "Why?"

"It's the Land Rover I bought Lexi for her...last birthday. She didn't even get to drive it."

"It's too difficult for you to drive," Blake said softly. "I understand. It must be hard."

Cam stared down at her hands for a long moment and then squinted at the rising sun. Blake's quiet presence was a comfort and Cam suddenly felt the need to explain things to her.

"The night she died, we were on our way to dinner to celebrate her birthday. I was freaking out because she'd taken so long to get ready. I was worried our being late would ruin the surprise I had planned for her." She looked over at Blake. "Believe it or not I used to be rather uptight. A real stickler for things like schedules and being on time. That's why we were arguing that night. Because I was freaking out over her taking too long to get ready. Stupid stuff like that, like being a little late to a damn party, it doesn't really matter in the grand scheme of things. That's why I don't stress the small stuff now. It's a waste. And it cost me everything."

She looked back at the rising sun as Blake came to her. She touched her arm.

"I'm sorry, Cam," she said.

She didn't say anything more, just stood there next to her, allowing her to feel. Cam felt the warmth of her hand through her shirtsleeve, and instead of it crushing her with the guilt she'd tossed and turned with half the night, it seemed to give her strength. She took a deep breath. "Anyway, I haven't driven the Rover very much. Just enough to keep it serviced. But now I think it's time."

"Are you sure?" Blake asked. "I—could borrow Sloane's SUV and we could—"

"No, I need to do this."

Blake dropped her hand.

Cam turned and unlocked the garage door and yanked it upward. She started to make her way to the driver's side door.

"Please be safe," Blake said, turning away.

Cam halted. "Did you—want to come with?"

Cam waited for what felt like ages before she faced her again.

"You want to go on your own. I understand."

"Blake—" She had wanted to go alone. It was why she was leaving early. She knew Blake would be up, but she'd hoped she'd be out on her run so she could escape unnoticed, because she didn't know how she was going to feel when she saw her again. The guilt she'd felt the night before had gnawed at her insides, leaving her raw and confused. She'd feared that seeing Blake would only make it worse and she didn't know how to tell her that. She didn't want to hurt her, but she didn't want to hurt either. She didn't know what to do.

The way she'd reacted at the sight of her coming across the sand and the surge of strength she felt from her touch changed things a little. And the obvious concern Blake seemed to have for her, tugged at Cam. She didn't want to let her walk away. She didn't want her to go, just as she hadn't hours before. But when she thought about the Rover and Lexi…

It was going to nearly kill her to get in and drive it on her own. She didn't want to put Blake through another emotional breakdown.

"Thank you, again. For everything."

The crestfallen look that came over Blake was unmistakable and Cam hated herself for it. Somehow she was fucking everything up despite trying to ensure that neither of them got hurt.

Blake simply nodded. Then she turned and walked away.

CHAPTER THIRTY-FOUR

It was dusk when Blake approached Tomas's room at the end of the hall. A nurse came out as Blake reached the door, and Blake was about to say hello, when she heard Cam's voice coming from inside the room. She'd waited all day before riding in with Sloane to see Tomas, wanting to give Cam the space she seemed to have wanted. But Blake, apparently, hadn't waited long enough.

She heard Cam speak again, and she didn't want to pry, but she needed to know if Cam intended to stay.

"Excuse me," Blake said to the nurse, catching her before she got too far away. "Do you speak English?"

"Yes."

Blake pointed at the door, which was partially ajar. "Do you know if the woman with the short, dark hair is going to be leaving anytime soon?"

The nurse came back and looked inside.

"Santi? I don't know. She's been here all day."

"You know her?" Did Cam know everyone in this part of Mexico?

She shrugged. "She's been here all day and she bought us all lunch. Everyone on the day shift knows her now."

Blake stared at her in disbelief. But she didn't know why anything she heard about Cam surprised her anymore. Cam was undeniably a very gracious, well-liked person who did a lot for people. The nurse further verifying that wasn't what amazed her, it was how she was feeling in response to that verification that was astonishing.

A loud gasp, followed by a short shriek, came from the room. The nurse and Blake both pushed the door open farther. Cam was standing next to Tomas's bed in the firm embrace of a woman and three children. They were smiling through tears, all of them talking at once.

"What's going on?" Blake whispered to the nurse.

The woman listened for a moment, then returned the door to its previous position.

"Sounds like Santi has offered to cover any medical costs and to help support them until he recovers." She leaned in and listened some more. "They are very grateful."

Blake could hear their gratitude through the emotion in their voices. Her own heart was full and heavy with the weight of Cam's generosity.

The door was pulled open without warning. One of the children blinked at Blake and the nurse, who quickly excused herself and hurried down the hall.

"Uh, hi," Blake said as everyone turned to look at her.

"Hola," the young man holding the door said.

Cam said something and the woman hugging her came to Blake, arms wide, and clung to her affectionately as she escorted her into the room. She spoke quickly and motioned toward Cam and then to Tomas, who gave Blake a tired but genuine smile.

Blake nodded, unsure how to respond.

"She's glad you're here," Cam said. "They've been wanting to thank you."

"Oh. I—tell them—"

"Don't try to tell them it's not necessary. They won't accept that."

"Oh." Blake took the woman's hands and squeezed. "De nada. De nada."

She beamed at Blake, nodded, and enveloped her in a tight hug. She waved over the children who embraced her too. Blake smiled at them and at Tomas, who looked better than she'd expected. Then she glanced at Cam who appeared sentimental.

"That's his wife, Alicia," Cam said. "And their children, Gabe, Pedro, and Izza. They are good people," Cam said. "A very close family."

Alicia led Blake to Tomas, who thanked her and told her how he was feeling, most of which was translated by Cam. Blake discussed his condition with him, learned what his doctors had said, and reassured him he was going to be okay. She was so happy he was doing so well.

When his eyes grew heavy a few moments later, Blake gave his hand a squeeze and said good-bye. Alicia took her place and brushed his hair with her hand and kissed his face.

Blake said good-bye to the kids and quietly walked to the door. Cam joined her, reaching for the handle before she could.

"I didn't mean to interrupt your visit," Blake said. "I thought—"

She stepped into the hall as Cam held the door for her.

"He needs to rest," Cam said. "So, don't worry about it."

Blake's phone alerted her to a text. She pulled it from her back pocket, read it, and sighed. "Damn it, Sloane."

"What is it?" Cam asked as they made their way toward the main entrance.

Blake was texting back. "I don't know. She's acting crazy."

Another text came in response to hers. She dropped her hands. "What the hell?"

Cam questioned her with her raised brow.

"She says she can't come and get me like we had planned. Something about—being tied up and she can't get away any time soon. I don't know. She's not making a lot of sense."

Cam made a noise like she wasn't surprised.

"What?" Blake asked.

"She messaged me about an hour ago and asked if I was still here at the hospital. And if so, for how much longer. I told her I was leaving around seven."

Blake checked the time on her phone. She slid the device in her pocket and rubbed her temples.

"I can't believe her."

Cam laughed. "They are clever, those friends of yours."

"They're insane." They exited through the main doors and stepped out into the night. Blake stopped at the curb and searched for a cab.

Cam looked back at her when she realized she wasn't next to her. "You coming?"

"No, I'll just get a cab or something."

"Why?"

"I'm—pissed and embarrassed. I can't believe the extremes they'll seem to go to to—"

Cam cocked a single eyebrow. "Throw us together?"

"Yes. And I don't want to intrude on you."

Cam came back to her and took her hand. "Come on. I can use some company, so you aren't intruding. As for Sloane and McKenna? You can chew them out when we get back."

"I can't wait," Blake said, falling into step next to her, trying her hardest not to melt at the simple feel of her hand in hers. What would walking on the beach with Cam hand in hand be like? Would it be as nice as this? She imagined it would be even better.

They reached the Land Rover and climbed inside, both buckling up. Cam pushed the button to start the engine and pulled out of the parking lot. Blake was uncertain at how Cam was going to be on the ride home. She'd been distraught earlier about having to drive Lexi's vehicle and though she seemed at ease now, Blake wondered if she truly was.

"Are you feeling better today? After having rested last night?"

"If you could call it rest."

"I wasn't referring to our—"

"I know. But even after you left, I didn't get much sleep."

Cam tightened her one-handed grip on the steering wheel and Blake tried to get a better look at her expression, but the interior glow from the dash wasn't sufficient enough for her to discern subtleties.

"I do feel better knowing Tomas is doing well. Seeing him today helped a lot."

"You really care about him and his family."

Cam glanced at her. "They're my friends and they're good people. So, yes I care."

"You care a great deal," Blake said.

Cam didn't respond for a few seconds. "What do you think of the Rover?" She was making an attempt to sound lighthearted and she even smiled.

"It's very nice. It still smells new." She ran her hand along the side of the leather seat.

"Think Tomas and his family would like it?"

"I—don't know."

"They only have one vehicle right now. Tomas's little truck. The kids usually have to ride in the bed when they all go somewhere together. Makes me nervous. So, I'm going to give them this."

"Do you think they'll accept it?"

Cam laughed. "I'm sure Tomas will fight it just like he always has when I've offered to get him another car, but right now it's needed more than ever. With his mother, his in-laws, and his wife's aunt now living with them, they really need another vehicle. A bigger vehicle. So, if I show up with this and give it to Tomas in front of the whole family and explain why it is they need it, I think Tomas will accept it. He'll say it's too fancy and too expensive, I'm expecting that. But I'll just tell him he can sell it and buy something more practical if he wants. Spend the difference on other things. Whatever he wants to do. I just want to make sure this goes to someone special for a good cause."

"Do you think he'll sell it?"

"They'll drive it for a while. Enjoy it. After that, I don't know for sure. They're very practical, so they'll probably sell it. But then again, Tomas is sentimental. He likes this car and he knows what it represents to me."

"It wouldn't bother you if he sold it?"

She seemed to think for a moment. "If you'd asked me that before today I would've said yes, there's no way I'm getting rid of it, much less selling it. But after…yesterday and my drive in it this morning, I feel differently. It's time to let this go. It's not doing anyone any good sitting in my garage. Giving it to Tomas would be what Lexi would've preferred."

Yesterday.

Was Cam referring to their passionate consummation on the couch, or what she went through with Tomas's accident? It could be, she surmised, both. But Blake's mind was fixated on their encounter. It had been replaying in her mind relentlessly. Her body craved her, as if what had transpired between them had only planted a seed of desire, and every moment since, the yearning that sprouted from it grew bigger and thicker, spreading out into her body, invading every crevice until she could feel the ends pressing into the tips of her fingers and toes. She could feel them now, urging, pushing against her skin.

Blake shifted her focus back to Cam's generosity and change of heart over the car.

"Lexi sounds like she was a lot like you in wanting to help people."

"She was."

"I'm glad you've found a solution. You seem more at peace than you did earlier this morning."

"I am, thanks." She leaned back and exhaled and Blake could sense her relief at her decision.

"It's very generous of you, Cam. Giving this to Tomas and helping him with his bills while he recovers. It's very kind."

Cam looked at her. "How do you know about that? About the bills?"

Blake met her gaze as a tiny surge of panic surfaced. "I'm not supposed to know that, am I?" She tucked her hair back over her ear as she waited for Cam to say something. But she didn't say anything. Blake explained. "I overheard you talking to Tomas and his family at the hospital. The nurse that had been in the room with you, translated for me when she came out. I shouldn't have asked her to tell me what was being said, but I heard all the commotion and…well, I'm glad I did." She watched Cam closely. "It allowed me to see another side of you. One that I had seen glimpses of and knew was there, but really loved seeing completely. You not only give your time and your love and loyalty to people, but you give your money and things that have value to you. That's not something I see every day."

Blake saw her swallow and she shrugged just before she spoke.

"Money—doesn't mean to me what it used to. It's not everything. Not what life should be about. And I have more than any one person needs, so I help others when I can."

Blake smiled warmly at her, but she knew she couldn't see it. It didn't matter though. Cam had touched her heart and she longed to reach out and take her hand in hers. Cam, however, focused on the road, and they drove the remainder of the two hours home in comfortable silence, with Blake leaving her to her thoughts.

When they neared the turnoff to the dunes, Blake glanced over at her and found her staring at her.

"Why haven't you said anything about my writing?" she asked.

Blake was totally thrown. She just looked at her.

"Everyone else has asked me things and commented. Even Sloane. But not you."

"I wanted to respect your privacy."

Cam studied her. "I appreciate that. But is that the only reason? You usually aren't shy about sharing your thoughts and opinions. I thought for sure you'd have something to say about what I do. Even if you've read some of my work and disliked it, you'd say something." She grinned toward the road.

"I haven't read your books," Blake said.

"Maybe that'll give you something to look forward to. So you can razz me about how silly and unrealistic they are."

She was joking but Blake couldn't bring herself to laugh.

Cam questioned her again. "No? Maybe not. They're probably not your thing. Just like the romances."

Blake stared out the window into the darkness, thinking about Cam's question. She hadn't read any of Cam's work, but she had heard of her and her books. Her own mother was actually a fan. And Sage had done nothing but talk about her since the night of the beach fire, filling in the gaps of her knowledge.

Cam was successful, popular, and apparently, a very good writer. And, according to Sage, rather wealthy. But Blake didn't care about any of that. Her success wasn't what crawled into her chest and made her ache with a torturous sweetness and excitement. The way she felt went a whole lot deeper than that, but until now, she hadn't been able to fully discern it.

They pulled off the main road and Cam changed the setting on the Terrain Response system to sand as they began the drive through the dunes. Blake tried to keep her focus on the well-packed dirt road, but that insistent desire growing and twisting inside her made it impossible. Her heart raced and she had so much she wanted to express to Cam but knew how difficult it would be to get a private moment to do so back at the beach.

She closed her eyes, gripped the door, and tried to steady her breathing. And then she spoke into the dark silence between them.

"Pull over."

Chapter Thirty-five

Cam seemed confused by Blake's request.

"Please," Blake said. "Pull over somewhere discreet."

Cam's eyes widened slightly in the dim light, but she kept driving straight ahead. Blake was about to protest and ask again when they came to the road that paralleled the houses. Instead of turning right, toward Sloane's and her own home, she veered left and drove until they reached the desolate beach where Blake had found solace on some of her runs.

Cam pulled off the path and put the car in park. She kept her eyes forward.

"You're going to tell me you're leaving soon," she said.

Blake stammered. "Uh—no—that wasn't what I had in mind."

"But you are leaving soon, aren't you? Javier told Tomas you were very interested in his building but that you called Alejandro today and put everything on hold. Said you needed to think some things over."

"I do." Blake wasn't ready to have this conversation. And the way things had gone with Cam earlier that morning, she hadn't been so sure she'd even have to worry about it much when the time did come to say good-bye. It would've been hard for her, but with Cam's distress and distance that morning, she'd thought Cam might've even welcomed her good-bye.

Now it seemed she'd been wrong. Things had changed within a span of hours. Would she ever be able to read her? Or was the fact that she couldn't one of the reasons why she was so intrigued by her?

"I do have a lot to think over, Cam. But I'm not going anywhere anytime soon so I still have plenty of time to do all the thinking I need in the weeks to come."

"What is it you want to talk about then?" Her tone was soft, like she was anxious about what Blake might say.

"Your writing, the way I feel—"

Cam laughed and shook her head. "Okay, lay it on me."

"Why do you think I'm going to say something offensive to you about your writing?"

Cam gave her an incredulous look instead of answering.

"Because of what I said about reading romances? You don't write romance do you?" From what she knew, Cam wrote books that were considered more science fiction, with dystopian plots.

"No, not typically. But now—" She stopped. "You had some rather strong opinions about romances, and some rather strong opinions about me. It isn't a far leap for me to think that you might have some equally strong opinions about my books."

"I haven't read them."

"You hadn't read the romances either, but you still had your opinions about them. You've also had some very strong opinions about me in general. You weren't very fond of me. I was just a woman in dirty jeans and work boots, with calloused hands, who liked to hammer nails and fix things. Beyond that, there wasn't much more to me."

"You forgot rude, smug, and annoyingly imperturbable." Blake meant it to be funny, but Cam didn't seem to take it that way.

"Did I? My mistake then."

"I did think some of those things, Cam. And I admit, at first, I didn't think there was much else to you. I didn't *want* to think that there was much else to you. I was physically attracted to you and that bothered me, so I was intent on completely ignoring you. Needless to say, that was impossible."

Blake gave a short laugh.

"I saw you reading on your patio and I became curious, wondering if there were things about you I hadn't yet seen. And as I spent more time with you, infuriating as some of those times were, I began to see you. I saw that you were deep and introspective, and very intelligent, as well as kind and caring to those in need. Learning that you were a writer confirmed what I'd already discovered. And it was, if I'm honest, the final nail in the coffin. I mean, my God, Cam, I was already a goner and that just pushed me over the edge. I didn't need to have read your work to be affected. I already knew all I needed to know about you. And if I had read your books, I would never say anything negative to you about them."

"You wouldn't share your opinions?"

"I would. But not the way you're thinking. Even if I didn't like something, I wouldn't be rude about it. That's *if* I didn't like something, and I don't think that's possible. Not if your writing is anything like you. And as for your dirty jeans and work boots? Cam, I could've been in a coma and somehow my body would've reacted to you walking around wearing that. That was…never a deterrent."

"Do you understand what I'm trying to say? You being a writer has only intensified my attraction. Every additional thing I learn about you, or see you do, does the same. That's what I wanted to talk to you about. This probably isn't the best place to do it, with this being Lexi's car and all, but I wanted to be sure I had you one-on-one, with no interruptions."

"I'm not bothered by the car, now. I'm at peace with it."

"So, this is okay? Sitting here alone with me?"

Cam turned off the engine and faced her.

Blake reached for her hand, held it delicately.

They were enveloped by the dark, and even after her eyes adjusted, Blake could barely make out the contours of Cam's face. Her exact expression could not be seen.

Cam held her hand tighter.

"The romance," she said. "You read it, didn't you?"

Blake laughed a little. "You're not going to let that go, are you?"

"Not when I suspect I'm right."

"All right, fine. I read it. Go ahead and gloat."

"I'll only gloat if you tell me what you thought."

"In that case, I won't tell you."

"It was hot, wasn't it? You liked it." She brought Blake's hand to her lips and kissed it. "Be honest."

"I—yes, it was hot."

"And?" Cam continued kissing her hand, reawakening that craving she'd had for her all day long, one tiny little caress at a time.

Blake closed her eyes, the sensation rushing through her like it had before and her thoughts about the book came pouring out.

"I thought about you and how the two main characters were so similar to us. I thought about the things you'd said about the book, and for some reason, knowing how the very words I was reading made you feel, made the story so much more visceral for me and aroused me so much, I had to sneak away to someplace private to read it. I... didn't want to be interrupted."

Blake opened her eyes and though she couldn't see Cam clearly, she could envision the way Cam's eyes were looking at her, dangerously afire.

"You thought of me?" Her voice was husky and Blake heard her breathing shallow.

"Till the very last word."

"It excited you to know that it turned me on just like it was doing you?"

"Yes."

"What did you do while you were alone? Why didn't you want to be interrupted?"

She moved closer and Blake could feel the warmth of her breath near her cheek.

"You really want to know?"

Cam inched in farther. She whispered, "I'm dying to know."

"I did to myself what we did together last night."

Cam laughed softly and kissed her just below her ear, causing her skin to come alive with gooseflesh.

"Tell me," she said. "In detail."

Blake heated, both with longing and a little embarrassment. "I'm not the writer. Details are your territory."

"You're capable," she said, kissing along her jaw. "More than capable." She laughed again and Blake felt her hand on her waist. "Remember, I was there for your story by the beach fire. And I was there with you...last night." Her mouth was now close to Blake's, the air between them growing hot as they both fought for it. "You aren't suddenly shy now, are you? You weren't last night."

"I was...aroused. Lost my inhibitions."

"You aren't aroused right now?"

"I'm—yes. But I'm not—"

"Being stimulated? I think I might be able to help you with that." She pulled away and climbed into the back seat. "Come here."

Chapter Thirty-six

Blake found her outreached hand in the dark and maneuvered over the console. Cam then tugged her onto the seat next to her and leaned in. She quickly lifted up the hem of her shirt and then, just as quickly, unfastened her bra, freeing her breasts. Blake sighed at the heat of her hand as she cupped her.

"By the way," Blake said. "Your hands aren't calloused. But I wouldn't care if they were. Soft, rough, right now I wouldn't—care." Her voice caught as Cam ran her fingers over her nipple, electrifying her.

"Soft or rough, you wouldn't care?"

"No."

"What about warm?" She scooted lower, her breath now tickling Blake's chest. "And wet? Like this."

Cam's hot mouth enveloped her breast, and it might as well have enveloped her clitoris it felt so good. Blake's breath was momentarily stolen, but as Cam began to lightly suck her, she clenched her shirt and cried out.

"Cam! Oh, my God, you—" Cam was pulling her in and then releasing, sometimes forcefully, sometimes gently, while her fingers teased her other breast. Over and over, she methodically played her, until Blake was clenching her legs together and trembling uncontrollably.

"Cam," Blake said. "Please."

Cam stopped and Blake felt the aching absence of her mouth. "Will you tell me what you did when you were alone with your book?"

Her fingers traced Blake's erect nipple, exciting the surrounding skin, tightening her breast in sweet agony.

"Yes," Blake managed. "Anything. Anything to get you to stop—or to get more. God, I want more. More than this. Please."

"Then tell me," Cam said, once again moving lower. "You were where? In the house?"

"Mm, the bedroom. The others were gone, on walks or on the ATVs."

"And what did you do in the bedroom?" She lightly kissed her where she'd sucked, teasing.

"I—got my book and got onto my bed."

"Did you undress?"

"No. I was too afraid someone would suddenly return."

"What did you have on?"

"My bikini."

"Keep going," she said.

Blake started to speak but was jolted back at the feel of her tongue circling her nipple.

"Cam—I can't I—" She felt Cam's hand trail down to her waistband where she unbuttoned her pants. A second later, she slid into her panties and found her flesh.

Blake rocked back as she quickly explored her, groaning wickedly when she found her excitement. She coated her with it and then began stroking her cleft.

Blake pulled at the back of her shirt and lifted her hips as her eyes rolled at the pleasure shooting up through her.

"You were saying?" Cam stroked her slowly, carefully, as if she were searching for the correct pressure and speed needed to keep Blake at a level of ecstasy she could handle enough to speak.

"You were reading," Cam said, at her ear.

"Mm, I was reading. And I thought of you—of us. The way we argued—the way I—wanted to dislike you and forget about you but I couldn't. I was so attracted to you—wanted you. We were so much like those two characters. And when I got to the first love scene—I thought of you. Imagined you wearing that blue robe, with your hair and skin wet, fresh from the shower. And I—slipped my hand in my bikini bottoms and touched myself."

Cam heightened her stroking and surprised her with a hungry kiss. Blake clung to her and brought her other hand to her face, holding her, meeting her tongue with her own as she met her giving hand with the eager pulse of her hips.

Cam took her close to the brink of climaxing before she slowed again and halted the kiss.

"Did you come fast or did you take your time?" she asked breathlessly, her lips still touching Blake's as she spoke.

"I climaxed quickly at first, unable to resist. And then I started again and took my time."

Cam moved back down to her breasts, this time breathing on the one her fingers had teased. "You drew it out," she said, kissing the center of it like she'd just done her mouth.

Blake arched into her swirling tongue and knotted her fingers in her hair. "Ye—yes. I wanted it to last. Wanted to imagine being with you as long as I could. When I got close, I stopped."

"How many times?"

"Three, four times. I don't remember."

"And then?"

"And then, I couldn't take it anymore. And—I—"

"Tell me. Tell me how you came." She took her in her mouth again and changed the rhythm of her stroking.

Blake fought for control, but there was none to be had, the pleasure too great, too intense, too unbelievably fucking good.

"I gave in and I—made myself come. So hard. So—Jesus, Cam. Like now. I'm going to come so hard now, Cam. You're making me come." She clenched her eyes as Cam sucked her and stroked her into a pleasurable oblivion where she called out her name again and again, digging her fingers into her scalp and back, desperate to keep her there, giving to her as she pulsed into her mouth and hand for what felt like an eternity before she finally stilled.

Cam eased away from her, her hand still nestled between her legs.

"I've got to get you more of those books. A lot more."

Blake laughed, deep and throaty. She gently tugged on her hair, bringing her up to her. "Now that I've admitted I enjoyed one, I guess it would be silly to try and refuse."

"You can still read them secretly if you'd like. But I would appreciate you giving me all the details later."

"About the book or about what I got up to while reading it?"

"All of it."

Blake kissed her, long and soft, relishing the careful probing of Cam's tongue. Cam was so deliberate, taking her time, as she began moving her hand again between Blake's legs. She started slowly there as well, carefully, like her kiss, and massaged in a circular motion.

Blake's audible reaction was swallowed by Cam and her tongue, and she responded like the noise was sustenance, the fuel she needed to keep giving, and her kiss and touch both became frenzied.

In seconds, Blake was climbing toward another climax, but she didn't want to come, not yet, not again, not without Cam. With all the strength she had, she shoved her away, severing their connection. Blake hurriedly pounced on her, wanting the return of that pleasure and the capability to give it to Cam.

She fumbled with her pants and Cam laughed at first but then seemed to sense Blake's seriousness and fell silent. When Blake finally unsecured the button and zipper and curled her fingers over the waistband to pull them down, she paused.

"Is this okay?" Their environment and its impact were still something Blake had concern over.

She heard her gasp for breath.

"If you don't want to, I understand."

"No."

Blake heard her swallow.

"I'm okay." She lifted her hips and helped Blake lower her pants. Then Blake lifted her shirt and, after grazing her fingers along her chest, unfastened and removed her bra.

"I wish I could see you," Blake said, angling herself toward her on the seat. She traced her fingers down her neck to her breasts, where she held them and brought them to attention with the purposeful movement of her thumbs. Her breasts were small, with large areolas, and Blake resisted the urge to take them in her mouth, and instead, enjoyed pebbling their smoothness with the tease of her thumbs. Cam let out a shaky sigh and covered Blake's hands with her own, obviously approving of Blake's decision.

"Now I really wish I could see you," Blake said. "See your face."

"This...the dark. It heightens our senses. I like it."

She encouraged Blake to increase her touching by guiding Blake with her own hands.

"It's been so long," she said. "I forgot how—good it feels."

Blake leaned in and whispered in her ear. "I'm so glad, Cam. So glad I can make you feel good. But touching you like this and hearing how much you're enjoying it, is driving me crazy. I can't hold back much longer."

"You don't have to."

"I want to make it last for you."

"I want it to last, too. But that's not going to be possible. I don't know if it's because it's been so long for me, or if it's because it's you. Whatever the reason, I feel like you do. I have no control over what my body wants. And it wants you, Blake. Now. So, please, don't hesitate. Because it will be pointless. Because I won't let you."

"Oh, my God, Cam," Blake said, taking her face in her hands. She kissed her until she could no longer think or breathe, and then she tore away and pressed her back into the seat and shoved her hand inside her panties and just about died at how hot and slick she was. Cam reacted to her touch with a sharp cry and inched farther down on the seat, giving Blake better access.

"Yes," Blake said, loving how much more of her she could feel. "Open yourself for me."

"Blake," she said, as Blake explored her, purposely avoiding her most sensitive spot. "Touch me." She grabbed her hand and tried to move it upward.

Blake slid up to her clit, grazed it. "Here?"

Cam tensed and tightened her grip. "Yes."

Blake framed her clit and stroked her side to side.

"God, yes," she hissed. "Like that."

Blake kissed her neck again, this time using her tongue, occasionally lingering and sucking. She felt Cam arch and she groaned with her chin tilted toward the ceiling.

"You like it like this?" Blake asked.

"Uh-huh."

"How about this?" She stroked her up and down, squeezing her between her fingers.

"Fuck! Yes, oh God." She struggled for breath and Blake changed again to a circular motion.

Cam nearly came up off the seat and groaned. "Faster," she said, digging her nails into Blake's arm.

Blake complied, getting wetter by the second. "Like this?"

"Yes. Fuck. Oh, God—yes." Her body tensed and she clung to Blake's back. Blake knew she was close to climaxing. She stopped her pleasurable assault just long enough to dip her fingers into her.

Cam stiffened. "Why did you stop?" She sounded like she could hardly speak.

"I just wanted more lubrication." She coated her fingers and slid back up to her most needful spot. "See?"

Cam shuddered and she seemed to melt. "Yes," she said. "Oh, yes, I definitely see."

"Just relax. I'm not going to stop again. I know what you like and I'm going to give it to you." She fell into the same rhythm as before. Slowly at first. Building Cam's pleasure.

"Make me come?"

"Yes, I'm going to make you come."

Cam rested her head back against the seat. She twitched as Blake moved faster.

"I'm going to make you come hard, like you did me. Are you ready?"

"Ye—es."

Blake lowered herself to her breast and took almost its entirety into her mouth and sucked her. Cam cried out and held the back of her head.

"Ah, Blake. Like that. Fuck. Ah, it feels so good."

She lifted her hips and Blake moved even faster, sucked her hard and listened with delight at Cam's cries in response.

"Make me come. Blake—make me. Oh, God. Now. Ah, fuck yes, now. Blake—"

Her cry was powerful, as was the shock that went through her body, arching her into a rigid stillness and then ravaging through her with convulsions.

Blake stayed with her, sucking and touching, making sure Cam took all she could get from her, ensuring her orgasm was as close to earth-shattering as it could get. And Cam took it all, voicing illegible words, clinging to Blake and grinding her flesh into her hand. She took beyond what Blake could've imagined and instead of falling back into the seat with exhaustion, she pulled Blake up onto her and kissed her vehemently while riding out the last few strokes from her hand.

Blake was so aroused, she shifted onto her thigh and started in on her own grinding, her flesh so hungry and full feeling, she thought she might burst if she didn't get release. Their kiss continued as their mutual pleasure met and fell into place side by side. And it wasn't long before Blake was moaning into her, on the edge of climax, about to spill over when Cam surprised her and bucked into her furiously, tearing her mouth away and coming again with short, loud, cries.

Blake came then, fast and furious, so moved by Cam's second climax she almost came out of her body. She shouted out her name over and over until Cam finally stilled and her own orgasm finally doused, the last of the flames inside her smoldering.

She fell against her and Cam wrapped her in her arms. Neither of them spoke. They just held each other and breathed, existing in the moment.

A loud ringing came from the front of the car, an automated voice alerting that the caller was Sloane.

"Of all the times for the phone to get a signal," Cam said, as her cell continued to ring.

Blake nuzzled her neck and laughed. "At least it let us finish before it intruded."

"Finished? I wasn't anywhere close to being finished."

"Don't say that or I won't sleep tonight."

"I'll be tossing and turning right along with you."

The ringing stopped but then beeped, alerting to a message, followed by more beeps from texts.

"I wonder why she hasn't called my phone," Blake said.

"Yours probably isn't getting a signal."

Blake laughed.

"You know, we could just toss our phones out the window for a while," Blake said.

"I considered that. But what if it's about Tomas?"

"Oh, right. Good point." Blake kissed her. "Raincheck?" She laughed, mimicking McKenna.

"God, I hope so."

"We'll make it happen."

"Swear to me, we will."

"I swear."

They kissed again before Blake climbed off of her and dressed, hoping as much as Cam that they'd be able to deliver on that promise.

CHAPTER THIRTY-SEVEN

Cam pushed the button to turn off the engine and looked over at Blake. Cam smiled, Blake looking a lot like she did the previous evening after they'd made love, with her messy hair and flushed face. Her eyes were clear and vibrant, with lids that looked heavy with calm. Even her blinking was slow. And when her smile came, it was lopsided in a satisfied, yet still somewhat amorous, kind of manner.

"Would you like to come in?" Cam reached for her hand. They'd just pulled into the garage, beckoned home by Sloane's phone call. She'd called Cam to see if Blake was with her, because, funnily enough, she couldn't get through on Blake's phone, the signal, apparently not working. She and McKenna were worried and wanted to be sure Blake had connected with Cam at the hospital, which was, Cam suspected, their plan all along.

Cam hadn't yet responded to the voice mail or texts. She and Blake had both decided to let Sloane and McKenna sweat a little. Served them right for setting them up like they had.

"Of course, I would *like* to. But should I? Should we…?"

The quiet ride back to the house had seemed to give Blake pause.

"Why don't you come inside and search for your answer there?" Cam skimmed her lips across Blake's inner wrist. She straightened as if Cam had kissed her along her spine.

"Sloane and Kenna are worried. They won't quit calling until they know I'm safe."

"Then Sloane shouldn't have left you. They had to have considered that we might not actually cross paths in this little plan of theirs."

Blake laughed. "You have no idea the lengths they go to sometimes. And with this, with you and me...I'm sure Sloane somehow, someway, made sure we would at least cross paths. She probably timed dropping me off perfectly to coincide with you leaving."

"Still, she couldn't have been certain we would agree to ride home together."

"I'd say she was pretty certain about that. After all, we did end up in the car together, didn't we? I hate to admit it, but all in all, their little scheme worked. The only hiccup was them not being able to get through to me to make sure I was, indeed, with you."

"Let 'em worry a little while longer." She ran her tongue along the edge of her palm where she'd teased with her lips. Blake inhaled and trembled.

"Cam."

"Please?"

"God, what you do to me. I couldn't say no to you if my life depended on it."

Cam grinned. "Let's go."

Blake hesitated for only a second before she nodded and they exited the car. Cam closed and locked the garage and then took Blake by the hand to run along the side of the house that wasn't exposed to Sloane's. They climbed up the steps to the patio and Cam cussed, first at the spotlight-like illumination of the patio light, and then with the keys.

The dogs barked as she unlocked the door, and she shushed them and allowed them out for a quick potty break. She left the door open a sliver for them after she pulled Blake in behind her. She didn't turn on any additional lights. Just left the lamp by the couch and the one in her den on. She didn't want to call any attention whatsoever to their presence.

All she wanted was Blake.

And she wanted her all to herself.

Cam entwined her fingers in hers and kissed her softly on the lips. Blake leaned into her slightly and sighed, the kiss seeming to be as blissful to her as it was to Cam. When they parted, however, the concern Cam had seen in her earlier was furrowing her brow.

"I'm fine," Cam said, trying to smooth the worry from her forehead with her thumb.

"Are you sure? With everything…you know…that's happened? Tonight even?"

She was referring to what they'd just done in the back seat of the Rover. She was offering her a way out if she needed it. But Cam didn't need it. She hadn't, and wasn't, feeling anything negative about their time in the car. Her mind had been, and continued to be, focused solely on Blake. So much so, she'd been thrumming with desire for her again before they'd even pulled into the driveway. She'd even devised a plan on the short drive home, on how they could secretly enter the house without being seen.

"I'm positive." Cam stretched a little on her toes to kiss Blake on her forehead. She'd never been with a woman as tall as Blake and she found it sexy. Her height alluded to her strength, and Cam couldn't help but wonder how that strength would match up against her own. She was pretty strong with all the physical labor she did, but Blake just might have an edge on her. She found the possibility of that, too, sexy, and she was curious to test that out at some point.

"I don't want you to go," Cam said, trying to convince her with her eyes as well as her words.

The dogs nosed open the door and trotted inside, bringing with them the sound of voices. Loud, calling, female voices.

Blake closed her eyes and rubbed her temple. "We've been found."

Cam peeked out the door and saw Sage and Rylee approaching the patio.

"Come back tonight," Cam said, tugging her close.

"Sneak out? In the middle of the night?" She laughed. "Cam, I—"

"You're right, it's crazy." She chuckled a little. "I'm getting carried away. Getting a little crazy myself." She started to back away, but Blake grabbed her forearm.

"This whole thing is crazy," she said. "But it feels so good I don't really give a fuck. How's that for crazy? You're not the only one acting out of character here."

They heard the women clamor up the steps.

"Hello!" Rylee called out.

Blake tightened her grip. "I'll sneak away every chance I get. I just don't know when or how often that will be."

Cam plucked the key hanging on the hook by the door.

"Here." She placed it in her palm and gently closed her fingers around it. "Come anytime. Night or day. Even if I'm not home. In case you need some more 'alone time.'"

Blake's lips tilted mischievously, and Cam almost slammed the door and carried her away to the bedroom, to hell with Sage and Rylee. But Cam wasn't the only one who wanted to keep their passion private. That was Blake's wish too.

"Yoo-hoo? You guys in there?" Blake released Cam and eased open the door.

"We're here."

Cam stood next to her and smiled. Blake's friends seemed too excited to pay close scrutiny.

"We heard the dogs so we hurried over to see if you came home with Cam," Sage said.

"We've been kind of worried," Rylee said. "No one's been able to reach you."

"Oh? Guess I better get home then." Blake escorted them back out the door, walking alongside them.

"Sloane's been calling and texting," Rylee said.

"Huh. Must be my phone."

"We don't always get a signal out here," Cam added, watching them go.

"That must be it," Blake said. "Good night, Cam. Thanks for the ride."

Cam lifted her hand in a wave. "Night all."

Sage and Rylee kept talking, asking after Cam, but Blake explained that she was tired and led them down the steps. Cam closed the door and ran her hands through her hair in exasperation. How was she going to calm down after her time with Blake? She was on her mind, on her skin. The taste of her on her tongue.

She wished suddenly that she was a runner, like Blake, so she could just take off down the beach and run until she collapsed in sheer exhaustion.

But I'm not a runner. I'm just a...

Writer.

She crossed to her den where she kicked off her shoes and sat at her desk. She cracked open her laptop and reread what she'd last written in her new story and picked up where she left off. The emotions swirling inside her flew out through her fingertips, into the keyboard and onto the screen. She didn't have to pause to search for words or feelings, or to speculate about how her characters would behave in any given situation. It all just came.

And she didn't have to pause to think about why.

Because she knew.

She was *living* it.

CHAPTER THIRTY-EIGHT

Cam opened her eyes and took in her surroundings. She was in her den and her head was in her arms on her desk. She must've fallen asleep. She sat up and glanced at the pewter clock on her bookshelf. It was just after six. Dawn had not yet broken through the windows. She stood and stretched, and the dogs, who were crashed out on their beds behind her, didn't pay her much mind. Byron, at least, lifted his head to consider her before he returned to his slumber.

She made her way into the kitchen and started a pot of coffee. She couldn't remember how long she'd written for, or even really what time she'd even started. What she did remember was Blake. She must not've been able to sneak away after all. Cam was disappointed, but as she headed for the shower, she thought maybe Blake staying away might've been a good thing. They'd both needed some sleep and had Blake shown up, sleep most definitely would not've entered the equation.

She soaked under the hot water for as long as she could given the limited water supply, and allowed it to work her back and shoulders. She heard the dogs bark for a couple of seconds, or thought she did, but the noise was gone so quickly she didn't give it further thought. When she emerged, feeling revigorated but pleasantly relaxed, she slipped into her robe without bothering to tie it, and ran a comb through her wet hair. Then she walked out of the bathroom to return to the kitchen, yearning for her first cup of coffee.

"Good morning."

Cam's heart jumped to her throat. Blake was standing across the room behind the couch.

"Jesus Christ." She clenched her chest.

"I'm sorry, I didn't mean to scare you. But whether I spoke up to announce my presence or not, I knew you would be startled."

Cam laughed and flattened her palm against her pounding heart. "Startled. That's not exactly the word I would use."

"I guess you didn't hear the dogs when I came in?" She had on gray leggings, running shoes, and a thick hooded jacket. She seemed nervous, and she didn't seem to know what to do with her hands. Cam couldn't figure out why until Blake glanced at her and her eyes quickly ran down her body before darting away.

Cam looked down at herself, saw that her robe was open and instinctively tugged it closed. "I heard them but I didn't pay attention." She tied her belt, securing the robe. "They didn't bark for very long."

"Once they saw it was me, they got a little excited and started battling for affection. Barking was no longer the focus." She glanced back at her, flushed, and laughed softly. "That uh, didn't help any."

"What didn't?"

"You closing your robe."

"Oh."

"I don't think anything will." She met her gaze and this time, held it. "Help, that is."

"Do you need help? Want…help?" Cam walked toward her, her first cup of coffee already forgotten. She was confused by Blake's nervousness in seeing her nude. But beyond her confusion, there was a little amusement, and she was very determined to discover the root of Blake's unease.

"That depends."

"On what?"

"On you and whether you're comfortable with my being here. Because if you're not, then yes, I'm going to need help. You're going to have to shove me out the door."

"Why would I be uncomfortable? You seem to be the one who's…off a little."

"I walked in on you pretty much naked and scared you half to death. So, yes, I'm a little off."

"I'm fine," Cam said. "I was 'startled' as you say, but pleasantly so. My heart is still racing, but now it's racing for a different reason."

Blake's demeanor appeared to change quickly as she listened to Cam, as if she'd finally found what she'd expected to find when she first walked in the door. Cam could feel the heat coming from her newly confident stare, and she knew, without a doubt, that Blake's heart was racing just as quickly as hers.

"I guess I don't need any help then," she said. She moved toward her. "If you're not going to shove me out the door."

"If I were you I'd be more worried about me holding you captive."

"What do I have to do to make that happen?" She stood before her and reached out and loosened her belt. The robe fell open and Cam shuddered, but not from the chill of the air hitting her moist body. But from the feather-like graze of Blake's fingers as they ran up her stomach to her breasts, where they tantalized and teased, carefully avoiding the centers.

Cam tried to keep her composure, but Blake was burning a trail along her skin and singeing her with her eyes.

"You know what? I think I do need help. Because I don't know what I want more. To keep standing here looking at you in that robe like this, only able to get a small, but very enticing glimpse of your beautiful body, or to open the robe and see you completely. What do you think I should do?"

Cam trembled as Blake's fingers dropped to her thighs and caressed there, moving up and then down, like she'd done to her torso.

"I don't care as long as—you keep touching me."

"Then we'll keep the robe on. Because I love the way you look in it. And I'll just...gladly work around it." Her hands left her legs and returned to her chest. She inched open the lapels of the robe and exposed her breasts. Cam saw the hunger that overcame her as she lightly brimmed them, causing Cam to hiss as the sensation shot down between her legs.

"Oh, God, how I've wanted to see these," Blake said. "Feeling them last night, imagining what they look like, didn't do them justice."

Cam laughed a little, the sound hitching with nerves and arousal. "They're small."

"Mm, they're beautiful." She circled the centers with her fingertips, seemingly fascinated. "Perfect."

She knelt and snuck her tongue out to trace the path her fingers had taken.

"Blake." Cam held on to her, desperate for the strength to remain standing.

Blake answered by taking her in her mouth completely, tugging on her just enough to make her wet and begin to throb. And for a second, Cam thought she was going to explore that for herself when she once again lowered her hand to graze along her thigh. But she only toyed with her, skimming her center externally, careful not to dip inside and touch where she ached the most. Then she moved her mouth to Cam's neglected breast, did the same as she'd done the other, but this time, she didn't lower her hand to tease her. This time, she drew away from her breast, knelt down to where she'd touched her, and breathed upon her before she made contact with her lips, sending Cam into a frenzy.

Cam panted, struggled to speak and to stand as Blake's feather-like movements continued everywhere but the place where she wanted it most. It wasn't long before Cam had her hands knotted in her hair, trying to guide her, while pleading with her to show her some mercy.

"Jesus, Blake. For God's sake. I'm dying."

"That's what I'm going for," she said. "I want you to want it so bad you feel like you're going to die if you don't get it."

"I do. I do. Christ."

Cam clenched her eyes, unable to watch. But what she felt next made her eyes fly wide open. Blake had snuck her tongue into her hidden flesh and begun to explore. Slowly. Tentatively. Enough to make Cam tense and shudder and tighten her fingers in her hair. But it was not near enough to satiate her need.

"You're fucking teasing me again," Cam breathed.

She heard Blake laugh as she drew her tongue away and then started in again, this time grazing her clitoris. Cam nearly buckled, and she swallowed hard, desperate for air.

She stumbled backward, seeking the wall that framed the entryway to the kitchen. When she found it, she braced herself and tried to catch her breath. But Blake was right back at her, on her knees between her legs, easing them apart and exposing her flesh with the gentle outward press of her thumbs. Slowly, painfully slowly, she began carefully licking her clit, as if she were purposefully trying to send sporadic shockwaves of pleasure up through her. Short, fierce shockwaves that had her crying out and slamming her head back against the wall, and then in the next instant, had her looking down at Blake, begging for more, her body shaking uncontrollably.

"Blake, I can't stand anymore," she said gripping her head so tightly her fingers ached.

"You can. I promise you can."

"No—Blake. I mean I literally—cannot stand here anymore."

Blake pulled away just enough to look up at her, and then she lifted Cam's right leg and encouraged her to rest it on her shoulder. Cam tried to argue, but Blake would have none of it, and as soon as she started kissing her way up her inner thigh, Cam wasn't able to argue.

"Lean on me as much as you need to," Blake said. "I'll support both your legs if I have to."

Cam soon had no choice but to oblige as Blake kissed her way back into her flesh and full on attacked her with an overzealous tongue. Cam opened her mouth to call out, but her voice was lost, eaten up by the ecstasy raging through her. It was all she could do to breathe, everything else was an impossibility, overtaken by the feel of Blake's slick, velvet assault between her legs. And as she pressed against her, cinching her tightly to the wall, holding Cam's leg securely on her shoulder, she went at her harder, as if she had Cam right where she wanted her, pinned against her mouth, unable to move, to escape, even if she became desperate to do so. And Cam was already there, at that point, feeling like she couldn't take another fucking second of the pleasure Blake was bestowing upon her. But her involuntary struggle to free herself was futile, and it only made Blake moan and push her tighter against the wall.

Cam clenched her jaw and fought for another few seconds until Blake changed her technique and went from frenzied licking, to deep, sensual, tongue swirling kisses, and deliberate, deep pulls of Cam's clit into her mouth.

"Oh, fuck," Cam rasped as the new sensation flooded her. She was suddenly no longer wriggling to escape. Now her body could not only handle what Blake was doing to it, it fucking loved it, taking it in, all that it could, like it would never, ever, be able to get enough. Cam could not remember anything ever feeling that fucking good.

The pleasure washed over her, invaded her, warm and powerful, and her hips began to slowly thrust, as her body fell into a composed, but eager rhythm for more. She relaxed her hands and caressed Blake's head and face, the feel of her flexing jaw exciting her further.

She watched her feed on her through hazed eyes, disbelieving the moment was real. Was it?

"Blake," she whispered. "Is this—really happening? Am I—? Are you—? How can it be—so fucking—" Her head and her eyes lolled back then and she came, her body arched into Blake, thrusting powerfully but silently, as everything Blake had been giving her collided and bunched and exploded outward, tearing her apart as it burst out of her. She couldn't focus, couldn't think, wasn't even sure if she was still holding on to Blake or not. She just kept coming, like it was fucking eternal, her body moving in that same controlled motion, allowing for the insanely sweet pleasure of that orgasm to be milked for as long as she could hold out. When her body finally did give, the flood of pleasure was still flowing, and she jerked and shook as she fought to pull away. Blake finally showed her the mercy she'd needed before and let her. An unknown amount of time passed before Cam registered Blake's soft voice, calling her name.

Cam blinked and nearly fell to the floor as Blake released her leg to stand. She took Cam in her arms quickly, bracing her. She helped her to the couch and eased her down and sat next to her. She was touching her face, brushing back her hair. Cam blinked some more, and she came into focus. She was smiling, her lips swollen and dark from their exertion. She looked just as pleased as Cam felt.

"How did you—what did you—?" Cam couldn't complete her sentences. Blake had just ravished her. That, she knew. In what was obviously expert-like fashion. That she knew too, but she didn't know how to question her about it at the moment. Because it seemed Blake had not only left her body spent and reeling, she seemed to have done the same to her mind.

She grinned and then leaned in and softly kissed her.

"Mm, it was wonderful," she said. "You were wonderful. And you taste fucking beyond wonderful." She touched her own lips with her fingertip and a satisfied look gleamed in her eyes. "I'm going to keep you on me for the rest of the day. So I can get a taste of you whenever I want." She pulled the blanket off the back of the couch and draped it over Cam.

"You—what you did to me…"

She stood and then knelt over Cam to kiss her once more. "Shh, we'll talk about it later." She straightened. "Kenna is expecting to walk with me this morning. I need to go work up a sweat so I can use running as my alibi when I go back to the house to get her. Although, you did work me up quite a bit already. So, it probably won't take much to convince her." She fingered her lips again and then touched Cam's face before walking backward toward the door. She said good-bye to the dogs, who appeared to be just as delirious as Cam, and then disappeared out the door after giving Cam one last grin.

Cam sat in silence and stared in a daze at the closed door. Her mind and body tingled, and she fell back against the couch and closed her eyes and allowed herself to be carried away in the wake of bliss Blake left behind.

CHAPTER THIRTY-NINE

Blake was curled up on one of the comfy chairs in Sloane's living room, happily reading another one of McKenna's romances, when Sage walked in and handed her another book. Blake took it slowly, searching her face for a clue, but she only saw a woman with poorly hidden excitement behind her eyes. That excitement broke free as Blake finally looked at the cover of the book.

"I bought it for you in town," Sage said, bouncing on the balls of her feet. "It's her first one. And it was so popular she continued with it and created a series."

Sage's mood was infectious, and Blake had to pretend not to be as affected as she read the title and Cam's pen name. While she was able to keep her display of emotions in check, she wasn't as apt with her actions, and she flushed as she caught herself running her fingers along the raised lettering of Cam's name.

"Kind of surreal, huh?"

Blake placed the book in her lap. "What do you mean?"

"That Cam wrote that. Wrote all seventeen of them. And she's right next door." She sank down on the couch and held a throw pillow to her chest like it was a teddy bear. "And hot. And single."

"Is she?" She cleared her throat, her voice faltering. Thinking of Cam always left her reeling, but today, it was more than just her desire for her causing the turmoil. Actually, her desire for her, her ache to be with her, was what was making the turmoil all the worse.

"Hot? Um, yeah."

"No, I mean…how do you know she's single?" They all knew of Cam's singlehood, but Blake was playing coy, hoping to throw Sage off scent.

"Where have you been? Sloane and Kenna have been trying like hell to hook you up with her. Rylee wants her. We've all done nothing but talk about her since the first day we got here. I know you haven't been that clueless."

Blake tried to feign memory loss. "I've had a lot on my mind with the clinic and everything."

Sage drew her bare feet up and sat lotus style. She looked reflective, like the thrill she'd initially had in discussing Cam had settled some. "I'd heard rumors that she was single, from fans, but I didn't give them much credit. The one about her losing her wife in a car accident seemed the most unbelievable to me." She pulled at the decorative frayed edge of the pillow. "But now that I've met her... and seen how she's so withdrawn, I'm beginning to think it might be true." She looked at Blake with what appeared to be an invitation to confirm her suspicion.

Blake wasn't comfortable discussing Cam's personal business, but she was relieved to hear that Sloane and McKenna had not divulged anything about the accident to either Sage or Rylee.

Blake chose her words very carefully. "She's a very private person, Sage. So, if what you're saying is true, and she has suffered a tragedy like that, then she would probably want to keep that, especially something like that, very private, along with the rest of her life. You can understand that. Right?"

Sage didn't have malicious intentions in her quest for knowledge about Cam. Blake knew her well and knew that her motivation was her insatiable curiosity. But she did like to gab, so Blake was trying to appeal to her big heart, hoping it would override her tabloid-like drive to discover and spread gossip.

"Put yourself in her shoes. Try to imagine, if you can, that you're not an extrovert, but rather someone who is more reserved and introverted. And you're a writer, which is a very solitary occupation, but you're good at it and your words reach a lot of people, and those people want to know you. So, you share some details of your life with the public, but not much else, hoping people will respect your need for privacy. Now, imagine you lost a loved one, the person closest to you in the world, in an accident. Would you want thousands of people knowing the details of that, flinging questions at you, flashing their cameras and intruding upon you during your grief? And probably for years afterward?"

"No, I wouldn't. That would be terrible."

"If it would be terrible for you, imagine how difficult it would be for someone like Cam. Can you understand now, why she may be so withdrawn, why she's so private?"

Sage seemed to be thinking over what Blake had said. The usual exuberance that was almost always evident on her face, especially in her cherub-like cheeks, was noticeably absent.

"It did happen to her, didn't it? No, don't tell me. I don't, I shouldn't know." She pulled her hands down her face, stretching the skin. "Oh, my God, I feel so bad for her. And I've been such a freaked out fan around her." She didn't wait for an answer. "I'm just so impressed by her work. I love it. Love her books. And she *is* hot, Blake. I'm human and I can't help but notice that. You can deny her looks all you want, but you aren't fooling anyone. Because like it or not, you're human too."

"I haven't denied…her physical…attractiveness." Denying Cam's attractiveness would be an obvious aversion, which would lead them all to suspect something more. She kept a straight face but couldn't quite manage to sit still under the scrutiny of Sage's stare. She shifted and Cam's book started to slide from her lap. She caught it quickly and then fumbled with it and got a glimpse of Cam's photo on the back. It was a *really* good photo. She franticly tried to find a more secure spot to put the book. When she couldn't, she returned it reluctantly to her lap and rested her hands on it.

Sage, apparently, had seen the whole thing, and Blake could tell by the crinkling of her eyes, that she'd seen the very thing Blake was trying to hide.

A huge smile cracked her face and she tossed the pillow at her and laughed. "I knew it! I freaking knew it! You've got it for her."

Blake threw the pillow back at her. "That's not what I said."

"You might as well have. You're so nervous right now, you'd probably faint if you turned that book over and looked at her picture again."

Blake rolled her eyes. "I would not."

"Then do it."

"No."

"See?"

"I'm not going to do it because it's stupid. One of your dramatic assumptions."

"You won't do it because you know I'm right. You'll blush like you always do when something gets to you. And Cam…she gets to you."

"Honestly, Sage, when are you going to give up the drama?"

But Sage moved right on, ignoring her. "We've all been wondering what you two have been up to the past few days."

"Her friend fell off a roof," Blake said matter-of-factly. "I'm a doctor and I helped out. We both wanted to check on him. I don't know why you guys are reading more into that." She couldn't hold her gaze and instead unintentionally glanced down at the book on the armrest. It wasn't Cam's, but she'd been thinking about Cam as she'd been reading the steamy romance. She hurriedly placed it on top of Cam's book in her lap. But she felt herself blush regardless.

She braced herself, waiting for Sage to notice and say something.

Sloane and Rylee walked in the back door though, saving her.

"Hola, ladies," Sloane said, tossing a football in the air and catching it with the same hand. She and Rylee had been down on the beach throwing the ball. McKenna emerged from the bedroom where she'd been napping. The noise must've woken her.

"Everyone about ready for dinner?" She walked up to Sloane, caught the football in mid-air and gave her a kiss.

Sloane promptly grabbed her ass and pulled her to her. "Mm, I love the way you smell when you've been sleeping." She nuzzled her neck and McKenna squealed. Sloane kissed her again before she answered her.

"We need to set a place for one more," she said, heading for the fridge for a cold bottle of water. She threw one to Rylee who settled onto the chair across from Blake.

"We do? For who?" McKenna asked.

"Cam."

Blake perked, as did Sage. Her eyes were wide behind her glasses and Blake knew she was dying to inquire further, but she managed to refrain.

"You're kidding," McKenna said. "How did you convince her to do that? We about had to bribe her to get her to come over here the very few times she has."

"I didn't. She sort of invited herself."

"Now you're really pulling my leg," McKenna said.

Sloane drank her water and then shook her head. "I'm not, babe. She's really coming and she really invited herself."

Blake had seen Cam in passing yesterday and today, but someone had always been with her when she had.

They hadn't been alone together in over forty-eight hours, and Blake knew Cam's request to come to dinner was in light of that fact. It seemed the urge to be together was wreaking havoc on her as well, and Cam was probably thinking that if they couldn't be alone, then at least they'd be together over dinner, face-to-face and able to interact.

Blake's skin burned uncontrollably as she imagined Cam walking through the back door. She knew she had to be as red as a beet. She gathered her books and headed for the bedroom, hoping no one would see her. But McKenna called after her.

"Blake, you okay with Cam joining us for dinner?"

Thankfully, McKenna's question threw her off kilter and the heat in her face dissipated. She turned and found McKenna behind her.

"Of course, why wouldn't I be?"

"I just wanted to be sure."

"Why are you asking me now when you never have before?"

"If I'd asked you before, you'd have protested or made yourself scarce. Tonight, however, I thought there'd be a good chance you'd say it was fine. And I was right." She smirked a little, wiggled her eyebrows, and turned to head back to the kitchen.

Blake retreated to her room, closed the door, and started digging through her clothes for something to wear. McKenna's probing hadn't surprised her. She'd been on her like white on rice since the night she and Cam had returned home from the hospital without returning their calls or texts. They hadn't forgotten that, and they hadn't forgotten that she and Cam had ended up alone at Cam's without letting them know they'd arrived.

They knew something was up and McKenna had been stuck to her like glue, wanting to walk with her in the mornings and the others wanting to hang with her the rest of the time. In all the madness, Blake hadn't been able to get to Cam. Even her attempt to sneak out at night had failed when Rylee had woken from her slumber on the sofa bed as Blake had slipped outside to go "sit under the stars."

Being away from her this long was wearing on her nerves and Blake had even considered sneaking out her window later that evening when everyone was asleep. She was that desperate to be with her. She needed to touch her and hold her. Now more than ever. She didn't have much more time, and she desperately needed to talk to her about that. The pain of having to do so had made staying away today easier than it normally would've been.

She just didn't want to do what it was she absolutely had to do.

She dressed in a daze and pushed her thoughts back to Cam and the evening at hand. She wanted tonight to be special and she wasn't going to let dread ruin it.

She wondered whether or not they'd be able to hide their powerful attraction over dinner. She had to downplay everything, even her outfit, so she wouldn't appear to be overdoing it. But she also had to show interest in Cam, just as any friend would and engage in casual conversation. She could do that, sure. She could do that standing on her head. She just didn't think she could do it while looking at her. Would anyone notice if she spoke to her while looking elsewhere? There was a strong possibility that they might.

She applied some makeup, made sure it wasn't too noticeable, and then eyed her bottle of perfume. Should she? That would be noticeable and McKenna would definitely wonder why she'd put some on for a casual dinner at home with friends. But Cam did seem to like it. A lot actually. The way she devoured her wrist and neck, like she couldn't get enough of her. If Cam liked it that much, then she'd most definitely notice it and that was all Blake focused on as she sprayed a little on her wrists and on her neck just below her ears. Where Cam liked to kiss her. She wondered what kind of reaction Cam would have when she caught the scent. Would it be too subtle for Blake to see? She hoped not.

She spent the next half hour thinking about that as she sat on her bed, taking turns tracing the letters of Cam's name on her book and staring at her author photo on the back. She opened the pages to read once, but then decided not to. She wanted plenty of time and plenty of peace when she sat down to do that.

At the moment, those two things were seriously hard to come by.

CHAPTER FORTY

After checking herself over in the mirror one last time, Blake emerged from her room for dinner. As she walked into the living room, she listened closely, wondering if Cam had yet arrived. She found her answer as soon as she reached the living room and could see out the windows. Cam was on the patio, with Sloane, Sage, and Rylee, holding a bottle of beer as she listened to Sage, who, from what Blake could tell, was very animated in whatever tale she was sharing.

Blake hurried on to the kitchen, to where McKenna was, and tried to behave as if it were any other evening, and Cam wasn't standing just outside the window in a black sweater and tight, faded jeans that ended in rolled cuffs at her shins.

She cleared her parched throat as she stood next to McKenna at the stove.

"What's on the menu tonight?" Blake asked.

McKenna was stirring a big pot of creamy noodles. "Shrimp fettuccine Alfredo." She stole a glance at Blake and then stared at her fully. "Ow, look at you."

"What?" Blake said, already feeling the flush beneath her skin. She ran her hands over her camel-colored sleeveless sweater and dark jeans, worried that she'd overdone it.

"Nothing," McKenna said lightly.

"No, really, what?" Now she was worried she didn't look good enough.

McKenna stirred the noodles after pouring in the steaming shrimp.

"Do I not look good? Is it the sweater?"

"You look fantastic." She sucked some Alfredo sauce off one of her fingers and then dumped the contents of the pot into a big serving dish. She winked at Blake as she picked up the dish with both hands. "Get the door for me?"

They crossed to the back door and Blake snuck a peek at Cam. She was smiling, and her hair was being teased by the breeze. Blake slid open the door for McKenna and forced herself to keep her eyes on the task at hand.

"Cam's here," McKenna said just before she stepped through to the patio. "But I'm pretty sure you're already aware of that." She winked at her again and set the dish down in the center of the table.

Blake wanted to retreat to the kitchen, needing a brief reprieve to get herself together, but the table was set, complete with everything, even drinks. And before she could come up with another excuse, Rylee saw her.

"There she is," she said. "The evening's complete now."

Blake smiled softly as everyone looked at her. Including Cam, who had lowered her beer and stopped laughing. Blake didn't keep her focus on her long. But it had been long enough to see Cam's eloquent eyes openly take her in.

"Where you been, B?" Sloane asked.

"Just in the bedroom. Why? Am I missing something?"

"Other than entertaining our guest? No," Sloane said.

"I didn't realize everyone was out here."

"I don't think she heard me call her the first two times," McKenna said. "But she's here now, so let's eat."

They all sat around the table and Cam took the seat one over from Blake, with Sage in between. It was an optimal spot in which to see each other completely, but Blake grew nervous for that very reason. She could still feel Cam's heavy stare, and when she looked at her, she felt the full weight of it from across the table as Cam continued to study her.

Blake tried to hide her nerves by offering Cam a warm smile.

"It's good to see you again, Cam. How have you been?" She grabbed her beer and drank, her voice sounding too high-pitched for her liking.

"I've been all right," Cam said. "How about you?"

She sounded surprisingly calm, given the intensity of her stare. But cool and casual was what Cam did best. Little did anyone know the magnitude of passion she had hidden inside.

"Not too badly," Blake said, trying casual on for herself. It sounded completely contrived to Blake, but no one seemed to notice. Cam, however, grinned slightly and then wound some noodles around her fork.

"This looks great, McKenna," she said. "Thanks for having me."

"It is great," Rylee said after swallowing. The others agreed.

McKenna seemed pleased. "I'm glad everyone likes it. And, Cam, we're thrilled to have you."

"And we love that you just up and decided to join us," Sloane said. "Anytime you want to come over, feel free."

"Thanks," Cam said.

"So what have you been up to?" McKenna asked her.

Blake forked a bite of shrimp and noodles and ate as Cam answered. She wanted to appear busy as she took her turn in consuming Cam with her eyes. The black sweater wasn't snug, but it was fitted enough to show off her lean form and small, taut breasts. The color of it set off the rich cobalt of her eyes and the thick waves of her dark hair. And her skin looked more appetizing than anything Blake had ever eaten.

"I've mostly been out visiting Tomas. He's doing really well, but he's having a hard time accepting that he can't do much for a while."

"Have you been writing?" Rylee asked. She lowered her fork when Sage burned her with a stare. "Oh, sorry. I didn't mean to pry," she said.

"No, it's fine," Cam said. "I have been writing. Quite a bit actually."

Sage squealed and gave a tiny, controlled clap. "Can you tell us about it? Or do you want to? I should ask."

"It's different," Cam said. "Something new for me."

"It's not science fiction?" Sage asked.

"Not this one." She took a sip of her beer. "This one is more emotional, more dramatic. It's about the dynamics between people as they experience love and loss and life together."

McKenna sighed and looked wistful. "Sounds good to me."

"Are you going to publish it?" Rylee asked.

Cam swallowed a bite of food. "I haven't really thought about it. I'm just so glad to be writing again."

"You're enjoying what you're doing," Blake said.

"Very much so," Cam said, meeting and holding her gaze.

"That's the most important thing," Blake added.

"It is."

"You must be very happy then."

"Thank you, I am."

"Well, you definitely look happy," Sloane said.

"Can I ask what inspired you to write this new piece?" Sage asked.

Cam covered her grin by quickly bringing her beer to her mouth.

"Frustration," she said, returning the bottle to the table. "Anger. Pain. Longing. Desire. All of it. I hadn't felt those things in a very long time, and I'd forgotten how powerful they are and how you aren't really living if you aren't allowing yourself to feel them."

"You're feeling them now?" McKenna asked.

Cam was staring into the tabletop, her fingers playing with the sweat on the beer bottle. Blake was sitting on edge, heart fluttering and skipping beats. Could everyone else understand what Cam was saying? Or was it just her? She gripped the edge of the table, waiting.

"I am," Cam said.

There was a long silence and Blake's pulse was so high she worried she might grow dizzy and fall from her chair. Cam was talking about her. About them. She was sure of it. And she was sure her friends knew it too. How could they not? Their cover was probably blown but she realized she didn't care. At that moment, she was so moved by Cam's words, so overcome with emotion and desire, she was ready to shout out her feelings for Cam to the world. And after she did that, she was going to shove everything off the table and crawl over to her and ravish her right there in front of everyone.

"That's terrific," McKenna said, breaking Blake's trance. "I'm so happy for you, Cam."

Sloane leaned over and patted Cam's shoulder. "We all are."

Cam blinked from what Blake had assumed was her own trance. She glanced up at Blake, scanned her face quickly, then down to her hands which were still holding tight to the table. She straightened and then swallowed as her eyes returned to Blake's.

She can see everything I'm feeling.

She knows I want her.

Oh, God this is torture.

Blake released her grip and forced herself to return to eating. Cam did the same, eventually tearing her gaze from Blake to rejoin the conversation. But every now and again their eyes would meet as they caught each other secretly admiring the other. It was the most erotic meal of her life and it didn't seem to matter that they were surrounded by other people. Blake couldn't help but stare at her, couldn't help but notice every single, subtle movement. Like the way Cam's mouth enticed her as the fork slid out from her lips. The way her jaw flexed as she chewed. The slight movement along the column of her throat as she swallowed. Then Cam brought the beer to her mouth and pursed those sweet lips for a drink, and after Blake watched the rise and fall of her throat again, her gaze traveled to Cam's fingers wrapped around the bottle. Those long, lean, talented fingers. She recalled how those fingers felt on her skin and how Cam's lips often followed close behind, tasting where her fingers had touched. Blake finally had to close her eyes to sever the stirring her mind was creating, and when she opened them she found Cam staring right into her.

"Dinner was great," Cam suddenly said, wiping her mouth with her napkin. "But I should get back and see to the dogs."

"Wait, no," Sage said. "You can't leave yet. This is our last meal together as a group."

Blake's heart fell to her feet.

Sage, shut up.

Shut up.

"Sage," Sloane said. "Cam doesn't have to stay because of that."

"No, but I thought she might want to." Sage looked at Cam. "We're leaving day after tomorrow."

Blake's fingers burned she was squeezing the table so tightly. Pure panic besieged her.

"I didn't know," Cam said. "You and Rylee will definitely be missed. Things will go back to boring the second you two leave." She smiled at them both and Sloane laughed.

Sage shook her head. "It's not just us, Blake's leaving too. She's riding back with us."

Oh, God. No. Fuck. She wasn't supposed to find out like this.

Cam blinked again and her smile faded. She shifted in her seat. "I didn't know that either."

"Tomorrow night we're going into town, so this will be our last dinner here together at the house," Sage said.

"Why don't you come with us tomorrow night, Cam?" McKenna said. She was treading carefully, Blake could hear it in her tone. She'd obviously picked up on the drastic change in Cam's mood.

The others also encouraged her.

Blake remained quiet, stiff as a statue, dying inside.

Cam smiled but it was cordial and nothing more. She pushed her chair back and stood. "I'm afraid I do have to go for tonight. And I don't know about tomorrow. But just in case I can't go, I'll say my good-byes now." She extended her hand and shook Sage's and Rylee's hands and then she held her hand out in front of Blake.

The pain in her eyes was piercing and Blake lost her breath. Somehow though, she managed to take her hand and Cam dropped it almost immediately.

"It was very nice to meet you all. You are all…unforgettable." Rylee laughed and Sage appeared to be swooning as Cam wished them a good night and stepped out into the sand.

Blake stood, unable to watch her walk away. She grabbed what dishes she could and hurried into the kitchen. She was running water into the sink to begin scrubbing them when she felt a hand on her shoulder.

"Blake."

Blake stilled. "Not now, Kenna, please."

"Go to her."

Blake closed her eyes. McKenna *did* know. When she knew for certain, Blake wasn't sure. It could've been as little as sixty seconds ago, or days before.

"Kenna. I can't talk about it."

"I'm not asking you to. But you do need to talk to Cam. You must." She turned Blake around to face her.

"I didn't want her to find out like this," Blake said. "I've been meaning to talk to her, to tell her. But we haven't had a chance to be alone and honestly, I didn't want to do it. I was hoping we could at least have tonight. One last night of happiness before I had to tell her I have to leave now…"

"Go."

"What if I only hurt her more? She's been through so much, Kenna. And you saw her face just now."

"You can't let it end like this, Blake. Even if you finally decide to go ahead with the clinic and plan on moving down here, you can't leave her like this. It's so sudden."

"I know, that's why I didn't want to do it. I just told her the other night I wasn't going anywhere anytime soon and now I'm having to tell her otherwise. It's hurting her, Kenna. I can already see it and it's hurting me too."

"All the more reason to go talk to her." She looked over her shoulder at their friends on the patio. "Go now. Out the front door. I'll tell them you went for a run."

Blake started to protest but the window to flee without being seen was closing. She nodded, having no further words to try to explain her trepidation. Then, as she saw her friends begin to gather up the rest of the dinnerware to come inside, she hugged McKenna and hurried out the front door.

CHAPTER FORTY-ONE

C am paced in front of the fireplace, the bottle of wine she'd grabbed sitting open and chilled to perfection on the end table next to the couch. The elegant glass she drank from was beckoning, but she couldn't bring herself to drink. Nor could she cry, or get a fire going, or scribble down thoughts in her journal. All she could do was pace and run her hands through her hair as her restless heart pounded, desperate to keep the advancing, resolute pain at bay.

The dogs barked and rushed to the back door. The way their tails were going, Cam figured Blake was headed up the stairs. A moment later, there was knocking and Cam stalked to the door and yanked it open.

Cam opened her mouth to speak, but the sight of Blake standing there in that sleeveless sweater Cam was sure she'd worn just for her, with the dying sun a golden backdrop illuminating her breathtaking beauty, caused Cam to react on instinct, and instinct alone. She took her hand, pulled Blake inside and slammed the door.

She could tell by the look on Blake's face she was startled and confused.

When she tried to speak, Cam pushed her against the wall and smothered the words with her mouth, plunging into Blake hungrily, pressing her body to hers, ensuring she couldn't move.

Blake made a noise, a muffled plea, but Cam responded by edging her feet apart and undoing the button of her jeans with a hurried hand. She tore them open and went for the zipper, shoving her pants down as best she could. Blake's pleas softened from alarm to approval. She raked her nails up Cam's back, beneath her sweater, and Cam made a noise of her own. Blake's desire sparked to life then, and she kissed her back vehemently, her own tongue meeting and matching Cam's. Her hands moved from Cam's back to her front where she shoved up on Cam's bra, freeing her breasts. Then she stroked and played her nipples, and Cam did the same to the soft skin just above Blake's panty line.

Cam broke away from her mouth before she went any further. Blake told her everything she needed to know with her eyes, and Cam eased her hand into her panties and into her slick folds. Blake inhaled sharply, widened her eyes, and then pinched Cam's nipples. Cam cried out in sweet torture, flames shooting through her. She rubbed Blake harder, played her swollen clit, and watched as Blake moaned and her breath hitched. She was trying so hard to control herself, and when she tilted her head back against the wall, jerked her hips, and bit her lower lip, Cam laughed wickedly and attacked her neck. Blake answered with a firm tug to her nipples and Cam cried out again, lost all resolve, and slid her fingers up inside her.

Blake's cry was loud enough to ring Cam's ears, and the noises that followed were deep, and throaty, and laced with the pleasure that was obviously surging through her. She tugged on Cam harder, elicited another cry, and laughed herself as she leaned in and licked Cam's lips.

"Fuck me," she said.

Cam plunged farther into her, and she released her hold on Cam and dug her nails into her shoulders and then up into her scalp as Cam began to fuck her, gliding her fingers in and out, again and again, stopping every so often just to look at her face, leaving her hinged, her fingers up deep inside, Blake clenched and was pulsing down around her.

Cam burned the image of her face into her mind, while the feel of being encased in her burned its imprint into her brain. Then she fucked her some more, her mouth next to Blake's, their lips touching and parting, their breathing hot and shared. Cam wanted to breathe her in and hold her there forever. Tried to with every quick breath she garnered with the thrust of her fingers.

Blake began to call her name and Cam fucked her until she could call no more, her head lolling back helplessly, eyes unfocused and glazed. Her hips kicked hard and fast against her, demanding the incessant rhythm of Cam's fingers. A rhythm that increased in both speed and pressure. Blake's body went into a frenzy, fucking Cam with its entirety as her hands threaded and pulled at Cam's hair. And then she came, screaming out into the oncoming night, screaming for Cam, for more, more, more. Cam felt the flood of her climax gushing down her fingers and she pumped her until her voice caved, her head fell forward, and her body went limp. She collapsed against Cam and Cam held her, easing herself from between her legs.

She walked her to the couch, sat her down, and slipped off her shoes. Then she removed her jeans and panties. Blake blinked at her as if she just regained consciousness.

"What are you doing?" She was hoarse and it turned Cam on almost as much as her screams.

Cam opened her legs by sliding her hands under and around her upper thighs and pulled her to her.

She started trailing kisses on her warm skin, already able to see the glistening of her dark pink center.

"Cam?"

Cam answered her silently, working her way to her flesh, where she wasted no time in delving in and taking her with hungry lips and heavy tongue. Blake jerked and sighed, and then fell back against the couch, relenting with surrendering moans to the return of pleasure. Her hands returned to Cam's hair, massaging and tugging, as her body writhed and began to move in motion to take advantage of Cam's generous mouth and for a long while, the only sound to be heard was that of Cam feasting, and Cam took her sweet time, relishing every second, loving the satin feel of her flesh. And when she delved lower, and got a taste of the hot silk of her arousal, she went at her like she was starved, first priming her with deliberate licks to her outer rim, then plunging into her and drawing it out to saturate her tongue.

Blake went crazy, opening her legs farther, clawing at her and yanking on her hair and sweater in an attempt to get her closer. She panted for more, bypassed begging altogether, and went straight into demanding. Cam thoroughly enjoyed her reactions, almost as much as she did tongue-fucking her. But her own desire began making demands and she couldn't resist giving Blake what she wanted most. She moved back up and paid worship to her full, swollen clit, assaulting it with swirls of her flattened tongue before taking it in her mouth to finish her off.

She sucked her and pulsed her with her tongue at the same time and Blake came almost instantly, coming up off the back of the couch, tearing at Cam's head, screaming with strangled, throaty cries. She forced her flesh into Cam's face, fucking her fiercely with wild, uninhibited thrusts of her hips. She fucked Cam so long and hard and furiously, that when she finally came down, she did so with raspy cries and pleas of sweet surrender, begging Cam to stop, and when she did, she really, truly began to cry.

Cam rose and embraced her and they fell back onto the couch, wrapped in each other's arms.

Blake started speaking, started apologizing about having to leave so suddenly, but Cam didn't want to hear it. She couldn't bear to hear it.

"Shh," she placed her finger to her lips. "Not now. Not tonight."

Then, she closed her eyes and nuzzled Blake's neck, inhaled her scent, and held her like she never wanted to let her go.

CHAPTER FORTY-TWO

Cam sat on her couch, staring mindlessly at another sunset. She never thought she'd see one she didn't like, but this one, vibrant and radiant as ever, would've chilled her to the core, had she still had one. As it was, she sat unaffected, broken and hollow, staring into the blur that the room and sunset had melded together to become.

Blake had left hours ago, claiming she needed to go pack. Cam had been able to keep her most of the day, after spending a long, restless night together, making passionate love. They'd spoken very little, preferring only the sounds and sighs their lovemaking elicited, often times spending endless minutes at a time doing things to each other with the sole intention of bringing forth those sacred sounds. Cam had kept trying for those sounds long after Blake had lost her voice completely, wanting to capture any last audible breath she could. And when there was finally no more to be had, Cam plied her with pleasure simply to feel and inhale what ragged breaths she could still exude. Blake, she'd sensed, was trying to do the same. Whether they were wrapped up together on the couch, tangled up in her bed, writhing on the blankets in front of the fire, they just could not seem to get enough of each other, and Cam knew she'd never forget the image of Blake undulating atop her, riding her fingers, her beautiful body arching as she came in the flickering firelight, her beautiful face overcome with passion and pleasure.

She would never forget it, and unfortunately, that just might be what finally did her in. She eyed the wine once again sitting next to her, her ever faithful companion. And yet again, she couldn't bring herself to drink it.

The dogs barked and ran to the door. She knew it was Blake. Could feel that it was Blake. But she didn't move, didn't react. Her heart and mind seemed still. Unaffected. They remained that way even when she heard Blake knock. And when Blake entered on her own a minute later, Cam's ambivalence remained.

Blake closed the door softly and stood quietly. The dogs were trying for her attention, but she only greeted them briefly. Cam saw all of this without directly looking at her, her stare into the blurry oblivion keeping her rapt.

"Cam?"

Her voice was like the softest grain of sandpaper. Noticeably uneven but not overly rough. Her vocal cords had had some time to recover. Her nerves, however, were evident, and they seemed to be considerable, and it occurred to Cam that Blake needed reassurance, but she couldn't do anything further with the realization.

"Cam?" Blake came toward her. Cam was aware of it, but she startled anyway when Blake touched her.

"Cam, look at me." Blake tilted her chin, ensuring she did.

Those eyes.

Those beautiful sea glass eyes.

Cam inhaled sharply as all the pain and reality that she'd somehow been fending off, set in. She winced, her struggling lungs trying to inhale again. "You're leaving," she let out.

Blake knelt before her, took her hands in hers. "I didn't know that I'd have to leave this soon. Honestly, Cam I didn't. I was just as shocked and heartbroken at hearing that as you were. I didn't want to tell you at dinner, or at any time, really. Cam, I don't want to now. I don't want to do this."

Cam smiled at her through pooling tears. "It's okay."

"No, it's not okay. We should've discussed this sooner, whether I was leaving now or weeks from now."

"It doesn't matter." Cam brought Blake's hand to her mouth, breathing in the scent on her wrist. She drew it into her lungs as she tasted it with her lips. She closed her eyes. "I don't ever want to stop breathing you in."

"Cam—"

Cam opened her eyes. "But I have to. And it's okay."

"No. Cam it's not. I don't want to leave you, especially not this soon. But my father called yesterday morning. I'm needed back at the practice as soon as possible. Otherwise, I wouldn't be leaving like this."

"But you would still leave eventually."

Blake seemed to search for a way to respond. "Yes, but—"

"You have things to think about. With the clinic, your family's practice, your life."

"Yes, but, Cam—"

Cam kissed her palm. "I understand. You have a life. A big life. In Phoenix. Mine is here."

Blake looked anxious, confused. "What are you saying?"

"I'm saying it's okay. I'm saying I understand. I'm saying..." Cam closed her eyes again. "Good-bye."

Blake tore her hand away and cupped her face. Cam opened her eyes and found Blake staring into her.

"I have a lot to do, a lot to consider and think about, but that doesn't change how I feel about you. I want to be here. In Mexico. Working in my clinic. That's still what I want. And now, there's you, too."

"That may be. But ultimately it doesn't matter."

"Why are you saying that?"

"Because one of us needs to face reality."

"Which is?"

"That this can never work."

"What can't?"

"You and me. You have a great big life ahead of you. In Phoenix, Mexico, wherever your dreams may take you. My life is simple. And it's here. On this beach, with my dogs. And we're so different. You—I drive you crazy. Would ultimately drive you crazy."

Blake dropped her hand from her face. She stood. "I know what you're doing."

"I'm letting you go."

"You're pushing—damn near shoving me away."

"I'm being realistic."

"You're running. Hiding. You're scared."

"No."

Blake came at her, forced her back against the couch and straddled her. She took Cam's hands and placed them on her face. "Tell me you don't have feelings for me."

Cam's voice left her as the warmth of Blake's body took precedence.

"What I feel—doesn't matter."

Blake leaned in. "Yes, it does. It's what's got you so scared. Tell me you don't want me, Cam. Want this." She kissed her. Lightly, delicately, her lips taking their sweet, sweet time in tasting hers.

Cam couldn't help but respond and she yearned to cling to her, to melt into her. But instead of balling Blake's shirt in her hands and tugging her closer, she gently pushed her away.

"I can't deny our attraction. I'm not even going to try. But that's all this is. It couldn't ever be anything more. For us to think otherwise, with our differences, personal and professional, and the distance between us, we would both end up getting hurt." Her voice faltered just as she finished and her throat felt like it had caved in.

Blake stared at her long and hard and then climbed off of her. "You're afraid I won't come back." She faced the fireplace, as if relating to its cold, desolate emptiness, ran her hands through her hair, and then looked at her again with obvious anger. "I told you, Cam, I want to be here. I want my clinic, I want...you."

"We don't always get what we want. Things happen. There's no guarantee—"

"Look, I understand that you're scared. And I understand why. But for someone who has prided herself the past few years on appreciating the little things in life, the important things, like love, while refusing to worry about all the rest..." She shook her head. "You need to do what you told me to do the day we first met. You need to take your own advice. And live in the moment. Live in the now. Because life is short, Cam. I would think you would know that better than anyone."

She waited a moment and when Cam didn't speak, she seemed to deflate. "Maybe someday you'll be able to live like you preach. Because I think that you want to be able to do that more than anything. And I'm hoping someday you can. Good-bye, Cam."

She turned and walked to the door, kneeling quickly to give the dogs a tearful kiss good-bye. Then she was gone and Cam was alone.

Once again alone.

Chapter Forty-three

Cam awoke at her desk and realized she'd fallen asleep again while writing late into the night. She rubbed her face, which was sore on one side from the press of her spiral notebook, which, she noticed as she glanced down, she'd drooled on as well as slept. She ran her finger over the finger pad of her laptop and woke her computer. She was relieved to see her document had saved and that she'd actually been able to get more done than she had been able to in the last couple of weeks. She pushed back her chair and stood.

The dogs followed her into the kitchen where she made herself some coffee. Then the dogs trailed after her out onto the patio.

She stood at the wall and looked down the beach as dawn broke in the east. Her heart sank as she envisioned Blake running along the sand, the dogs happily ambling alongside her. Her mind did this to her every day. Bringing Blake to her the way she'd seen her almost every morning. Jogging toward her in her tenacious manner, like a soldier on a mission, the dark, wet sand absorbing her footfalls, the gray light of dawn behind her. But Blake never reached her in these visions. She always slowly faded before she got to her. An apparition that vanished into the mist of the sea, crushing Cam with a new, different sense of loss. Not the loss of what had been and would never be again. But the loss of what never had the chance to be.

She sipped her coffee and watched her dogs play at the water's edge. For the first week or so after Blake left, they, too, had seemed to be expecting to see her every morning. And they, too, seemed bogged down with sadness at her absence. She wasn't sure how they were all getting through, the hours of each day dragging on and on. But somehow they were making it, one minute at a time, inhaling and exhaling, but doing little else. A routine that, at one time, had been their norm when Cam had plowed through her grief over Lexi.

Her writing, which had been feverish with Blake there, had lagged and almost ceased completely when she'd left. After a few days of wallowing however, and staring at wine she couldn't bring herself to drink, Cam had picked up her pen again and began writing down her feelings. She'd then poured those into her manuscript, weaving them into the story, understanding her characters and their pain and journey now better than ever.

Her agent, Irene, seemed to agree. She'd called after reading the draft Cam had sent her and raved about the new direction she'd taken in her work. She'd encouraged her to keep at it and to come up to Phoenix for a meeting soon to discuss it further. So far, Cam had put her and that meeting off. She wasn't yet sure what she wanted to do with the manuscript. If anything at all. And Irene would try to talk her into selling it. Cam hadn't produced anything new since the accident and Irene was antsy to get Cam back out into the public eye. Her fans were, according to Irene, restless, confused, hungry for more of her work. Irene wasn't concerned that the new manuscript was outside of her usual genre. She'd said if anything, Cam would gain a whole new fan base in addition to the one she already had. And that there were many successful authors who wrote and published in different genres.

Cam sipped more coffee, placed the mug on the ledge and walked down to the beach. She walked through the cold sand, hands in her pockets, inhaling the chill coming off the hissing sea. Her flannel sleep pants weren't very thick, nor was her long-sleeved Billabong shirt. But the dawn air didn't bother her. She liked how it felt as it spread throughout her chest and settled into her bones.

She didn't venture far from the house before she stopped and stared out at the ocean. For an instant she thought about stripping out of her clothes to wade out into the Sea of Cortez and dive under the waves to swim and swim until her body screamed for air. At which point she'd surface, suck in giant gulps of oxygen, and then go back under to stroke and kick against the weight of the water again, lost in the dark peace of its silent cocoon.

How far out could she swim? How long before her arms and legs and lungs could take no more and she'd succumb to that dark, quiet, peace?

Would I fight it?

If I pushed myself to that point, to the point of exhaustion and my body began to fail...would I fight those last few seconds when the end was inevitable? Would I try, kicking and flailing for the surface? And if I did, would it be because of instinct? That desperate, innate need for air that every human has, or would it be my own conscious, purposeful doing? My own want and will to live rather than something instinctual and involuntary?

It would be me. My own want and will to live.

She was sure of that. There had been a time, not so long ago, when she wouldn't have been so certain. Now, however, she was.

But why?

Why would she want to surface and suck in that priceless, God-given air?

What was driving her to continue?

Hope?

She didn't think of the future. Didn't dream or want for anything specific.

So why did she think her desperate scramble for the surface would be stemmed from her own conscious will to live?

"Cam?"

Cam turned, startled to hear anyone on the beach at that hour, or really at all. There were very few residents visiting their oceanside homes at present.

McKenna came to stand next to her, her smile looking somewhat hesitant. "Am I intruding? You looked so deep in thought."

"I—" *Was. But I was starting to scare myself.* "Just appreciating the splendor of the sea."

"It is something," she said. "I could get lost in it forever if I wasn't careful." She hugged herself and it reminded Cam of Blake and the way she'd often done the same to ward off the cold sea air. She had to glance away from her, the memory too unsettling.

"I didn't expect to see you guys back so soon," Cam said. Sloane and McKenna had left for Phoenix not long after Blake, and though they hadn't said when they'd planned to return, Cam had assumed it wouldn't be anytime soon, given it was off season.

"It's been a month," McKenna said. "If you can believe that."

I can. Feels more like an eternity. "Hard to believe," Cam said. She felt McKenna turn to look at her.

"How have you been, Cam?"

"I've been all right." It was her standard response as of late and her friends didn't question her further, though she suspected they wanted to. So, for the most part, she stayed cooped up at home.

McKenna knelt and scratched Bingo's head as he bounded up to say hello. "Your little guys seem well. Happy. How about you?"

"Happy enough."

"Ah."

"Ah, what?"

"You're not so happy."

"I didn't say that."

"You didn't have to. Not with words anyway."

Cam looked at her. "I forgot how you are."

"How I am?"

"Insightful."

She laughed. "You don't have to be so polite, Cam."

"Okay, fucking psychic. And I'd say nosy, but you seem to sense things without even trying to pry. But, yeah, at other times, you can be nosy too."

She cracked up. "That's more like it. Tell me how you really feel. Seeing as how we are past pleasantries and neighborly politeness? I'd like to think we're really friends at this point."

"We are," Cam said, meaning it. McKenna was a friend. Could quite possibly become a good one. The same could be said for Sloane. There was just one thing Cam had to consider in having the two of them as friends. And she didn't want to think about it.

"I don't want to discuss how I am. Not beyond what I already said. I'm all right. Let's leave it at that."

"For now?" McKenna tried.

Cam couldn't help but laugh. "It's so easy to see how you and Blake are such good friends. You're both so God damned determined and relentless sometimes." She stiffened as she realized what she'd said and who she'd said it about. She angled away from McKenna's direct view and pretended to search the sand for shells. She found a few small pebbles and began tossing them out into the water. She was done with this conversation now and she hoped McKenna, with all her insight, would take notice and leave her be.

She didn't want to go back there, couldn't afford to go back there.

She'd moved on from Blake and all the feelings she encompassed.

She'd begun anew again.

She took a few steps forward and looked down at the water as its chill enveloped her bare feet, biting into her skin.

The sensation took her breath away and sent her blood thrumming, forcing her mind to awake and fire.

She watched the water creep toward her again and she took a step back, literally and figuratively, to get a new perspective.

Have I really moved on?

Have I really begun anew?

Chapter Forty-four

"We're relentless about things we care about," McKenna said, coming closer. "Things that are important to us."

Cam tossed another rock, trying to dismiss her own questions on the subject. If and when she did seek the answers to them, she'd want to do it privately.

"We don't like to let go," McKenna said. "Especially if what's important to us is a person. Someone we care deeply for."

"Sometimes you have to let go," Cam said, wiping her hands and then shoving them into her pockets. "Sometimes you have to know when to say when."

"And sometimes, Cam, you can't. Even if you want to believe it's the right thing to do. Even if it seems like the right thing to do. In those instances, when you think you're doing the right thing, for whatever reason, and you find that you just can't let go, no matter how hard you try, then that's a clear sign that what you think may be the right thing isn't the right thing after all. No matter how noble or well-meaning you think it is."

"I know you're well-meaning right now, McKenna," Cam said. "But I told you, I don't want to talk about this."

"I am well-meaning. And I'm not listening to you, am I? I'm not shutting up or leaving you alone about this. Because I care. I can't stop caring about you or this. If I could, then that would suggest that the right thing is being played out. But I can't stop. Because the right thing isn't being done. Well-meaning or not."

"I don't know what she's told you," Cam said. She was starting to get upset, pissed that McKenna wasn't respecting her wishes and annoyed at all her well-meaning gibberish. "But I did more than just what I thought was right. I faced reality. One of us had to." She started walking back toward her house, not caring in the least if McKenna thought she was rude. In her mind, McKenna was being rude by pushing the issue.

"She hasn't said a word," McKenna said, hurrying after her. Cam didn't slow her pace. "She never would. And she didn't have to."

"Yeah, the whole psychic thing," Cam said.

"She's my dear friend and I know her very, very well. You want to call it psychic, go ahead. Call it bullshit for all I care. It doesn't bother me. But what does bother me is seeing my dear, good friend hurt. And seeing my new, dear friend hurt. Needlessly."

Cam closed in on her patio. She whistled for the dogs who were farther behind her than she'd realized.

"She's working herself to death, Cam. Even sleeping at the practice some nights. She won't talk to anyone. Won't spend time with anyone outside of work. Her folks are worried. Her mother has come to me asking me if she's sick and just not telling anyone."

"She's probably upset about the clinic," Cam said. "And having to tell them about it. She's been anxious over that for a long time." Cam started walking up the patio steps. The dogs rushed up alongside her.

"She's given up the clinic, Cam."

Cam froze.

"She dropped everything. Told Sloane and everyone else she was no longer interested. That it was a pipe dream and ridiculous."

Cam took in a big breath and tried to control her reaction. "That's her choice, McKenna."

"You know as well as I do, that is not her choice. You know that isn't what she wants."

"Blake does exactly what she wants," Cam said. "She's the most stubborn, willful, and determined woman I've ever known."

"Then you should know what it is she's doing."

"She's doing what she wants."

"Just like you are?"

Cam continued up the steps.

"You're both so full of shit you can't see what's right in front of your face. What everyone else within a fifty-mile radius of you can see. Or...what I think...I think you can see it. Both of you. And you feel it. And that's why you're both doing your damnedest to stay away from each other. You tell her to fuck off. She leaves. And now she's giving up her life's dream so she won't have to be anywhere near you."

Cam spun on her heel. "You're blaming me for her choosing to not to pursue her clinic? Christ, McKenna, that's low. That's really low."

"Cam, she's giving it up because it would mean she would be here. In Mexico."

"So? She wouldn't be near me. She'd be close to town."

"To Blake, Cam, it would be too close. Don't you see? She'd be too tempted. She'd be able to *feel* you. She'd want to get in her car and come to you. Blake is a very stubborn woman, Cam, but when she loves...she's all in and it's the one thing she cannot control. Despite her wanting more than anything to be able to. She can't come back. She won't come back. Cam, she's already told us she's never coming back to our place. She hasn't said why, but I know why. Being anywhere close to you and not being able to love you, to be with you, it would hurt her too badly."

"So, what am I supposed to do?" Cam said. "Move?"

"Don't be a jerk, Cam. It isn't you and I see right through it."

Cam threw up her hands. "Then I'm lost. I don't know what you want me to do."

"I want you to do what's in your heart. I want you to face your true reality and feel it and deal with it whether it scares you or makes you uncomfortable or drives you insane. Blake, I have a feeling, tried to do it. I know that woman's heart and what I saw in her that last time she came to you was love. And it was real. And for whatever reason, you turned her away. And she won't push you on it, Cam. She's not like that. She's very strong in many, many ways, but she is human and rejection sucks, I don't care who you are."

"It can't work," Cam said, but her voice was weak, telling of her own lack of conviction.

"If you love each other, it can work. It will work. Because you will both make it work."

Cam shook, the cold suddenly penetrating. She stared beyond McKenna and out into the sea. She thought about diving down under the waves again and swimming as hard as she could until her lungs felt like bursting.

"I'll leave you be now," McKenna said. "I would apologize for upsetting you, but I'd only half mean it. I don't want to cause you any pain, but at the same time, I do want to cause you to feel. And if pain is a part of that picture, then it is. I care about you, Cam. And I care about Blake. This is the last I'll say about this to either of you, regardless of what you do."

She walked away and left Cam staring out at the sea, where she was imagining pulling at the heavy weight of the water with her arms and kicking against it with her legs. Her lungs were burning, her muscles on fire, desperate for air. She could see the glimmer of the surface from the dark depths, but the depths were calm and comforting and offering her peace and solace from any more pain. They were tempting her, encouraging her to give in and let go. To stop trying, to relax her body and just sink, down, down, down. But she looked up at the pale glimmer of light. Where the surface was, where life was. And she saw Blake. Saw her swimming at her from just below the surface, her hand outstretched. And Cam felt a surge of life explode inside her and she swam harder, wanting, needing to get to her. And when she reached her and she touched her hand and shot up out of the water to suck in the wondrous air, she realized she wasn't there. She was alone, treading water, gasping for breath. But it felt so good to breathe. To be alive. To feel the cold of the water, the chill of the air, the ache in her body. And she knew then, that though she'd chosen to swim because she'd seen Blake, the thrill and rush of life was so good she knew she'd choose to swim for herself from now on, regardless of who was or was not waiting for her at the surface.

Because there was no guarantee who or what she'd find as she emerged from the depths to take in air. But one thing was for certain. There'd be absolutely nothing there if she chose to never surface again.

CHAPTER FORTY-FIVE

Blake took two sips from the heatable Campbell's soup container she'd grabbed off her desk, grimaced at the now tepid tomato soup, and tossed it in the trash before heading back out into the main hallway of the Livingstone family practice. Another attempt at eating down the tubes. She blamed lack of time, but truthfully, she didn't try to make time. Her angry, growling stomach had become less of a nuisance lately, as if it had learned that protesting resulted in nothing.

Blake crossed to the main hub of office operations where the three medical assistants they employed were headquartered behind a rounded counter. One assistant passed by her with a patient in tow, another was pecking away at a computer with her two index fingers, and the other, Yvonne, her medical assistant, rose from behind the counter, handed Blake her small laptop, and breezed past her toward the exit.

"New patient in two," she said. "I'm going for lunch. Rubio's. You want your usual salad?"

"No, thanks. I'll grab something around here."

"Soup?" Her young face was crinkled with the sarcasm that had drenched her question, her top lip curling upward just enough for Blake to see her braces.

Blake adored Yvonne, and most of the time, her knowing Blake so well worked out fine. It helped them remain in sync and work effectively together. But at the moment, their close rapport was annoying her. "Maybe."

Yvonne rolled her eyes. "I'll bring you a salad. You don't want it, don't eat it. Someone else gladly will."

"You better hope so," Blake said, walking toward exam room two. "I wouldn't want you to waste your money." Yvonne mumbled something Blake couldn't make out and Blake wished again that everyone would just leave her alone and let her do her job. Her mother was constantly on her case, questioning her health and state of mind. Her father, who was more like Blake, respected her privacy and left her alone to her face. But he voiced his worries to everyone else and it seemed everyone in the practice was focused on her, asking when she last ate, slept, took time to herself. She didn't understand the problem. She was doing what her family wanted. She was working hard and busting her ass to be able to take over the practice. What was the problem?

She knocked softly on the door to exam room two, wondering if she should even take a lunch at all after she saw this patient. She decided against it, knowing if she did she'd end up thinking about Mexico and the clinic and...Cam. She'd rather work than dwell on what she couldn't have.

She walked inside the room. "Hello," she greeted politely. She didn't glance up completely before turning to close the door behind her. Then she opened the laptop, focused on the awakening screen, and moved toward the small counter where she normally sat. "I'm Dr. Livingstone." She set the computer down and smiled over at her patient.

Her heart stopped.

She started stepping backward, her hand over her throat. She hit the rolling stool and nearly fell.

"Cam." She blinked at her rapidly, the sight of her too fantastical to be real. The way she looked was equally as fantastical. She was wearing a dark, designer skirt and matching jacket. The blouse between the two was as crimson as her lipstick. Her black as night hair was styled with a wet look and it set off the glimmer in her matching irises. She was made up and dressed to the nines. From her perfectly arched eyebrows, alluring smoky eye shadow and her seductively mascaraed eyelashes, to her well-tailored suit and her shiny black designer heels. The sheer shock of her presence was enough to bowl Blake over. But seeing her like that, like the absolute drop-dead gorgeous woman she was, left Blake feeling brainless. "What are you—" She searched for words. Stammered. "I don't—you're—here."

"I have an ailment," Cam said. "And I heard you're the best doctor around these parts."

Blake waited for a grin to crack her well-poised face. A playful lift of her eyebrow. But neither showed. She appeared to be just as serious as she was sexy, and Blake wasn't sure what to make of her presence. So she persevered in the best way she knew how. As a concerned physician.

"If you're not feeling well, I can get someone else in to see you."

"I want to see you."

"I—it wouldn't be professional for me to see you."

"I don't really care."

Blake fought again for the stability and formality she'd always had in precarious situations. This situation, however, seemed to be far more formidable than any other she'd faced before. Her heart was pounding and adrenaline was racing through her, enough to make her hands tingle like they should be moving to save someone, like *she* should be moving to save someone. Just like she used to feel when she did her rounds in the ER. And yet Cam was sitting there on the examination table, luscious legs gracefully crossed, not showing the slightest sense of injury or illness.

So why do I feel like I'm about to jump out of my own body?

"I'll go get another doctor in to see you." It would be her mother. Her father had already left for the day to tend to his sick brother. Her uncle was gravely ill, and his condition was the reason why she'd had to return home so suddenly. She thought briefly about how she would explain to her mother the reason why she couldn't treat Cam, who was, ironically, one of her favorite authors.

"I won't see anyone else."

"Cam, I can't—"

"No one else can help me."

Blake clamped her mouth closed. "Pardon?"

"No one else can help me, so there's no need to go get anyone else. I won't see them because it's pointless. So, it's either you or... no one."

No one else can help her?

"I don't know what you want me to do."

"I want you to help me."

Blake forced down a swallow and cleared her throat. "Okay. How is it that I can help you?"

"I told you, I have an ailment. I hurt." She pulled her burning stare away from Blake as if what she'd just said was somehow too revealing. Blake took a step closer, alarmed.

"You're in pain?"

"Yes." She whispered like it was difficult to get the word out and her gaze remained fixed on the wall.

Blake crossed to her, full of concern.

"Where is the pain?"

Cam was quiet. She eased out of her suit jacket and placed her hand on her chest. "Here." She finally looked at her and her eyes were large and glistening. "I hurt right here."

Blake started to speak, to question whether or not she meant that literally, but then stopped, realizing it didn't matter. If Cam felt anything like she did, then she was hurting in every way possible, the cause something that even modern medicine could not fix. That kind of pain was very real and she wanted to help her in any way she could.

Blake struggled with her stethoscope, her instinct as a physician still piloting her. Regardless of what was causing her chest pain, Blake needed to examine her. Cam, however, reached out and stopped her. "No. Not that way. I don't want you to listen to my heart." She took her hand and placed it on her chest. "I want you to feel it."

Blake's breath shook as she looked into her eyes and felt the subtle thudding of her heart.

"Can you feel it?"

"Yes."

"Can you feel how fast it's beating?"

"Yes."

"It's because you're touching me. Because you're here with me. Can you feel that?"

Blake swallowed. "Yes."

"Can you feel how it aches when you aren't touching me? When you aren't with me? Because it does, Blake. It hurts so badly sometimes I think it's going to give out on me completely. For a while, I was hoping it would. That way the pain would be gone. But I don't want to live like that. I don't want to walk around without a heart, with a hollow chest. I want to feel. Even if it's awful and agonizing. Because there are moments when it's worth it. Like now. Like the way I feel when I'm with you. And I don't ever want to give that up."

"Cam, I—"

"Don't," she said. "Don't speak. Don't think. Not right now. Just feel."

She pressed Blake's hand firmer against her chest. "Feel me, Blake. Feel my love for you." She reached out with her other hand and cupped Blake's jaw. The heat of her palm and the soft caress of her thumb caused Blake's body to melt and she made a small noise as she exhaled and fell into the lure of Cam's gaze. Cam pulled her to her and they stared into one another without saying another word. With just the beat of Cam's heart between them.

CHAPTER FORTY-SIX

When Blake saw her red lips part and beckon, with her heart beating beneath her hand, encouraging her, she moved in to take those lips with her own.

But just before she reached her, Cam whispered, "I love you," and Blake nearly fainted as she captured her mouth, the words so good and so sweet, she wanted to taste them to see if they could taste anywhere near as good as they'd sounded. She found her answer quickly, and disbelieving of the impossibility of how delectable Cam and her words were, she took more of her, sucking the sweet words from her lips, chasing them with her tongue. She couldn't believe how she'd forgotten what kissing Cam was like, how delicious she was, how warm, how soft, and how skilled and agile she was in kissing her back, as if she, too, were rediscovering her all over again.

The taste of the lipstick was new and it, along with how fucking amazing it looked on her, drove Blake to near madness, and she literally wanted to consume her. She felt Cam's heart careening wildly beneath her hand as their kisses deepened, and she realized she needed to feel more of her. She broke their kiss and sought for breath as her fingers hurriedly unbuttoned her blouse.

"What are you doing?" Cam asked, sliding her hand along the back of Blake's neck, her lips lightly touching Blake's as she spoke.

"I'm doing what you asked me to do." She undid the last button and pulled the shirt from her skirt and spread the front open, exposing a matching red lace bra. "Dear God," she breathed, taking in the sight of her bronzed skin, the beautiful dip along her collarbones and the firmness of her chest.

"What I asked you to do?"

"Yes," Blake said, skimming her fingers along the outline of the lace. "I'm helping you."

Cam shivered and grabbed her hand. "Here?"

Blake met her gaze. "That's what you want, isn't it?"

Cam glanced at the door.

"Am I not helping you? Did I misunderstand?" Blake tilted her chin so Cam was once again looking at her.

"You didn't misunderstand. I just didn't think you'd want to do anything like this...here."

"Are you being serious?"

"Someone could walk in. This is your office, where you work—"

"You came here, without my knowing, dressed like this, looking like this, saying the things you said and you didn't think I'd want you right here and now?"

"I'm meeting my agent for lunch at a nice restaurant. I needed to look nice—"

Blake pulled away. "Well, you definitely do, Cam. There's no denying that. I guess I did misunderstand, because I thought that maybe you'd—I don't know—done all this for me."

"I'm here, aren't I? I could've made the appointment for another time. A time when I didn't need to look so nice."

"You are confusing the hell out of me."

Cam grabbed her hand and tugged her back toward her. "I was hoping my looking nice would help to...entice you into forgiving me. Or at the very least would make you listen to what I had to say. So I did make the appointment at this time purposely. I did do this for you. It was you I thought about when I chose this outfit."

"It worked. You got me. But just so you know, it wouldn't have mattered how you looked."

"But it helped, right?" She raised her eyebrow and tugged her closer.

"It helped a little too much. Because now I want you, would do anything to have you, and you're slamming on the brakes. You're killing me."

The grin that Blake had been searching for moments before showed itself.

"You aren't the only one suffering."

"If you're suffering, then why are you grinning?"

She shrugged. "I don't know." Her gaze flicked back to the door. "Does that door have a lock?"

"No. But my medical assistant is out for lunch." Blake trailed her fingers along the edge of the bra again. "Does that comfort you any?"

"Not really."

Blake laughed. "Cam, you're worrying. It's not like you."

"This is your office. Your parents work here. It's not like you to *not* be worried."

Blake laughed again. "I know. But here we are." She leaned in and delicately kissed her neck, causing her to shudder. "You're anxious and I'm calm. The irony." She traced her fingers down to Cam's bare thigh and ran them up under her skirt, causing a sigh and a shudder this time.

"Blake," Cam let out. "What if your mother walks in?"

Blake kissed her ear. "Then I'll introduce you."

Cam laughed but gripped her shoulder as Blake continued to place kisses along the side of her neck and down to her chest. "That's not quite the introduction I had in mind when I imagined meeting your family."

"You actually imagined meeting my family?"

"I've been imagining a lot."

"Mm. But not this? Getting it on with me in an examination room?"

Blake kissed her breast through her bra, used her tongue to tantalize her through the lace. Cam gasped and tangled her hand in her hair.

"Oh, I imagined it, I just didn't think you'd want to do it."

Blake peeled the cup of the bra down. "Well, I do. So what are you going to do about it?" She took her already puckered center in her mouth and Cam cried out quickly before stifling herself.

"There's not anything I can do about it, is there?"

"Other than tell me to stop, no." She teased her nipple with her tongue while her fingers continued to tease her upper thigh.

"I—can't."

"I didn't think so." Blake straightened, kissed her deeply and hurriedly helped her hike up her skirt. Then she lowered herself back to her breast as her hand returned on its quest along her thigh. Cam started to speak, probably to voice more worries, but Blake licked her nipple and distracted her. "Don't speak. Don't think. Just feel."

Cam looked down at her and Blake gave her her own version of a wicked grin as she pressed her fingers against the hot flesh hidden behind her panties. She rubbed her carefully at first, while she continued to tease her breast with her mouth. Until Cam was knotting her hair in her hands again and crying out softly repeatedly, her hips urging for more.

Blake rose back up to her ear and said, "I love you," as she eased her panties aside and snuck her fingers into her slick folds, quickly finding and feeding her hungry clit with firm strokes. Cam made a sharp cry of helplessness and clung to her, her body moving against Blake's erotic assault, seeking all that it could.

Blake spoke more words of love in her ear and devoured her neck. Then she watched her for a few moments as she made love to her, taking in the expression on her face, the pulse beating in the vein on her neck, the slick feel of her core in her hand.

"I love you," she said again, giving it to her harder and faster.

"I—love you, Blake." She clenched her eyes. "Oh, God, I love you." And she came then, loudly, and Blake covered her cries with a searing kiss while Cam came in her hand, her body convulsing. She felt so wonderful as she climaxed into her, so beautiful, so hot and slick, Blake slid her fingers up inside her and fucked her until she came again, her body bucking, her flesh rubbing against the heel of Blake's hand. Cam moaned into her mouth and their tongues danced and dueled for as long as Cam's body fed. When she finally stilled, Blake kissed her softly before breaking their connection so they could both garner breath.

"I came for you," Cam said.

"Yes, and it was beyond fucking beautiful."

"Blake. I mean I came for you. Came here for you. To see you. To tell you how I feel. I—miss you. Want you. Want to be with you."

"Cam I—I don't know what to say. So much has happened here—"

"I don't expect you to do anything. I just wanted you to know how I feel. How badly I do want to be with you. How much I do love you. I couldn't go on with you not knowing."

A quick series of knocks sounded at the door and Blake felt Cam stiffen and she tugged her blouse closed.

"Doctor?"

It was her mother's medical assistant. Blake turned her head to yell at her. "I'll be out in a second."

"I need the smaller blood pressure cuff. I think it's in there."

"In a second." She turned back to Cam who looked panicked but far from ashen. She had the color of a woman full of fire, one that was still a long way from being properly put out. But for the time being, Blake had to give up her attempts to do so. "Well, that was a nice, final little thrill." She gave her another grin.

"I think I really am going to have a heart problem after this."

"Well, it's a good thing you have a doctor then."

"I thought you said you couldn't treat me?" She was buttoning her blouse.

Blake stopped her with one hand while the other toyed with her as it was still inside her. She elicited another gasp before she slowly removed herself from her.

"You know what? I don't really care."

"What has happened to you?" Cam asked, touching her face.

Blake kissed her and placed a finger to her lips. "You."

Chapter Forty-seven

Four Weeks Later

Cam finished putting some of the final touches on the latest chapter of her manuscript and closed the laptop, feeling a sense of satisfaction as she rose to stretch. The light in the room had dimmed considerably and she was surprised to see how late it was as she glanced at the pewter clock on her bookshelf and looked out the window to the sea. She'd worked longer than she'd realized and the overcast day had given way to the darkening approach of late evening.

The dogs stirred at her feet as she made her way into the kitchen to retrieve a bottle of water. She eyed the wine fridge next to the refrigerator and felt nothing. The urge she'd had to drown in wine in order to get through had left her weeks ago and she hadn't even wanted any at meals either. Not even when she went to see her aunt and uncle for their weekly meals. Last Saturday she'd had a beer, but only because her uncle had brought her one as they'd sat out on the back deck of their home to visit.

She hadn't really needed anything as of late.

Maybe that was because she didn't feel like she had anything to try to make it through.

Life was...well, just good. She didn't have everything she wanted, but she had a lot, and the gratefulness for that alone had sort of settled over her psyche and left her feeling content and relaxed. She was finally feeling more like herself. Her friends and loved ones had noticed and even the dogs seemed to be in a better state of mind.

She left her water on the counter and led the way to the back door. The dogs scurried ahead of her onto the patio and then looked back for permission before taking off down the steps.

"Go ahead."

They took off and she smiled after them and hugged herself in the strong breeze. She stared out at the churning, charcoal gray sea as it began to meld into the shadows of night. She'd missed the sunset but she wasn't overly disappointed. It, like the wine, didn't feel as necessary to her happiness as it once had. She knew there'd be another again tomorrow and she didn't worry about whether or not she'd be there to see it. If she was then she'd take the time to relish it like she always had and appreciate each and every color as they burst forth to shine before melting down into the horizon. If she wasn't there to see it, then she wouldn't have anything to worry about at all would she?

She took life as it came, one thing at a time, one moment at a time. The rest…was just filler. Things a writer would add to a book that the reader might enjoy, but they weren't absolutely vital to the plot.

The dogs barked from the water's edge and then sprinted to the left, kicking up wet sand like they were on the run for their lives. She walked to the steps and peered after them, curious as to what would cause such a commotion. Her breath caught as she found the source, and for a second, she questioned her sanity. For a long while she'd envisioned Blake running toward her from down the beach at dawn, but that had been a dream. Blake had always vanished before she reached her. And those were dreams she'd had at dawn. This was evening. And that was…

She descended a step and blinked.

"Blake."

She wasn't dreaming. It really was her. Walking toward her in jeans and a sweater, with the dogs dancing at her feet.

Cam hurried down the steps and through the cold sand. Though she didn't have to run far to reach her, she was still breathless when she came to a stop before her close to the whispering waves of the sea.

"You're here," Cam said in disbelief. "What—?" She shook her head, unsure what to question or even what to say she was so surprised. She'd last seen her a month ago when Cam had gone to

Phoenix to meet Irene about the book. The book she'd since sold and was now under contract with. But that was not what Cam remembered most about that trip. It was seeing Blake again that had really left its mark on her. They'd spent two passion-filled days at Blake's home making love and trying desperately to get as much of each other as they could before they had to part. They'd talked about seeing each other again, but those plans hadn't been fleshed out yet. Or at least not to Cam's knowledge anyway.

Blake tucked an errant strand of hair behind her ear and grinned. "Surprised?"

Cam stammered. "Uh, yeah."

"A bit lost for words?"

"Somewhat, yes."

"Is your heart pounding out of your chest?"

She reached out and placed her hand on Cam's chest. Cam covered it with her own.

"You tell me."

Blake inched closer and touched her face. "It is. Just like mine did when you surprised me. I'll never forget walking in that room and seeing you sitting there like that. Looking the way you did. Never."

"And I'll never forget this."

"I suppose not."

The wind blew her hair again and pressed the maroon sweater against her body. Her cheeks tinged a shade lighter than her sweater when Cam traced her fingers along her neck.

"What are you doing here?"

"You mean other than surprising you? I came to close the deal on the building and to hire someone to start the renovations."

Cam wasn't sure she'd heard her correctly. Last she knew Blake was once again leaning toward making her dream of the clinic a reality, but she was unaware she'd made up her mind completely. "Blake, that's—Jesus, that's great."

"It's a shock, I know. And I've been dying to tell you, but I wanted to surprise you. Kind of like you surprised me."

"You've succeeded. More than succeeded. I can't believe it. I'm so happy for you." Cam was smiling so hard her face hurt. She could see the light in Blake's eyes, the heavy weight of the world gone. She was all about making her dream come true now, no matter what obstacles she might face in doing so. It was her dream and any difficulty she would face would be worth it, the fight to make it through more meaningful and the end result all the sweeter. She was going to be happy now, Cam could see it in her, really, truly, happy. Doing what she loved. What she felt she was meant to do.

"You're happy for me?"

"Happy? I'm ecstatic! You should see the way you look right now. Just seeing you glowing like this makes me happy, much less your good news."

"I'm happy too. But not just for me. Not just because of the clinic. But for us. I'm happy for us. I'd be lying if I said I didn't think about that when I made this decision. I couldn't help it. I can't help it. I think about you and about us all the time. I know that probably makes you uncomfortable because you said you wanted me to base my decision solely on me and my dream in case we don't work out. And mostly, I have, Cam. But you were part of the equation too. And if for whatever reason we don't work out, I won't be upset with you. How could I? You've only helped me to make the decision to chase my dream. I could never resent you for that. Besides," she stroked Cam's cheek and inched even closer, "I'm not worried about us working out. I can only think about how good it's going to be to try." She kissed her, lightly, delicately, like she was afraid Cam would vanish if she pressed too hard. "Because it's going to feel so incredibly good to try."

Cam licked her lips, the feel and taste of Blake still lingering. The kiss had been a tease, a promise as to what was to come.

"Yes, it will," Cam agreed.

"Hey! Lovebirds!"

They looked up toward the voice. Sloane was standing in front of her patio with her hand on her hips.

"You coming for dinner or what?"

Cam laughed. "I had no idea any of you had even arrived."

"We were purposely stealthy." She moved the hand she had on Cam's heart and stroked her arm, eliciting goose bumps. "God, I'm freezing and you're in short sleeves. You're not ever cold."

"I get cold," Cam said. "Just rarely happens when I'm with you."

"You're saying I make you hot?"

Cam smiled and stilled her hand. "That would be the understatement of the century."

Blake laughed and tilted her head toward Sloane. "With that in mind, what should we tell them about dinner? Kenna started cooking the second we arrived. You know how she is."

Cam looked back up to Sloane who held her arm out and raised a shoulder, waiting for an answer.

"Think they'll forgive us if we skip out on dinner?"

"Do we care if they don't?"

Cam took her hand and tugged her toward the house. Her house. "Absolutely not. After all, this is exactly what they've been wanting. They don't have a leg to stand on."

"Good point." Blake hurried after her and they jogged up toward the house.

Sloane was calling out to them, still trying to get an answer. It only made Cam laugh harder. They reached the bottom of the steps and Blake stopped them. Cam faced her.

"What is it?" Cam asked, noticing the soft seriousness that had overcome her.

"I didn't even ask you if this is okay with you. If this is still what you want."

Cam held her hands and looked deep into her eyes. Night was falling all around them and the sea was gently hissing just beyond. The chill of the breeze blew against them, the scent of salt and sand rich and alluring. It wasn't like her dream. It wasn't dawn and it wasn't warm. And Blake couldn't stay indefinitely. Not yet.

But it was real.

It was life.

And it was pretty fucking terrific.

Cam answered her with a kiss and told her all the things she couldn't possibly say with words. Then she pulled away, saw the love in Blake's eyes ensuring she'd understood, and she tugged her up the stairs to continue to relay her feelings to her without words.

Words, for the moment anyway, Cam decided to save for her books.

Because some things couldn't be conveyed through words.

Some things could only be conveyed through the heart.

THE END

About the Author

Ronica Black lives in the desert Southwest with her menagerie of animals and her menagerie of art. When she's not writing, she's still creating, whether drawing, painting, or woodworking. She loves long walks into the sunset, rescuing animals, anything pertaining to art, and spending time with those she loves. When she can, she enjoys returning to her roots in North Carolina where she can sit back on the porch with family and friends, catch up on all the gossip, and relish an ice cold Cheerwine.

Ronica is a two-time Golden Crown Literary Society Goldie Award winner and a three-time finalist for the Lambda Literary Awards.

Books Available from Bold Strokes Books

Bet Against Me by Fiona Riley. In the high stakes luxury real estate market, everything has a price, and as rival Realtors Trina Lee and Kendall Yates find out, that means their hearts and souls, too. (978-1-63555-729-9)

Broken Reign by Sam Ledel. Together on an epic journey in search of a mysterious cure, a princess and a village outcast must overcome life-threatening challenges and their own prejudice if they want to survive. (978-1-63555-739-8)

Just One Taste by CJ Birch. For Lauren, it only took one taste to start trusting in love again. (978-1-63555-772-5)

Lady of Stone by Barbara Ann Wright. Sparks fly as a magical emergency forces a noble embarrassed by her ability to submit to a low-born teacher who resents everything about her. (978-1-63555-607-0)

Last Resort by Angie Williams. Katie and Rhys are about to find out what happens when you meet the girl of your dreams but you aren't looking for a happily ever after. (978-1-63555-774-9)

Longing for You by Jenny Frame. When Debrek housekeeper Katie Brekman is attacked amid a burgeoning vampire-witch war, Alexis Villiers must go against everything her clan believes in to save her. (978-1-63555-658-2)

Money Creek by Anne Laughlin. Clare Lehane is a troubled lawyer from Chicago who tries to make her way in a rural town full of secrets and deceptions. (978-1-63555-795-4)

Passion's Sweet Surrender by Ronica Black. Cam and Blake are unable to deny their passion for each other, but surrendering to love is a whole different matter. (978-1-63555-703-9)

The Holiday Detour by Jane Kolven. It will take everything going wrong to make Dana and Charlie see how right they are for each other. (978-1-63555-720-6)

Too Hot to Ride by Andrews & Austin. World famous cutting horse champion and industry legend Jane Barrow is knockdown sexy in the way she moves, talks, and rides, and Rae Starr is determined not to get involved with this womanizing gambler. (978-1-63555-776-3)

A Love that Leads to Home by Ronica Black. For Carla Sims and Janice Carpenter, home isn't about location, it's where your heart is. (978-1-63555-675-9)

Blades of Bluegrass by D. Jackson Leigh. A US Army occupational therapist must rehab a bitter veteran who is a ticking political time bomb the military is desperate to disarm. (978-1-63555-637-7)

Guarding Hearts by Jaycie Morrison. As treachery and temptation threaten the women of the Women's Army Corps, who will risk it all for love? (978-1-63555-806-7)

Hopeless Romantic by Georgia Beers. Can a jaded wedding planner and an optimistic divorce attorney possibly find a future together? (978-1-63555-650-6)

Hopes and Dreams by PJ Trebelhorn. Movie theater manager Riley Warren is forced to face her high school crush and tormentor, wealthy socialite Victoria Thayer, at their twentieth reunion. (978-1-63555-670-4)

In the Cards by Kimberly Cooper Griffin. Daria and Phaedra are about to discover that love finds a way, especially when powers outside their control are at play. (978-1-63555-717-6)

Moon Fever by Ileandra Young. SPEAR agent Danika Karson must clear her werewolf friend of multiple false charges while teaching her vampire girlfriend to resist the blood mania brought on by a full moon. (978-1-63555-603-2)

Quake City by St John Karp. Can Andre find his best friend Amy before the night devolves into a nightmare of broken hearts, malevolent drag queens, and spontaneous human combustion? Or has it always happened this way, every night, at Aunty Bob's Quake City Club? (978-1-63555-723-7)

Serenity by Jesse J. Thoma. For Kit Marsden, there are many things in life she cannot change. Serenity is in the acceptance. (978-1-63555-713-8)

Sylver and Gold by Michelle Larkin. Working feverishly to find a killer before he strikes again, Boston Homicide Detective Reid Sylver and rookie cop London Gold are blindsided by their chemistry and developing attraction. (978-1-63555-611-7)

Trade Secrets by Kathleen Knowles. In Silicon Valley, love and business are a volatile mix for clinical lab scientist Tony Leung and venture capitalist Sheila Graham. (978-1-63555-642-1)

Death Overdue by David S. Pederson. Did Heath turn to murder in an alcohol induced haze to solve the problem of his blackmailer, or was it someone else who brought about a death overdue? (978-1-63555-711-4)

Entangled by Melissa Brayden. Becca Crawford is the perfect person to head up the Jade Hotel, if only the captivating owner of the local vineyard would get on board with her plan and stop badmouthing the hotel to everyone in town. (978-1-63555-709-1)

First Do No Harm by Emily Smith. Pierce and Cassidy are about to discover that when it comes to love, sometimes you have to risk it all to have it all. (978-1-63555-699-5)

Kiss Me Every Day by Dena Blake. For Wynn Evans, wishing for a do-over with Carly Jamison was a long shot, actually getting one was a game changer. (978-1-63555-551-6)

Olivia by Genevieve McCluer. In this lesbian Shakespeare adaptation with vampires, Olivia is a centuries old vampire who must fight a strange figure from her past if she wants a chance at happiness. (978-1-63555-701-5)

One Woman's Treasure by Jean Copeland. Daphne's search for discarded antiques and treasures leads to an embarrassing misunderstanding, and ultimately, the opportunity for the romance of a lifetime with Nina. (978-1-63555-652-0)

Silver Ravens by Jane Fletcher. Lori has lost her girlfriend, her home, and her job. Things don't improve when she's kidnapped and taken to fairyland. (978-1-63555-631-5)

Still Not Over You by Jenny Frame, Carsen Taite, Ali Vali. Old flames die hard in these tales of a second chance at love with the ex you're still not over. Stories by award winning authors Jenny Frame, Carsen Taite, and Ali Vali. (978-1-63555-516-5)

Storm Lines by Jessica L. Webb. Devon is a psychologist who likes rules. Marley is a cop who doesn't. They don't always agree, but both fight to protect a girl immersed in a street drug ring. (978-1-63555-626-1)

The Politics of Love by Jen Jensen. Is it possible to love across the political divide in a hostile world? Conservative Shelley Whitmore and liberal Rand Thomas are about to find out. (978-1-63555-693-3)

All the Paths to You by Morgan Lee Miller. High school sweethearts Quinn Hughes and Kennedy Reed reconnect five years after they break up and realize that their chemistry is all but over. (978-1-63555-662-9)

Arrested Pleasures by Nanisi Barrett D'Arnuck. When charged with a crime she didn't commit, Katherine Lowe faces the question: Which is harder, going to prison or falling in love? (978-1-63555-684-1)

Bonded Love by Renee Roman. Carpenter Blaze Carter suffers an injury that shatters her dreams, and ER nurse Trinity Greene hopes to show her that sometimes love is worth fighting for. (978-1-63555-530-1)

Convergence by Jane C. Esther. With life as they know it on the line, can Aerin McLeary and Olivia Ando's love survive an otherworldly threat to humankind? (978-1-63555-488-5)

Coyote Blues by Karen F. Williams. Riley Dawson, psychotherapist and shape-shifter, has her world turned upside down when Fiona Bell, her one true love, returns. (978-1-63555-558-5)

Drawn by Carsen Taite. Will the clues lead Detective Claire Hanlon to the killer terrorizing Dallas, or will she merely lose her heart to person of interest, urban artist Riley Flynn? (978-1-63555-644-5)

Every Summer Day by Lee Patton. Meant to celebrate every summer day, Luke's journal instead chronicles a love affair as fast-moving and possibly as fatal as his brother's brain tumor. (978-1-63555-706-0)

Lucky by Kris Bryant. Was Serena Evans's luck really about winning the lottery, or is she about to get even luckier in love? (978-1-63555-510-3)

The Last Days of Autumn by Donna K. Ford. Autumn and Caroline question the fairness of life, the cruelty of loss, and what it means to love as they navigate the complicated minefield of relationships, grief, and life-altering illness. (978-1-63555-672-8)

Three Alarm Response by Erin Dutton. In the midst of tragedy, can these first responders find love and healing? Three stories of courage, bravery, and passion. (978-1-63555-592-9)

Veterinary Partner by Nancy Wheelton. Callie and Lauren are determined to keep their hearts safe but find that taking a chance on love is the safest option of all. (978-1-63555-666-7)

Everyday People by Louis Barr. When film star Diana Danning hires private eye Clint Steele to find her son, Clint turns to his former West Point barracks mate, and ex-buddy with benefits, Mars Hauser to lend his cyber espionage and digital black ops skills to the case. (978-1-63555-698-8)

Forging a Desire Line by Mary P. Burns. When Charley's ex-wife, Tricia, is diagnosed with inoperable cancer, the private duty nurse Tricia hires turns out to be the handsome and aloof Joanna, who ignites something inside Charley she isn't ready to face. (978-1-63555-665-0)

Love on the Night Shift by Radclyffe. Between ruling the night shift in the ER at the Rivers and raising her teenage daughter, Blaise Richilieu has all the drama she needs in her life, until a dashing young attending appears on the scene and relentlessly pursues her. (978-1-63555-668-1)

Olivia's Awakening by Ronica Black. When the daring and dangerously gorgeous Eve Monroe is hired to get Olivia Savage into shape, a fierce passion ignites, causing both to question everything they've ever known about love. (978-1-63555-613-1)

The Duchess and the Dreamer by Jenny Frame. Clementine Fitzroy has lost her faith and love of life. Can dreamer Evan Fox make her believe in life and dream again? (978-1-63555-601-8)

The Road Home by Erin Zak. Hollywood actress Gwendolyn Carter is about to discover that losing someone you love sometimes means gaining someone to fall for. (978-1-63555-633-9)

Waiting for You by Elle Spencer. When passionate past-life lovers meet again in the present day, one remembers it vividly and the other isn't so sure. (978-1-63555-635-3)

While My Heart Beats by Erin McKenzie. Can a love born amidst the horrors of the Great War survive? (978-1-63555-589-9)